THE BUTCHER
OF OXFORD

Jake Weston Mysteries, Book 2

Marko Realmonte

For Lorri, Bridget, and Thomas

"Reality is merely an illusion, albeit a very persistent one."

—ALBERT EINSTEIN

PROLOGUE

Every story is a love story...
but this one is timeless.

CHAPTER 1

The Magdalen Bridge

Casey Larson was gorgeous. His chiseled muscles are a mere by-product, a glorious afterthought, of his fierce dedication to the Oxford Rowing Club. He wondered how many of his privileges and favors would be revoked once the knowledge of his disgrace was out. His public humiliation would be brought about in the subtlest of British ways. Whisperings. A gradual but persistent frost. Invitations to balls and private dinners would cease to arrive. He'd become a pariah, like Shelley two hundred years before him, expelled from the finest university on earth, but for a far less noble cause.

He shrugged as he put in his EarPods and cranked up the dance music. A foggy, predawn workout wouldn't solve his problems but it just might clear the cobwebs from his head. *Cheater*, he overheard in the halls of Corpus yesterday as classmates averted their eyes. *So be it.* He reached up pulling his custom-made Oxford Shell from its perch in the boathouse.

Casey didn't realize that he was being watched from the shadows.

He placed the racing boat into the chilly water, rhythmically moving to the tribal beat reverberating in his ears. He might've been a dancer if his life had taken a slightly different course.

Padding barefoot back into the boathouse, the two made eye contact in the diffused orange glow of first light. He grinned and rushed in, arms wide for a hug, and saw the brief-est glint of steel too late. An upward slash from the polished blade and the killer cleanly, and deeply, cut Casey Larson's throat wide open.

The speed and precision of the deed, as well as the deadly accuracy, testified to a practiced hand. In one stroke the murderer had managed to sever both carotid arteries with the scalpel. Casey's face only registered a kind of smiling wonder and painless surprise as blood spurt four feet in front of him. He reflexively brought his hands up to the wound, spinning once and spraying the killer, the boathouse, the punts, and deck with deep arterial blood. He dropped to his knees, then fell prone with a thud onto the wooden planks. It took less than a minute for Casey Larson to die.

The murderer sliced off the victim's spandex shorts and jersey and bending down, inscribed a symbol into the muscled flesh of the naked young man's back.

His clothes and other belongings were placed in a small vinyl backpack. *Murder is a messy business*, the killer thought, silently entering the water and swimming away in the fog. *Messy and cold.*

◆ ◆ ◆

On that same morning, Timothy James Abbot was in disguise. He hadn't shaved for two days. The black stubble of his beard made a stark contrast against his pale English com-plexion. He wore threadbare corduroy trousers and a dingy gray thermal in his attempt to avoid the perception of Oxford privilege.

When he arrived at his favorite spot beside the River Cherwell it was still dark, the willows and other shade trees casting shadows across the water. Over the centuries the ori-ginal Magdalen bridge had been built and rebuilt, widened, and modernized. The eleven stone archways are of different dimensions, covered with moss and lichen. Its designer, John Gwynn, had originally envisioned decorating the balustrade with extravagant sculptures of sphinxes and other mythical creatures, but those ideas were abandoned in 1782.

Fog crept along the damp cobbles on little cat's paws, turning the light from the streetlamps into gauze. Timothy used the flashlight app from his iPhone to see as he set up the Vox amplifier, carefully connecting it to his violin, which was also camouflaged. No one would guess from the shabby, velvet-lined container that it held an instrument of immeasurable quality and value. The Allegretti violin.

He tucked his long dark curls under a woolen cap and dropped a few shillings from his pocket into the open case to encourage contributions from the audience the music would summon. Timothy watched the sun breaking through the thick mist and it is just at that moment that he heard the faint splashing. Someone had ventured out for an early, and rather chilly, swim.

Better you than me, mate, he thought, closing his eyes, and playing the opening bars of the *Mission Impossible* theme from memory.

Two hours later, Mr. and Mrs. Abbot had finished breakfast and were wandering about the Oxford Covered Market chatting with their artisan friends.

"Do go check and see if there is any rhubarb in season," Bea said to her husband. "I want to make some pies this weekend."

"It's only February, do you think any produce will be worth the effort?"

She shrugged. "That's why I'm sending an expert, my love. Buy whatever looks appetizing. I saw some purple sprouting broccoli as we were walking in."

He straightened his cuffs wordlessly and made his way

through the narrow lane. Mr. McNett, the local silversmith, winked at Bea when her husband's back was turned.

She went rushing to meet him. "Did you manage it, Payson?"

"Aye," he replied, chuckling. He reached under the counter and brought out a handsome walking stick.

"Oh yes," she whispered, smiling broadly. The handle was a silver eagle's head affixed to a dark polished oak cane. "It looks exactly like the photo. You do fine work."

"You say the original belonged to his grandfather?"

"Yes, lost ages ago, or perhaps it was buried with the gentleman, who knows? In any case, my old bird can certainly use a sturdy cane and he's much too vain to buy one for himself."

They laughed. "None of us is getting any younger."

"Truer words were never spoken. Keep it safe here and I'll pick it up before our birthday next week."

"Our birthday?" the silversmith asked.

"My husband and I share the same birthday," Bea gushed. "February twenty-fifth. We're both Pisces."

McNett blinked thoughtfully as if he was calculating the odds of such a thing. "Must be kismet for you two to be together. Don't give your hubby much of an excuse if he forgets to buy you something though."

Bea clucked her tongue. "Mr. Abbot may be getting on, but he has a memory like an elephant, and he wouldn't dare neglect me."

McNett nodded as he wrapped the gift in brown paper and tied it with a string. "Saw your boy while I was setting up in the wee hours," he whispered confidentially.

Bea looked confused. "Really? Where do you suppose he was off to?"

"You didn't hear it from me," he said while polishing a set of candlesticks with a soft cloth, "but word is a talented young bloke is playing the violin out near the Magdalen Bridge."

"Interesting," she said.

someone that wouldn't involve a revolver."

She swatted at her husband's shoulder. "I'll remind you, Mr. Abbot, that I've spent the majority of my life in Hackney."

Timothy's mind raced back to when he was setting up to play. There wasn't a soul around and it was still fairly dark. The river was hidden in a slowly creeping fog.

"No one was around. It's so quiet just before the sun comes up, even the sparrows seem to be holding their breath. Funny, I did imagine…"

It seemed silly.

"What?" Abbot demanded.

He laughed nervously. "I thought I heard someone swimming."

"Did you see them?"

"No. There was a mist over the water at that hour."

His mum stood and pushed past Abbot to put the kettle on. "Only a madman would get into that freezing river in winter."

Abbot and Timothy stared at one another, thinking the exact same thought.

CHAPTER 3

Vagabonds & Earls

Billy Redgrave was completely out of his depth. Seriously. His family connections had gotten him into Oxford but his lack of concentration was almost certainly going to get him sent down. Billy's father was the Earl of Rockhold, so since he would one day fill those shoes, he'd been placed on the track for a philosophy, politics, and economics degree. Naturally, each of the three prongs in that evil trinity could trip him up, but piling them one on top of the other just felt like cruel punishment.

Timothy came into the cottage looking like a vagabond. The boys shared the guest bungalow tucked behind the gardens of Brigsley Manor, near the pool. There was plenty of room in the manse, of course, but Timothy felt odd living under the same roof with his mum and stepdad. He was eighteen and needed his personal space.

The two boys bunked together at Eton the previous year and had a long, somewhat complicated history together. There was comfort in returning home to a familiar face when you are thrust headfirst into a sea of new people.

"Redgrave!" He grabbed a banana from a bowl on the table. "I've had an interesting morning."

"Would that explain your clothing?"

Timothy glanced down at his outfit and smirked. "I almost forgot about that." He stripped off his thermal and walked into his bedroom to find more suitable attire. "I like to play music for passersby on the street once in a while, and this thrift store chic helps with my illusion."

"A man of the people," Billy teased. "So those rags are your Clark Kent look?"

He came back wearing a paisley button-down and dark Ferragamo slacks. "All of my looks are mild-mannered." Timothy poured some Absolut Elyx vodka over ice and sat down in his favorite recliner by the fire.

"Well?" Billy asked, giving Timothy a questioning stare. "Your interesting morning?"

He took a hearty gulp of the Swedish vodka. "Someone was murdered near the Magdalen Boathouse, not more than a stone's throw from where I was playing this morning."

"Do you know who was killed?"

"No."

"Did you see who did it?"

"Nope."

"Then how do you know anything happened?"

He glanced toward Billy and allowed the fear to take shape for an instant, then he returned to watching the ice melting in the tumbler. "A lot of police showed up."

"Thames Valley or Metro?" Redgrave asked.

Four police agencies merged back in the sixties to form the Thames Valley Police, which was a separate agency from the University's Department of Security Services. It was a muddle with all the factions vying for authority.

"Don't know. Probably all of them. I don't think anyone has been murdered at Oxford since the nineties."

"I heard the helicopter."

Timothy finished his drink and laid back in the recliner. "Yeah, it was a proper circus."

In minutes he'd fallen asleep.

CHAPTER 4

The Yardies

It was well past noon when he heard the familiar double knock at the door and Abbot strode into the cottage on a mission. He quickly assessed the situation.

"Ah, good, you've changed your clothes. There's no time to shave, your presence is required at the house. We have visitors."

"Who?"

The former butler picked at some non-existent lint on his sleeve. "One of our old acquaintances from Scotland Yard, I'm afraid." He noticed the open liquor bottle and slightly frowned. "Have you been drinking this morning, master Timothy?"

"Yes," he admitted, "but I've also been sleeping."

"Well, you'll need to have your wits about you. This isn't a social call."

Brigsley Manor's paneled drawing-room was where Bea had chosen to plant the coppers down. She wanted to give the appearance that the Abbots were gentry and that the authorities were imposing on their hospitality, but the visitors seemed too thick to take notice.

DCI Bridges stood near a window next to a tall fellow

somber as a crucifix. "Listen, Detective Chief, we slept together, Casey and I, last Saturday night."

Abbot shook his head and put an arm around his wife.

"Of course you did," Bridges said.

The sergeant looked confused. "So you two are nancy boys?"

Timothy rolled his eyes. "It's rather more complicated than that..."

Bridges gave Timothy his detective glare. "And where did this liaison take place? Here?"

Tim nodded. "I share the back cottage with another boy."

"So there's a third lad in the mix?" Eddings asked.

"No," Timothy answered quickly. "Jesus, Redgrave has his own room. He's completely hetero."

Eddings turned and leaned in toward his boss. "Still the victim's DNA will be all over the premises." The cops headed toward the door.

"One thing more," he asked, looking into Timothy's eyes. "Do you happen to own a scalpel?"

"Don't be daft."

Abbot cleared his throat. "Um, DCI, I own several."

"What?" Bea said, alarmed.

"They come in quite handy," Abbot shrugged.

Bridges regarded the old gentleman carefully. "We'll need to take those with us if you don't mind."

"Of course," Abbot replied, calmly leaving to retrieve the knives. Eddings followed him out while the others waited awkwardly.

"Exactly what's wrong with this tie?"

Timothy smirked. "Nothing DCI. Did you borrow it from Forrestal or did you lose a bet?"

CHAPTER 5

The New Member

O riginally she wasn't meant to be at Oxford until the beginning of the Trinity Term, which was in April, but the conductor insisted that she begin with the orchestra early.

Oxford's storied history stretched back nine hundred years; the *city of dreaming spires* was designed to invoke a sense of awe and accomplishment. To Namika's eyes, it seemed oppressive. All the cleft stone and sculpted towers were created as a monument to England, or education, or whatever else these Anglo Saxons worshiped.

Namika Ito preferred simplicity, and she adored Japan.

Yet, here she sat with her overbearing mother by her side. There was no stopping her parents when the acceptance letter arrived. A member of the Ito family would attend Oxford. It was a matter of honor so her wishes were never a part of the equation.

The conductor greeted them warmly, even attempting a slight bow as a show of respect. Julian Adler. He was a well-built man in his late forties with a dimpled chin and bulging biceps.

There's nothing sadder than an aging peacock, Namika thought, looking at the man.

It was only his fifth year at Oxford so he was still attempting to make a personal statement with the student orchestra. He appeared rather vain and fey.

A few sharp taps of his baton alerted the attention of all the young musicians. More than a hundred people suddenly fell silent. "Ladies and gentlemen, it is with great pleasure that I introduce the newest member of the Oxford Student Orchestra— Miss Namika Ito."

Her mother nearly pushed her up and out of her chair, where she joined the conductor center stage, turning to face the students and deeply bowing.

"I'm sure we would all love to hear you play if you wouldn't mind Miss Ito."

"Sorry?" she whispered, the question drifting openly. Namika was employing an old trick by pretending that she wasn't fluent in English. It helped her avoid tedious conversations and also made it appear that she was at a disadvantage in social situations. Her mother was not amused by the pretense.

"Play violin?"

"If you would be so kind."

She took up her instrument in preparation and glanced over to the string section, seeing the beautiful dark-haired boy intently watching her every move. *It must be his position that I will be usurping,* she thought.

She launched into Paganini's Caprice Number One. An incredibly fast-paced, exacting piece of music that reminded her of the speedy fluttering of hummingbirds in the cherry orchard.

She performed the Arpeggio perfectly, and received a polite amount of applause, particularly from her fellow strings. Namika wondered if she would find any true equals in this group.

A friend would be too much to hope for.

CHAPTER 7

The Back of Beyond

He called her and she answered immediately. "How do you do that?"

"What?"

"You always answer your phone on the first ring."

"All I do all day is sit and stare at my iPhone waiting for you to call," she jested.

"Funny."

Dr. Leta Kelly was the best thing to happen to Carl Bridges in a long, long time so he was desperate not to screw things up. Everyone knows dating a cop has major drawbacks.

"Listen, I'm stuck in the back of beyond with a homicide, so I'm afraid I'm going to miss our date night."

"Where are you?"

"Oxford University. A lad from Corpus was killed yesterday morning."

"That's unusual," she noted. "I don't think there's been a murder there for decades. Are you sure it was deliberate?"

"Pretty sure. His throat was slashed from ear to ear."

"Messy," she said, unconsciously touching her neck. "I guess you won't need me to find the cause of death."

"No, but I do wish you were here helping me fend off the crowd. I've got the Thames Valley Police and a gaggle of eggheads from the Uni already making me crazy."

She laughed. "Well, keep a level head, Darling. People get jumpy when there's a murderer on the prowl, especially in sleepy hamlets like Oxford."

She was completely right, Carl thought. *If I'm going to get this solved quickly I need a team that knows what they're doing.*

He shot a text to the Kid instructing him to go to the pub the victim frequented— The Rusty Bicycle. It was time for a meeting.

to get back together with me? To change what happened that morning I met my gruesome fate at Ducker?"

Timothy steepled his hands as if in prayer. *If even part of what my dream of a boyfriend is saying is true,* he thought.

"I'd do anything, whatever it takes."

"Excellent!" Jake said, jumping around the drawing-room. "Boy, this place is nice, isn't it? I'm so glad I found it. Terrible about that murder though. You were pretty close when it happened."

Timothy crossed his arms and stared. "Mm-hmm."

Jake giggled and nudged Tim with an elbow. "He was a looker, that Casey Larson. What a bod. And you slept with him, you naughty boy."

"Bloody hell," Timothy shouted. "Were you?"

"Watching from the corner of your room. Quite a performance, I must say. Vicarious thrills for the dearly departed —but you should get a move on before the corpses start to pile up."

"Are you saying there's going to be more murders at Oxford?"

"Oh yeah," Jake said, "heaps more, I expect."

CHAPTER 9

The Rusty Bicycle

He had been interviewing people all afternoon and could use a pint. Bridges walked down Magdalen Road to check out the pub, hoping that the Kid had enough time to travel the distance. Oxford made him feel old— too many teenagers.

He passed a photo of Larson around the Rusty Bicycle and everyone recognized him immediately, everyone. *This lad was the life of the party*, he thought to himself.

"Can't believe he's gone," the bartender admitted. She was wearing a torn Rusty Bicycle tank top and had two full sleeves of tattoos to compliment her shaved head.

"He was a regular?"

"All the crew lads are. They like a good time those rowers, don't they? And they're always sharking for freshers."

"Hmm, and was he *sharking* for girls or boys?"

She rolled her eyes. "From what I could see, Casey liked to mix things up."

"So, he wasn't picky?"

She flinched slightly while drawing the detective's beer. "I didn't say that. He'd only make a move on the most beautiful person in the room. Birds of a feather, you know."

Bartenders love to gossip, especially in college towns. "Did he have any enemies?"

She tugged at a thrice-pierced ear. "Probably. Sooner or

later we all do."

"Got any names?"

"No. But you want my theory?"

This is going to be good, Carl thought. *The amateur sleuth at work.* "Certainly."

"Someone probably had a crush that got out of hand. I mean, people noticed Casey."

It wasn't the worst idea. "An ex who didn't want it to end?"

Her eyes narrowed. "Or maybe a little lord or lady who was too ugly to make the grade in the first place."

Bridges took his pint and turned around to survey the pub. He spied the Kid sitting in a back booth, eating a salad. Skip Loge. Boy genius.

Carl ambled over and sat down across from him. "Kid."

"Hiya' Bridges."

Loge wore geeky black glasses and a button-down shirt that didn't fit. "What were you and Carol discussing?"

"Carol?" Bridges asked, surprised. "Is that the bartender's name?"

The Kid scoffed. "Damn Chief, don't you even ask their name before you start grilling them?"

"I usually do." The DCI downed some lager. "I guess that haircut distracted me."

Skip continued to tuck into his food.

"What the fuck are you eating?"

The boy shut his eyes as if in ecstasy while Bridges watched him eat. Skip's nose was too big for his face and his head too large for his body. God has a wicked sense of humor.

"Ah, this is the Clean and Green. Quinoa. Asparagus. Peas. Roast cauliflower. Spinach. Radish. Avocado. Basil dressing. Pumpkin and sunflower seeds."

"Don't tell me, you're a vegetarian."

"Brilliant deduction, Detective Chief."

Bridges lowered his voice. "You know why you're here, don't you?"

The Kid nodded. "I read the file, such as it is. I gather you want me to help you catch a murderer before all of Oxford wigs out."

"What are your first impressions?"

"It happened fast. No sign of a fight. It's personal though. The killer certainly knew the victim."

Carl took another swig. "You and Carol agree about that part."

The Kid wiped his mouth with a napkin. "If you're going to slit someone's throat it's easier to sneak up on them from behind, grab hold of a shoulder and slash them by drawing the blade toward yourself. More control takes less strength and is not as messy. You slash someone's throat while you're facing them and there's a good chance you're going to get wet."

"And how do you know the killer was facing Larson?"

"Come on, Chief. The angle of the cut. This killer is right-handed too, slashing the victim from left to right." He pantomimed the motion.

"Well, that narrows it down," Bridges grunted. This boy is nineteen years old, basically the same age as the victim. Every agency tried to recruit him, from MI6 to the CIA, but for reasons undisclosed, he landed in the violent crimes division of Scotland Yard. "So, why aren't you enrolled here or at Cambridge?"

"I'm American."

"That's not an answer. Harvard or Yale then, a young guy like you should be in school, not working homicides."

He stared past the DCI and adjusted his glasses. "I don't need to spend a quarter of a million dollars to get a piece of paper that tells me I'm the smartest person in the room."

Carl grinned then continued watching the clientele in the pub, mentally ticking off possible suspects. "I'm not going to argue with your logic or the wisdom in that observation. But don't you feel like maybe you're missing out? You know, in the grand college experience?"

"Open your eyes, Bridges. Freaks like me have completely different grand college experiences than guys like Casey Larson."

"I think a mind like yours would be considered somewhat attractive in an environment like this."

He pushed his salad to one side. "Places like Oxford are bizarre. Everyone who attends here is exceptional or entitled. The best and the brightest, the richest, the famous, and the most beautiful. The well-connected, the rarely gifted, in a word: privileged. It's no great shock to me that this is a breeding ground for aberrant behavior."

"Well, you're the brightest person I've ever met, and the giant hole in your hypothesis is that there hasn't been a murder here in decades," the DCI mentioned.

Skip shook his head. "Murder is only the most extreme expression, and we're just scratching at the surface. Trust me, Chief, there's a ton of weird shit going on in Oxfordshire. That's what happens when you throw 25,000 exceedingly special people into a small town and they discover they aren't the unicorns they always believed themselves to be. I'll tell you something else about this case..."

"What's that?"

"Whoever did this knew what they were doing. This wasn't their first kill, and it probably won't be their last."

CHAPTER 10

The Introverts

He sat in the back of the chapel at St. Peter's College in utter darkness, carefully watching as the rehearsal broke up. It was Friday night and two girls were giving him special attention. One of the other violinists was whispering into his ear, but he took the beautiful harpist's hand while they were chatting.

Skip emerged from the shadows and made his presence known. "Excuse me," he said, tripping over a chair. The girls were startled by his abrupt appearance, but Timothy knew he was being watched.

"What can I do for you, Detective?"

Clever boy.

This made his task much harder. "I'd like a word alone, Mr. Abbot, if you can spare the time."

"Of course," he looked toward his friends. "I'll meet you guys there. Don't wimp out, Namika."

Timothy motioned toward the padded chairs and they sat.

"How did you know I was with the police?"

He shrugged. "I thought you might be a student when I first caught you following me yesterday, but you don't quite fit in, do you? Apart from being the proper age, of course."

"I'm not trying to fit in."

Timothy smirked. "Of course you are, you're an American."

"Is that obvious too?"

"Actually, yes it is. What's your name?"

"Skip Loge."

"Skip?" he repeated, teasing.

The detective sat back watching the boy. *He's perfect for this place*, he thought. *Talented, smart, beautiful. He inherited a pile of money from a deceased boyfriend just over a year ago.*

"So what do you have against Oxford, Skip?"

"What? Nothing. What makes you say that?"

Timothy winked. "You walk around here like you're looking at animals in the zoo."

"Ah, busted. This place is just a lot to take in all at once...it's...different."

"I'd have to agree. Oxford often feels like a parody of itself. We're all meant to be humbled by its grandeur. It can be intimidating if you take it seriously, which I don't, and neither should you."

"You are also distrustful of Scotland Yard?"

Timothy fiddled with the zipper on his hoodie. "Let's just say I question authority in all its many gradations."

"DCI Bridges and you have a history."

"Yes."

"Your ex-boyfriend was murdered and now another one of your lovers is killed."

"So it would seem."

"The odds of that happening..." Skip began and trailed off into silence.

"I didn't kill Casey, in fact, I rather liked him."

Timothy's hazel-green eyes started to mist over. He was proclaiming his innocence in a nearly offhand way, but it was straightforward and even slightly raw. *He's telling the truth*, Skip thought.

"I assumed you liked him, after all, you slept with him."

"That isn't always a prerequisite."

"Hmm, between us, I know you aren't the killer."

"So why am I attracting your attention?"

He silently debated how much information to offer, but Loge knew he could use an ally on the inside. "Off the record?"

"Sure."

"I think this killer knows his trade. The method was precise, personal, and arguably militant. You don't have the requisite skill set or the experience for it. And as I recall, your weapon of choice is a firearm. I'd be more suspicious of you if we had discovered Mr. Larson riddled with bullets."

Skip was a trained observer and he was mentally placing Timothy Abbot under the microscope. *He bites his nails and he's too thin*, he concluded. Is he nervous? Unhappy? Or maybe just stressed out from school. Money isn't the problem, not anymore. He's pale. He doesn't exercise or go outside enough. He's strikingly handsome—and now he'd caught the detective gawking.

"Why are you telling me this?" Timothy asked.

"Because I believe you and the killer are acquainted with each other. You should keep your eyes open."

"I always do, and I don't think this thing is over yet. You should catch this guy before the bodies start to pile up."

"What makes you think this is the beginning of a spree?"

Timothy peered into the dark shadows of the old church. "Call it a hunch."

Despite being a suspect, Skip found himself liking Timothy. He was unguarded, open, and remarkably unpretentious for someone who resides in the land of the entitled. Maybe that's because of his humble beginnings, they certainly have that bit in common.

"Where do you think I should focus my inquiry?"

Timothy cracked his knuckles. "The Oxford Rowers. They're big, strong, and not too bright—at least not compared to lads like us. Check the records, I'd bet more than a few of them spent some time in military training. Some of these boys have been marching in formation since before puberty. It's a popular boarding school elective and it helps them avoid doing community service or anything that might actually prove useful."

CHAPTER 11

The Lamb & Flag

"I'm glad I play the harp," Madelyn said, staring hard at the new girl. "Fewer interlopers."

A gaggle of musicians was crowded into the Lamb and Flag Pub, a five-hundred-year-old watering hole favored among bookish nerds and freshers. Namika hadn't uttered a word.

"Would you like a pint?" Tim asked her, but she shook her head no.

"Come on, have a drink with us. If you're going to make any friends it's going to be among the orchestra geeks." He wandered toward the bar to buy a round.

"Don't get any ideas," Maddy muttered to Ito, who simply replied with an inscrutable gaze. She shouldn't be jealous, with her perfect skin and violet eyes, Madelyn Drepa was one of the most beautiful girls at Oxford.

The twins joined the party. Sheri and Teri, identical in almost every way. They were pencil-thin blondes hoping to be doctors. They both played the flute. "He swings both ways," Teri whispered, giggling. Miss Ito was interested in this revelation. "Tim?"

"That's the rumor," Sheri answered.

"I don't think he likes girls at all," Turner said. Doug Turner, percussionist.

"What would you know about it?" Maddy asked. Drummers, even at Oxford, are thick as bricks. Doug's a handsome devil though. He was wearing a soft cricket jumper and tight white jeans.

"Anyone who passes up the chance to bed twin flautists must have a screw loose."

The sisters simultaneously blushed. "Who said he passed?" Teri placed an arm around her twin.

Timothy returned with a whole tray of pints. "What are we talking about then?"

"Sex," Turner replied.

"Don't believe anything these dodgy musicians are on about." He took one of the mugs and held it aloft. "To our newest member, may she never play the violin as well as I do."

"Hear, hear!" The harpist shouted, touching her mug to his.

Namika smiled and took a long pull of ale while Madelyn casually held Tim's hand.

"So, what's the story with you?" Turner asked, while she just stared blankly at the group.

"Douglas," Maddy said regally, "she understands every bloody word. Our latest addition just thinks she's too grand to have a real conversation with us commoners."

Timothy and Ito exchanged a knowing glance. "Don't look at me—I'd never give you away."

"Aha!" Turner shouted.

"All right, you tossers, Miss Drepa is correct. I understand every bloody word."

They all laughed.

"I knew it," Sheri said, turning to her sister. "We both did."

"Yeah, I'm sure nothing gets past you two," Ito deadpanned.

Leigh Wallace, a cellist, came to the table with her boyfriend Austin Smith-Fordham in tow. He's the hunky, blond captain of the Rowing Club.

"Guess you guys all heard the latest," he said, downcast.

"Can we please talk about something else?" Leigh muttered under her breath. She'd grown weary of the terrible news.

"About what?"

"One of our lads, a fellow rower, was the bloke murdered by the boathouse," Turner answered bluntly. "The cops are crawling all over the colleges looking for his killer."

Austin sat down next to Turner while Leigh hugged him from behind. "The worst thing about it is that they think it might have been one of his teammates."

"What?" Doug said, stunned.

"Can you believe that?" Austin muttered a sliver of anger in his voice. "I loved Casey like a brother."

The twins nodded in agreement. "Everyone loved him," Sheri whispered. "What did the cops want with you, Timmy?"

"Oh, yeah, they thought I might have seen something," he said, releasing Maddy's hand and standing. "I was practicing out near the bridge on Tuesday morning."

"You were?" She looked surprised, her violet eyes glittering.

"Did you know Larson?"

Timothy stared at his feet.

"We've bumped into each other."

CHAPTER 12

The Heart of the Buddha

I t took him a week to secure the appointment. The doctor only saw graduate students so he had to embellish his reason for an urgent meeting, and he had to drop the name Weston into the conversation, which Tim was reluctant to do.

He'd done scant bits of research on his own, but even the broad strokes are painfully hard to grasp. To say that quantum physics is slightly out of his field of expertise would be a gross understatement. He just didn't want to sound like an imbecile when he asked about time travel.

Tim rode his bike to the address at St. Antony's College hoping the ten-minute trip would give him time to gather his thoughts. He wondered if the whole experience with Jake wasn't some sort of fever dream, but oddly enough, when he consulted the Oxford directory there was a Dr. Pe listed—in Asian Studies.

This feels like a mistake, he thought.

A dark-haired young man in a pink bowtie answered the door. "Yes?" Even one word exposed a heavy Italian accent.

"I have an appointment with Dr. Pe, I'm Timothy Abbot."

"Please," the man gestured, opening the door wide. The outer office was austere. Uncluttered. A perfectly manicured white bonsai tree sat sentinel on a low table.

The Italian and Timothy watched one another. He sensed a slight animosity but couldn't imagine why. He usually made a pretty good first impression.

The inner door swung open and he was greeted by a smiling little man in a tailored silk suit. His round black glasses accentuated his almond-shaped eyes.

"Timothy!" he cried as if he were a long-lost relation. "Come in, come in."

The doctor's large office was a cabinet of curiosities. Bookcases lined the walls overflowing with dusty manuscripts and tomes. There were maps and tapestries, ceramic bowls, and carved wooden figurines scattered in a haphazard way everywhere you looked. A hat rack sat in one corner filled with dark bowlers and straw skimmers. Near his desk, a gold cage held two lovebirds.

He offered Timothy a seat and then clapped his hands. "Fausto," he chirped. "Bring tea! We mustn't let our guest think us rude."

"Sir, that's kind of you, but it isn't necessary."

"Nonsense," Pe said with a flourish. "You silly Englishmen drink tea every day yet you've never actually tasted it in your lives."

"I'm sorry?"

The Italian returned with a hand-painted porcelain tea service, setting it down in the center of the desk. "Thank you, Fausto. I will handle it from here." Tim watched as Pe carefully prepared the brew, and an odd sensation of deja vu tingled the back of his neck. Dr. Pe was so familiar to him. "This is Da Hong Pao from Wuyishan province. It has the heart of the Buddha."

He bowed his head as he handed the steaming cup to his young guest. Tim inhaled the pungent aroma and took a delicate sip. It was delicious.

"I thought you were Japanese, Dr. Pe."

"And so I am."

"But you drink tea from China?"

He tittered. "I'm not being unfaithful to my culture. I

drink wine from France, and my prosciutto is always from Italy. Great tea is great tea and the Chinese have been perfecting this art form for fifteen hundred years."

He held the teacup in both hands, allowing the rising steam to fog his glasses. "Do you speak Japanese?"

"No, sorry."

"Mandarine, then?"

"I'm afraid not."

He frowned. "Don't tell me you only speak English."

"Well, my French isn't terrible..."

A white lie. Timothy was lost when it came to foreign languages.

Pe shook his head. "I suppose that's a start. You don't look like my typical Asian Studies student."

"Do they have a typical look?" Tim asked, his curiosity piqued.

"Yes, usually Asian." They chuckled together. "We are all searching for lost connections to our past."

Perhaps the good doctor had already guessed the true intention of this visit. "Actually, I'm a musician."

"Musician!" he gasped. "What on earth do you want with me? What is this appointment about?"

Tim gently placed his cup down. "I wonder if you might speak to me regarding your work with infinitely diverging timelines and the multiverse."

Pe's expression betrayed him just for an instant and then he turned his back and regarded his small birds. He broke off a portion of an almond cookie and fed it to them.

"Did you get lost on your way to the Beecroft Building, young man? Quantum Mechanics isn't my field."

Pe was avoiding any further eye contact.

"Isn't it, though? Even as a hobby?"

He finally met the boy's gaze. "How did you get my name?"

Timothy stood and began exploring the cluttered bookshelves searching for clues. "You wouldn't believe me if I told you."

"Hmm, you'd be amazed at what I can believe."

Tim found what he was looking for among the shelves. *The Nature of Space and Time* by Stephen Hawking and Roger Penrose. He held it up. "Here's an interesting book for a professor of Asian Studies."

Pe shrugged. "Philosophy and science often stand close together, like silent chessmen, only the color of the squares is different."

"I have no idea what that means, but I do need your help," he admitted.

"To do what, Mr. Abbot?"

"To travel back in time and prevent the murder of my boyfriend."

"Ha!" he shrieked. "Is that all?"

Tim could feel his brief meeting coming to an end. "I'm begging you, Doctor. He was only seventeen. Jake had his whole life ahead of him. Our whole life together. We will pay any price."

They sat silently together for a long time, staring at the lovebirds.

"What you are asking is both dangerous and quite unlikely to succeed. You may end up being reunited with your partner in the grave."

"I'm willing to take that risk."

"Well, your timing is fortuitous. In two days Dr. Matthias Krage from Munich will be giving a lecture on space-time. March eleventh at seven in ther evening. He won the Nobel Prize for physics. I would advise you to attend."

CHAPTER 13

The Favor

Namika didn't truly know what led her to his house. Fear and desperation, she suspected. He will think I'm a twit and perhaps a fraud, she thought.

She asked one of the twins for his address. High Street. Before she could convince herself to walk away she was knocking on the red door of the Abbot's beautiful mansion. But no one answered.

It was a faulty plan. Misguided to appear at his doorstep unannounced. Frankly, she felt relieved. What was she thinking?

"Are you looking for Timmy?"

Namika turned on her heel and saw the curious, dark-haired boy in sweatpants smiling up at her.

"Yes," she admitted. "We are colleagues—musicians in the orchestra. I was told he lives here."

"Well, you've come to the right place. We live in the cottage in the back. I'm Billy."

She bowed but he jumped up next to her and kissed her hand like a prince in a fairytale. Caucasians are so brazen. "Namika Ito," she said, reclaiming her hand. "I haven't told him I'd be visiting. It's rude of me to come without an invitation…"

"Don't be absurd. Timmy needs more unexpected visitors in his life. Follow me."

They proceeded through a gate to the backyard where a beautiful garden was planted next to the swimming pool. There to one side sits a lovely brick cottage covered in carefully manicured vines.

It must be magnificent in spring, she imagined.

"Timmy," Billy called as they entered the flat. "I have a surprise for you!"

"You sound just like Jake," Tim said walking into the room wrapped in a towel.

"Namika!" he shouted. She quickly lowered her gaze. "Redgrave, why didn't you tell me I had company?"

Billy laughed. "Well, she's the surprise then, isn't she?"

Tim ran to the back room. A moment later he returned wearing skinny jeans and a black turtleneck but the blush was still on his cheeks.

"I'm sorry to disturb you," she offered, bowing her head reverently.

He smiled warmly. "You aren't disturbing anyone. Your visit is a pleasant treat. May I offer you something? A glass of Barolo?"

He was already reaching for the crystal decanter.

"If you are having some, that would be nice."

Timothy poured two stemless glasses and handed her one. They look into each other's eyes and he reaches out gently touching her glass with his. "To absent friends."

She took a sip of the dark wine. It tasted like cherries and chocolate. Billy yelled from the other room, "You should ask her to come tonight."

Tim looked at his guest and then turned toward the kitchen. "Mind your own business, Redgrave."

"You have plans for this evening?"

"Yes, and Billy's right, you should come along. It's a pub in town that has live music on Friday and Saturday nights. Jazz and blues. You would enjoy it."

"It sounds fun."

He watched her body language and she seemed jittery. He was trying to work out the purpose of her visit, but came up rather short. "So, Miss Ito, what brings you to my humble abode?"

Namika realized, sitting beside him, that her request was preposterous. "A favor, but now that I'm here I find myself too embarrassed to ask."

"In that case, you must drink more wine. *In Vito Veritas* — from wine, truth."

She beamed. He was so charming and also beautiful. "It's about tomorrow, our competition."

"Ah, I should have known. You are worried that I will beat you."

She looked directly into his hazel eyes. "Yes, you are a better musician."

"Ha!" he cried. "Tell that to Julian. He believes the gods have sent you directly to us from the east. I appreciate the compliment though. So, what's the favor?"

Namika worried that he would think less of her, but her fear of dishonor is far greater. "I'm begging you to let me win."

"What?" he asked, disbelieving. Timothy was caught off guard. "You can't be serious."

"If I lose my family will be disgraced. They expect me to be named soloist."

He slowly swirled the wine, examining the legs as they trickled down the Riedel glass. "What about you? Could you live with yourself knowing that I didn't try my best? What sort of a victory is that?"

She didn't blame him. It was the Western way of thinking. "It isn't about me."

He rose and poured the last of the wine into their glasses. "The hell it isn't! I rather enjoy being the soloist. Why should I pass that privilege to you? You don't even like the violin."

My God, she thought. *How can he possibly know that?*

"What?" Namika replied, incredulous. "The violin is my entire life."

Tim openly mocked her. "Please don't lie if you want me to be a co-conspirator. Your playing is wonderful, but it is an imitation of others. A skillful impression you learned to do expertly. A dear friend of mine found your efforts kind of robotic. Frankly, he thought it was soulless, believing your passion lies elsewhere."

Namika felt the tears coming. "Your friend is perceptive."

He touched her hand. "Why then is this important to you? This favor?"

"It's my mother," she whispered. Namika had nothing more to lose, he was already aware of her deception. "She is a dragon."

"Is she?"

"When I was fourteen years old I received a B in Organic Chemistry."

He blinked his eyes. "So?"

"My mother was so ashamed of my grade she lit her arm on fire with lighter fluid."

Tim looked horrified. "That's completely insane."

The pressure within powerful Japanese families was a difficult thing to explain to an Englishman. A vast cultural divide separated them.

"I'm begging you. I will be in your debt. And you and I will always know the truth. Is that not enough?"

After a long pause, he smiled at her. "Miss Ito, I'm inclined to grant your request, but I have a few conditions. First, tell me your true passion, if not music?"

It was Namika's turn to blush. "Sushi," she whispered. "I dreamt of being a great chef."

"Then why didn't you…"

She lifted a hand. "My mother thought it was menial."

Tim groaned, starting to get the picture.

"My second condition is that you be my date tonight. It's time you experienced some heartfelt music and had some fun."

Namika tilted her head, letting her long dark hair fall loosely on her shoulder. She would have gladly agreed to be his escort under any circumstances. "What is the name of this pub?"

CHAPTER 14

The Mad Hatter

Places often possess a vibe and in a town as serious as Oxfordshire a pub like the Mad Hatter was an oasis of light-hearted mirth. The wooden floors creaked with age and the chairs scraped when the patrons moved about the rooms. True musicians might comment that the acoustics weren't ideal, but no one had ever complained.

The drinks were often exotic and rather silly concoctions served in colorful fluted glasses. The long oak bar was always well lit with an assortment of Christmas lights and other festive decorations.

Timothy took Namika's arm as they entered. Billy and several other friends were already crowded around a table near the front. It was another busy Friday night.

Madelyn waved to him from the far back corner. She was entangled with a dread-locked fresher who was rather over his head with the amorous harpist. Drinks were brought to the table and more than a few winsome lads clapped Timothy on the back.

This must be one of his regular haunts, Namika thought.

"Do you prefer listening to jazz or blues?" he asked confidentially.

"If the vocals are good, I'd have to say blues."

He nodded and leaned back in his chair. "Good to know."

Although there were loads of fun clubs in Tokyo, she

was rarely allowed out with her friends. Live music for her had always been in stuffy concert halls. She glanced at her watch.

"When will the music start?"

Timothy took a final gulp of his drink, mustering his courage and taming the butterflies. "Any minute, I think." He stood. "Excuse me, Miss Ito."

Billy leaned toward her. "You're in for a treat tonight."

She whispered back politely, "Why is that?"

The lights in the main room began to dim. "Because he hasn't felt like playing for weeks."

She furrowed her brow and turned toward the stage, where Tim was holding a Fender Stratocaster electric guitar. An older black gentleman sat at the piano, and the boy she met days earlier, Doug Turner, was behind the drum set.

The spotlights hit him just as he was counting down and the trio launched into *Ain't Nobody's Business* with Timothy singing lead and, genuinely, wailing on the guitar. He looked right at her and winked. Namika was spellbound.

A half-hour later they were finishing up with a rowdy version of Muddy Waters, *Hoochie Coochie Man*. The crowd of students and other locals responded with sincere applause. Timothy seemed embarrassed by the adulation as he hugged his bandmates, grabbing a towel and making a speedy exit from the stage.

Moments later he was back at the table, wiping sweat from his neck and chugging a pint. People reached out to touch him, shake his hand, and bathe in the glow of his talent.

"Well?" he asked her.

She looked stricken. "Why didn't you tell me?"

He shrugged. "What? That I'm a pub musician in a jazz and blues band? Big deal."

"Great set," he heard from the owner standing behind the bar. Tim lifted his stein in response.

Turner joined them at the table. "We should go on tour, mate," he said, grabbing Tim's shoulder.

"Maybe you forgot we're both in uni, and Lincoln over

there is seventy-two." The piano player had settled at the bar and was chatting up a waitress.

"You're a fucking genius," Namika whispered sharply to her date. "I feel like an idiot."

"If it's got strings I can play it. That's my gift."

"And the singing? You sounded like Stevie Ray Vaughan."

"Thanks! He's my idol. I still watch his videos on YouTube."

Timothy felt a tap on his shoulder and turned to see Maddy swaying slightly on the floorboards. She was drunk. "Hey!" he said. "I saw you there in the back, but you looked preoccupied."

She placed her hands around his neck. "You were fantastic tonight."

"Ah, you're biased. Who's the new bloke?"

Madelyn waved her hand in the air like she was swatting away a gnat. "Nobody." She giggled and then nearly fell.

"Steady on," Timothy said, catching her by the waist.

She looked at Billy but couldn't quite place him. "You're not in the orchestra, are you?"

"No," he said, shaking her outstretched hand. "Timmy and I are flatmates."

"Lord Redgrave is one of my oldest and dearest friends," Timothy bragged. "I'd be lost without him."

"How charming." Madelyn quickly pulled Timothy aside and kissed him deeply in front of everyone. "I'll see you at practice."

Namika began putting on her coat. "I hope I'm not stepping on any toes by being here with you."

Timothy chuckled lightly. "Don't be ridiculous. Maddy and I are just good mates, and I think she's had a bit to drink tonight."

"I'm your mate and you don't kiss me like that," Billy jested.

"Well come here Redgrave and I'll give you some sugar,"

Tim said, grabbing his shirt.

"Get away! All you musicians are the same." Billy muttered, wandering into the dense crowd.

"Why do you even bother with the violin?" Namika asked when she had regained his attention.

Tim frowned. "Are you kidding? Because I love it, not to mention it's the violin, not anything else, that's managed to get me scholarships to all the posh schools I attended. I'd be washing dishes if it weren't for Mozart and the blue-haired ladies who support orchestras."

Namika inched closer, feeling the heat radiating off his damp shirt, and then she reached over and kissed him tenderly on the mouth. "Thank you," she said sincerely.

"For?"

"Opening my eyes."

Their knees were pressed against each other. "I knew you'd get it. It isn't the competition that's important, only the music. I'm going to let you have the solo spot, but you have to promise me you'll play from your heart. Find the passion. Anything less is a waste of our time."

"I will," she promised. "I wish this night would last forever."

Timothy softly traced his finger up and down her arm. "Would you like to come home with me?"

CHAPTER 15

All About Time

"Why am I going to this?" Billy asked.

Timothy watched him adjusting his necktie and waistcoat in the mirror. "Because I sat through an entire lecture on feminist economics with you when Barbara Bergmann came to speak."

"Yes, that was big of you. But this wanker we're going to see is a physicist, isn't he?"

"Exactly."

"And correct me if I'm wrong," Billy continued, "but neither one of us is studying physics at Oxford."

"Quite right."

He allowed his flatmate to straighten his tie. "So why are we going?"

Timothy grinned roguishly. "To pick up women, of course."

❖ ❖ ❖

A Nobel laureate like Dr. Matthias Krage would merit a fairly large lecture hall, but Timothy was surprised to find him booked into the Sheldonian Theater which can seat 750 people. Of course, the orchestra spent plenty of time there so it felt like a second home to the violinist. They took seats right near the front.

The physicist did manage to draw a respectable crowd with the theater more than half full. Dr. Pe walked past, giving Timothy the slightest acknowledgement as he removed his skimmer. It was a pretty geeky crowd. Tweed coats and thick glasses, open laptops, and unfortunate haircuts.

The man who took to the podium was the opposite of all the misguided fashion of Oxford. He was tall, refined and clean-shaven, with just the right amount of strategically-timed stubble on his jaw. The suit he wore was made of dark green silk and Italian design. Pretty daring for a scientist. His salt and pepper hair was swept back and had enough product in it to reflect the light. He also wore stylish, modern glasses.

"I know why you've come here tonight," he announced with a faint German accent. He seemed to be talking directly to Timothy. "You want to know if time travel is possible..." He paused dramatically. "Of course it is! I'd be willing to wager that a traveler sits among us right now in this lovely, old theater."

The crowd murmured nervously as Dr. Krage waited patiently for complete silence. "A group this large, and with our topic of conversation. Space-time, entanglement, mirror universes, parity transformations, and the grand mystery of time travel. It's only natural that a tourist from the future would be here to see if I get it all right. Wherever you are," he gestured broadly, scanning the room. "Welcome back."

He knows, Timothy thought. He could feel it deep in his bones. *He knows how to do it and he's probably done it himself. There's nothing theoretical about this lecture.*

Krage pressed a remote and an image was projected onto a large screen. The famous Dali painting with the melting clocks.

"Who can tell me the name of this artwork?"

Dozens of hands shot up. He called upon a gray-haired woman who reminded Timothy of an old librarian friend he had at White Oak. "It's titled, *The Persistence of Memory* by Salvador Dali."

"Exactly right. Melting clocks, in a bizarre outdoor land-scape. *La persistencia de la memoria*, which Dali painted in 1931. Every physicist worth his salt knows about the relation-ship between space and time. Relativity. Dear Dr. Einstein gave us that, but the missing ingredient in his theory of time travel is, as Dali is hinting at in his painting, memory."

Billy nudged Tim's arm. "This guy is good."

Krage motioned to the crowd. "With my heritage, I'm often asked if it is possible to travel back and murder Hitler in his crib. It can't be done, obviously, or it would have already been accomplished. Adolf Hitler was born on April 20, 1889. No one is still alive who can remember Austria during that period. No one with first-hand knowledge and memory, which is necessary for the trip. To travel to the past your memory must be vivid and specific. Hitler's legacy is safe today because everyone who might have changed it is already dead."

The doctor scanned the room to see if anyone had caught his half-truth. He knew you could travel to Berlin circa 1940 but that lecture couldn't be given.

A dark-haired girl in a lumpy sweater raised her hand. She had a curdled expression on her face like cream left out overnight. An obvious skeptic. Dr. Krage immediately acknow-ledged her. "Yes, Miss...?"

"Lutgert," she replied.

"You have a question so soon, Miss Lutgert?" He pro-nounced her name in a distinctly Germanic style.

"I do, sir. I think you may be having a laugh with us. Let's say I was able to travel back in time where I have ex-tremely vivid memories of my grandparents..."

"Ah, yes," Krage motioned to the rafters. "Another pet theory. Friends, I give you the Grandfather Paradox. In which, Miss Lutgert travels back and kills her grandfather, for reasons unfathomable to us all. In any case, with dear old grandpapa dead one of her parents would not be born, and so, Miss Lutgert would never have the pleasure of attending my lecture, and yet here she sits."

The crowd was amused, but the question remained. "First I must explain that unlike in novels or films, you cannot physically travel through time, but your consciousness can. The Hebrews had a word for the soul— *Neshama*, it is our divine spark, an energy that is uniquely our own. It is that energy that can if directed properly, enter a kind of temporal wormhole. An Einstein-Rosen Bridge, and for a brief interval, visit the past."

Another hand, this time a boy with his arm in a cast. "Yes, mister?"

"Morrow, sir. So it actually would be possible to kill your grandparents or even your parents?"

The physicist moaned. "Sadly, yes. Your present consciousness can inhabit your past body, and with knowledge of current events make changes, even drastic ones like you are imagining.

However, while Mr. Morrow is plotting the perfect murder via time travel, we must remember Everett's many-worlds interpretation. Imagine holding a handful of sand with thousands of individual grains, each one a universe of its own, similar in most ways to this one but with slight variations. Mirror universes. Your *Neshama* leaves this grain and travels into another. In that time and place, you kill your grandfather. You may, or may not, still exist in this universe when your spirit is pulled back to the present. There are variables.

Physicists such as Novikov and Deutsch have determined self-consistency principles. The multiverse can and does interact between planes, an observation I have termed the ripple effect, or *Time Harmonics*. Akin to dropping a stone in a still lake.

Yet, history, I have found, has a way of healing itself naturally. Destiny can and will find a way to remain intact. Events that affect thousands of people, say Vietnam or the moon landing, would take a monumental effort to change over many timelines.

And some have theorized that there are guardians who protect the past from over-meddling." He looked directly at Timothy at this juncture.

"Those rare beings are known as Time Menders, guardians of our most precious history and memories. The cunning folk who keep the big trains running. So for those of you enamored with the concept of the Butterfly Effect, I regret to inform you that it is utter nonsense. Only our tremendous egos would imagine that the slightest change we make in our tiny lives will have profound ramifications over the entire timeline of a universe and rewrite the pivotal events of history. That hypothesis is drivel."

His eyes washed over Timothy again and the boy had déjà vu so strongly that all of his senses seem to overload. It was a glint of true recognition as if they were lifelong friends. Dr. Krage had certainly guessed why Timothy was in attendance, or perhaps someone had mentioned him.

"And while we are debunking theories that hold no water, here's another: since your spirit is doing the traveling, not your physical body, it is impossible to meet yourself in the past and create some sort of temporal paradox. Your spirit is meeting your past physical body in a separate reality and inhabiting it for a short time."

Miss Lutgert raised her hand yet again. Dr. Krage was bemused by her persistence. "Yes?"

She crossed her arms defiantly over her nondescript chest. "You sound as if you've done what you've theorized here tonight."

"Do I?"

"And what may I ask happens to your present-day body while your spirit is traveling to another universe?"

"Excellent question. You sleep. This is why you can only travel for a matter of hours, not days."

"And what happens to your spirit in the past while the present one is crowding in?"

"Another practical question. Theoretically, your mind cannot hold two distinct *Neshama* simultaneously. You would go mad. So, that time, those hours spent traveling, would be missing when you returned to the present. A memory gap. Only a true Time Mender could hold more than one reality. If you remember cassette tapes as I do, you can tape over past songs with new ones, but in doing so you overwrite the originals. They are no more. And further, constant overwriting weakens the tape. Eventually, it will break."

It's confusing, Tim thought, but certainly promising. He raised his hand. Dr. Krage stood less than twelve feet away.

"Yes, Mr?"

"Abbot, sir. I'm wondering about the method. How exactly is your spirit unbound from your body, here in our universe?"

Krage looked directly at the boy and tilted his head slightly to one side. "There are many ways to dislodge our consciousness. In 1965 a man named Paul Twitchell founded a religion called *Eckankar*. One of the basic tenets is that the soul, the true self, can separate from the body and travel freely to other planes of existence. Many natural substances in the world can facilitate jolting our spirits from our bodies.

Of course, finding your way to a temporal wormhole or bridge to another universe and timeline would need a power source for propulsion, and a strong and accurate memory to act as a map. A beacon. And no one has yet published, or been able to prove, that such a bridge can be created," he lied.

He smiled directly at Timothy in a way that made it clear that he knew exactly how to manufacture that space-time bridge.

"Now I'll ask you a question, Mr. Abbot. Is traveling into the future possible?"

Timothy stood again and with an air of confidence replied, "Based on what you've told us tonight, traveling to the future would be impossible."

"And why is that?"

"Because no one has any memory of tomorrow."

Matthias Krage applauded. "Excellent. Yes, it all comes down to memory, that is the key. We must also remember that there is no single timekeeper for the universe. When something is occurring depends on your precise location relative to what you are observing. This is known as your frame of reference. You are a budding theoretical physicist, Mr. Abbot?"

"No, sir. I'm a musician."

That got a huge laugh from the assembly of nerds.

"Ignore that," Krage said quietly. "Music and mathematics are the only universal languages, forever entangled with one another. Music is, in fact, the physical manifestation of mathematics. They are twins of a sort. And music, as well as scent, can evoke powerful and lasting memories. A song can bring you to a specific moment in your life, as I'm sure we all would agree.

Our memory is primarily chemical, while our brain function is electrical. We, humans, are complex and miraculous machines."

At that moment Timothy noticed him shuffling in the back row, near an exit. Detective Skip Loge. *Was he tracking his movements, or perhaps just interested in the lecture?* Timothy waved just so the detective knew he had been detected.

"And isn't it true that we have all been time travelers in our lives?" Dr. Krage continued. "When we revisit our memories we journey to the past, and often this is accomplished in our deep sleep, our dream state, where theta waves dominate our brains. Perhaps someone down in one of the quantum labs of the Beecroft Building will invent a device that will have the ability to direct and focus that brain energy across the fabric of space-time."

He smiled kindly at Timothy. "We physicists, as well as some musicians, are in the business of making dreams come true. The universe has a plan, whether we can perceive it or not."

As they left the theater Billy draped his arm around

Tim's shoulder. "I have to admit I enjoyed that—the parts I understood, at least."

"I'm glad," Tim said. "I did too. I noticed that detective in the back row though. I think he might still be following me."

Redgrave inspected the crowd on the street. "That's a tad creepy. The break starts at the end of the week. You and your parents should think about coming to Scotland with my family. They'd love to see you again."

"You're thoughtful. I'll let them know."

The boys walked briskly down the cobbles of Oxford past the Radcliffe Camera. "It will be cold there, but at least it's far away from all this nonsense."

CHAPTER 16

Winners & Losers

Namika picked music that she believed Maestro Adler would appreciate. Brahms Violin Concerto in D Major, Op. 77. Interestingly, it was a piece the composer dedicated to his friend, another violinist, Joseph Joachim.

"Miss Ito, if you please," the conductor said, motioning toward center stage.

"Break a leg," Tim whispered.

As Namika played she thought of her handsome freckle-faced friend. She visualized the Mad Hatter and recalled his expression as he performed the blues, the sheer joy of making music. Then she remembered the brush of his cheek and the softness of his hands on her skin. He brought a gentle passion to the bedroom. An intensity that she attempted to bring with honesty and feeling into her playing. Closing her eyes, she truly felt Brahms' emotion, rather than simply playing the required notes.

When she concluded the concerto she heard polite applause from the musicians, but Timothy whistled loudly.

"Well done, Miss Ito," Adler said, turning wickedly toward the string section. "I'm afraid you have your work cut out for you this time, Mr. Abbot."

He stood and met the conductor's smug gaze. "Very true, Maestro. I believe I will pass the baton to Miss Ito. I hereby withdraw my name from the competition."

"What?" Adler said, disbelieving.

"It's as you said, Julian. That was a masterful perform-ance. I certainly don't have anything in my catalog that is com-parable. I'd only be embarrassing myself."

Timothy grinned and saw that the conductor was quite flustered. Julian's tiny power play had been thwarted by unex-pected generosity.

"You mean to say that you aren't even going to try to maintain your position?"

Timothy adjusted the strings on his gorgeous violin and shrugged. "It's a *fait accompli,* and change is often good. None of us know how long we will sit upon our lofty perches before someone comes along and knocks us off, right? Why a new conductor might even show up tomorrow and challenge you to a baton waving contest."

The orchestra quietly chuckled, but Julien glared at Timothy, the muscles tensed in his tight black tee. "What have you heard? What are you hinting at?"

"Nothing at all, Maestro. I'm happy for Namika, she de-serves this honor."

CHAPTER 17

The Ides of March

D r. Pe lived in a stately vicarage in Stow-on-the-Wold just outside Oxfordshire. He ushered Timothy in with great fanfare.

"So, you're quite determined, I see."

Timothy nodded bravely.

The entire house could be a first-rate museum of antiquities from the far east. Pottery and bronze pieces, full suits of odd armor, what looks like decorations from a tomb and every wall covered with gorgeous tapestries, and ancient artwork. Pe seemed to have a particular fondness for vintage photographs of scantily clad men.

He led Timothy back past a sitting room and through a cherrywood library filled with leather-bound books and cases containing other strange artifacts.

"You would never guess from looking at the outside of your home that it was like this on the inside."

"Hmm," Pe said, adjusting his thick round glasses. "The same might be said for each of us." He giggled as Timothy watched him take a marble mortar and pestle and begin to grind up various mushrooms, vines, and leaves. "Hand me that wine," he commanded. He then added a few splashes to the concoction.

"Is this safe?" Tim asked, but of course, he knew it

couldn't possibly be.

"Certainly not," Pe said sharply. "More than half of these ingredients are poison to a greater or lesser degree. But shamans have been using this in Bolivian caves for a thousand years."

Timothy didn't find that encouraging. The doctor continued to hum as he labored with the secret recipe. "Either way it's going to knock your spirit loose from your body, you can be assured of that."

"What if it doesn't work? I mean, what if I just pass out, or vomit, or hallucinate?"

The doctor shrugged his shoulders.

"Would you call an ambulance if I needed one?"

Pe looked closely at the young man before him and in doing so Timothy glimpsed the vast wisdom in the old man's dark eyes. "No, if you die I bury you out in the garden. My larch tree needs fertilizer." He giggled again. "You talk too much."

"Sorry. I jabber when I'm nervous."

"You want to see this dead boy again or no?"

"Yes, yes," Tim pleaded. In fact, he was fairly certain Jake's ghost was eavesdropping.

"In each life, we travel with the same tribe. A troupe of people that we recognize. Soul-mates, and partners. Sometimes they are our mother or father, other times friend or lover. Our hearts know them on sight."

Timothy nodded silently, sensing the profound truth.

"You'll be asleep for eight hours, maybe more because you are a scrawny chicken. When you wake up your spirit will be pulled back from whatever reality you visited. You will grow from this experience. Come, come."

They ventured toward the back of the house and into a sea-green tiled bathroom. A massive copper tub sat near the window looking out on the garden. Pe turns on the spigot and then begins dropping lavender clippings and rose petals into the steamy bath.

"So preventing Jake's death in the alternate reality will

save him in this one?"

Pe shrugged dramatically again. "Maybe yes, maybe no. The threads are certainly connected, they intersect as they weave through time and space. But who truly knows? Fate, destiny, life, death, the spirit world, and the physical plane. The universe has its reasons for the way life plays out. Entanglements, Mr. Abbot. Some might say your friend's life was taken from him before his true lifetime could manifest, so that bodes well for your quest. What you're doing today might be thought of as a correction, rather than an outright change."

"A mend," Timothy whispered.

Pe blinked at the boy. "Krage's ripple effect might yet save your friend." He trailed off in his explanation, never completing his thought, like footsteps dissolving along the seashore. Instead, the doctor began to hum while lighting candles and incense, then he unfolded a small tatami mat. "Remove all your clothes."

Timothy did as he was told.

If this was just an elaborate scheme to drug me and get me naked then you have to give the old boy credit for originality, Tim thought. He placed his belongings on a lacquered chair to one side.

"Sit on the mat and meditate. You must visualize the day. Feel it, hear it, smell it. Memory connects to your nose," Pe instructed.

Tim inhaled deeply.

"It must be important and vivid in your mind, see the moment in your deepest private history or God knows where you'll wind up, or when."

That might sound ominous but it was the easiest part of the process because each moment of that day was embedded in Timothy's psyche. His chosen destination was crystal clear.

The doctor left him sitting naked and cross-legged in the bathroom for half an hour.

"Time, time, time," Pe said finally, smiling at the irony. Tim watched him adding salt to the bathwater and testing the temperature. "Get in."

The water was incredibly soothing. Pe has added so much salt that Tim was floating in the deep copper tub. He began to relax, inhaling the pleasant smell of flowers and smoky incense.

Pe unhinged a black metal case and removed a smooth cylinder not much larger than a thermos. He began shaking it.

"What the hell is that?"

The doctor quirked his eyebrows. "The Device, of course. It will open the bridge. Don't worry, your spirit will find it easy enough."

Tim could see the thing vibrating in Pe's hand and it was also making a low humming noise. It didn't appear to have buttons or lights, or even seams.

"What's its power source? Batteries?"

"Batteries? Ha! Silly boy. Uranium, but only a small amount."

"Uranium!" Tim shouted.

"Relax, it can't escape. Only dangerous if you breathe it in or eat it. Perfectly safe, see."

He handed it to Timothy, who carefully examined it, turning it over in his hands. Whatever this machine was, it had been sealed up completely in a shiny steel casing. Tim felt it pulsing against his hand, and also heating up.

Pe took the device back and unceremoniously dropped it into the tub where tiny vibrations began to disturb the surface of the water. Timothy felt the slightest jolt of electricity. *Bloody hell.*

Pe then handed him a wooden bowl filled with the poisonous potion which looked as harmless as blackberry jam. "Eat all of this quickly," he commanded.

Tim shoved a heaping spoonful into his mouth expecting the taste to be terrible, but he found it wasn't half bad.

Earthy, and slightly nutty. The stuff would've been even better on toast.

Just as he took the last bite it started to kick in and the spinning began. Twirling. Like being on a crazy ride at Alton Towers. Every sound was magnified a hundredfold. The dripping of the tap sounded like thunder, and then the colors of the room swirled and began to melt together. The green tile of the bathroom turned pink and then suddenly orange, it pulsed with shades of blue and then morphed into bright magenta. Timothy didn't know how long he watched the prism of light dancing on the walls— An hour? A day? Time stood still and he floated in an ocean of light. He heard the distant but familiar ticking of a clock.

Then suddenly the world grew dark and he started to fall. Plunging and sinking through cold, bitter blackness. He heard a hissing, like air spilling out of a punctured tire, then he could see the stars. A lattice of twinkling lights, distant suns, and rotating galaxies. He had a brief, startling glimpse of infinity. A universe of possibilities.

He opened his mouth to shout but no sound came out. He was endlessly falling, end over end through the vastness of space. Tim shut his eyes tight, begging for stillness and willing the motion to stop.

And just like that, it did.

Tim was naked in bed, listening to familiar breathing. He rolled over and Jacob was there. Alive.

He slowly reached out to touch his blond hair, and Jake turned to face him. "Hey," he whispered, closing his eyes and smiling.

Tim fell into his arms. He was in their room at Brigsley Cottage and they were seventeen-years-old and together again. He hugged him with all his might. "I'm mad for you. You know that, right?"

Jake laughed. "You'd better be. I don't give all my boy-friends fancy violins for Christmas."

"What time is it?"

"Seven-fifteen. I expect Abbot to bring our cappuccinos at any moment."

This meant Timothy had until three o'clock to alter the timeline and change Jake's fate.

They heard two quick raps on the door and Abbot entered wearing a red and black velvet robe. He held a tray with two cappuccinos.

"Quite stylish, sir," Jake said.

He cleared his throat. "Well, it's rather much for my taste..."

"I wouldn't let her hear you say anything against it."

"Sound advice, master Timothy. It isn't a battle worth fighting." He handed each boy a cup and saucer.

"It isn't a battle he'd win," Tim whispered to Jake, and they laughed.

"I can hear every word," Abbot said, which made them giggle all the more. "And of course, you're correct."

Tim finished his coffee quickly. *Just the ticket*, he thought, giving him a jolt of caffeine after Dr. Pe's poisonous brew.

"This is delicious," he remarked.

"Thank you."

"But tell me why we can never have a cappuccino after dinner?"

Jake rolled his eyes. "Here we go. Why must you wind him up this early?"

Abbot tugged on the lapels of his outlandish robe. "Because we are not barbarians, and any self-respecting Italian would chase us out of their country if we attempted such an offense. Has your mother taught you nothing?"

Tim shrugged. "I guess we're a bit spotty on Italian beverage protocol."

"Thank goodness I'm here to fill in the gaps," the gentleman said.

"Truly. Thank God for you, Mr. Abbot."

CHAPTER 18

Boxing Day Redux

It's Boxing Day and Jacob had a dozen tasks ahead of him. He'd purchased a lovely silver flask for Coach Lir. It was a duplicate of his own. He also had the coach's initials engraved on it and then filled it with a rare Dalmore 62 Single Highland Malt Scotch which was sure to knock his socks off.

Abbot had been arranging papers all morning on the dining room table. Timothy was becoming a vice-president of the JP Weston Corporation, which might seem a rather brash move on Jake's part, but the vision he had still haunts him. If he was not long for this world then he wanted to know that he had taken care of Bea and Timothy. It's strange because as Tim signed all the contracts he looked rather unnerved.

"Are you a lawyer then as well as a butler?" Bea kidded. These two old souls had gotten as thick as thieves. No one would be surprised if they decided to get married. Love is ageless.

"I know my way around contracts and bank statements, Mrs. Ashlock."

Jake started to bag all the presents he'd be bringing up to the Aquatic Centre and he spied Timmy staring at him like an expectant puppy. "Do you want to come to London?"

"I thought you'd never ask. I'd love to ride along!"

"You don't want to stay here and play with your new toy?"

He shook his head. "Plenty of time for that later."

"Hmm, well, bring it along then. I'm sure the coach would love to hear you perform."

Abbot packed all the papers into his briefcase. "I'll electronically send copies of the contracts to the bank immediately."

"Brilliant, and what are your plans for today?"

He folded his apron and adjusted his waistcoat. "Mrs. Ashlock and I would like to see the Oxford property. Assess what needs to be done. Perhaps hire some local staff."

Bea took Jake's arm. "I'd like to move in next week."

That threw a wrench into the secret plan so he decided to tell them all his intentions. "That's fine, of course, but I was thinking we might all want to ring in the New Year together. Someplace warm."

Tim winked. "Australia?"

How the devil did he work that one out? Jake wondered.

"Yes, as a matter of fact. I'm weary of seeing all my good friends in foul weather. I was thinking about Byron Bay in New South Wales."

"Australia," Bea said, wistfully. "I've never been."

Tim put his arm around her. "That's where Chris Hemsworth lives—Mum fancies him."

"I think three out of four of us fancy him, and Abbot is probably on the fence," Jake teased.

"Master Jacob, really…"

"You'll never guess who's coming up the walk," Bea announced, scowling out the window.

"Who?"

"That killjoy of a headmaster and his wife."

Timothy rushed across the room and grabbed Jake's arm just as they knocked on the door. "Don't believe a word out of that bastard's mouth," Tim said urgently in his ear. "I'll explain it all in the car."

Curious.

"What a pleasant surprise," Jake said with mock sincerity while opening the door.

"We noticed how wonderful Brigsley looks," Kitty said, "and I just had to see how you decorated the interior."

Tim was staring right at Jake and slowly shaking his head. "We have Mr. Abbot here to thank for the decorations," Jacob replied. They all felt it, the tension in the air. This wasn't a social call.

"Weston, I wanted to wish you all the best at Eton next term," the headmaster said, extending his hand. "We will certainly miss you around here."

Abbot jumped in, waving, "Nothing has been finalized yet."

So, there's the bombshell. Did Abbot and Ashlock already know about all this? Jacob wondered. *How could they keep such a thing from me?*

Rothwell wickedly smiled, "I hate to contradict you, Mr. Abbot..."

"Then don't," Timothy interrupted. "You know what Sophocles wrote, don't you, Headmaster? No one loves the messenger who brings bad news. In fact, during wartime they used to shoot them," he paused for dramatic effect. "So now you've said what you came here to say, why don't you and your wife sod off. I'm sure you have other pupils to torture today."

Who was this guy and what did he do with Timothy Ashlock? Jake thought, starting to chuckle, but Rothwell was seething.

"Looks like you'll be moving back into St. John's house, Mr. Ashlock if we let you attend here at all."

He scoffed. "Either both Jake and I will be attending Eton, or we'll be back here at White Oak. No one splits us up, not even the high and mighty Paul Weston. So if you play your cards right you might hang on to a world-class swimmer and a brilliant musician, which is probably more than this rundown institution deserves."

Suddenly all the windows began to rattle and Kitty's eyes grew as big as saucers. "Restless spirits," Jake whispered.

"Come, Barbara," the headmaster said, ushering his wife out. He looked utterly confused.

As soon as the Rothwells were out of earshot the group was hysterically laughing. Timothy just stared at them.

"What?"

"Exactly when did you grow a pair of brass balls, Timmy?" Jake asked, trying to catch his breath. He had to embrace him.

Abbot cleared his throat. "I was waiting until after the holiday to discuss this with you, but that horrible man seems to take pleasure in stirring the pot."

He looked at the old gent and could see the news had been troubling him. "No worries, but what should we do about it?"

"Eton is the better establishment. I propose we do just as master Timothy suggests and attempt to enroll him alongside you."

"Leave it to me, Abbot. I know how to talk to Headmaster Fetterman," Tim replied.

Abbot tilted his head to one side. "Do you?"

Curiouser and curiouser.

"His house will be one of our first stops. I'll sort it."

CHAPTER 19

The Cruel Heart

He never wanted to let Jake out of his sight.

Could just tagging along with him to Stratford change the timeline? Things are already different since he isn't leaving by himself in a rage this time around.

Tim scribbled a note quickly at the table and placed it in an envelope while Jake grabbed his sack of presents and started making his way out.

"What's that?"

"Just a note."

He scrawled her name across the outside of the envelope so Jake read it as Tim tacked it up to the outside of the door.

"Samantha? Have you already made plans for today then?"

"Not at all, I just have a hunch she might be stopping by in a few hours."

Jake focused that razor-sharp power of perception directly at him and raised his eyebrows. "A hunch?"

"Umm-hmm," he mumbled.

"So you've penned a love note? Have you written her a poem?"

"In a manner of speaking. I've told her to fuck off and die."

Jake nodded. "Ah, so it's more of a haiku. You do have a

way with the ladies."

◆ ◆ ◆

They were less than a mile from White Oak when Jacob asked the question. "Do you want to tell me what's actually going on?"

Tim rested his hand on Jake's thigh. Pe has warned him not to say too much about the mission he's on or the method that brought him to this place and time. He doesn't know if he's risking creating a paradox or ripping the fabric of space-time by telling him, and he can't believe he's thinking such crazy thoughts.

"What do you mean?"

Jake glanced his way. "I don't know what the game is, Honey, but something is certainly up. You seem like an altogether different person. You told our headmaster to sod off, and that is not the Ashlock I know and love, not to mention that cruel note to a girl I thought you were keen on."

Tim sighed through his nose. He'd been in this alternate reality for about an hour and Jake could already see through his machinations.

"You're right, of course. Something is going on, but I'm not supposed to say anything. Do you like physics?"

"What?"

"Quantum physics. Mirror universes, relativity, time reversal, Schrödinger's cat, things of that sort. Does the subject interest you?"

Jake's eyes narrowed. "Of course."

"Well," Timothy mentioned, "you should study up on it. Seriously. I think there's quite a lot of it that isn't just theoretical."

"Another one of your hunches?"

"Precisely."

Jacob stared at the snow on the side of the road. "Hmm."

When they arrived at the Aquatics Center everyone was thrilled to see Jake. The effect he had on people was stunning. He was magnetic. Coach Lir loved the silver flask (not to mention the delicious contents) and Jacob thoroughly enjoyed himself playing Father Christmas and handing out the many small treasures he'd brought along.

Timothy showed off the stunning violin and played some traditional Irish folk music for the coach and the crowd of workers that gathered.

"That's quite a lovely fiddle," Lir said.

Jacob wore his lopsided grin, "And quite a lovely fiddler to boot."

Tim's cheeks flushed.

"So Coach," Jake said, watching four young boys doing the backstroke in the main pool. "It appears we may be attending Eton next term. Will that affect my training schedule?"

"It will make it a damn sight easier, I'd wager. The Eton headmaster is hiring me to coach some of their toffs. I could use you to show them how it's properly done."

"Tim and I are off to see the campus today. It's exciting."

"Drive carefully, lads. The roads are still icy."

When they were back in the car Tim put the Allegretti down in the backseat.

"I was thinking we should make a trip to Botany Bay after Eton," Jacob stated. "We could talk to Tommy's mom."

Tim stared at him as they sat in the parking lot of the Centre. "Have you ever considered the possibility that Tommy may have taken his own life?"

Jacob looked like he'd been punched in the gut. "Because

he was queer?"

"And being harassed by the fag-masters. He was frail and alone."

"But he wasn't alone," Jake countered. "What about Tyler? The boy he's waiting for at Brigsley."

"The boy who betrayed him. Stillman Tyler Rothwell."

"Rothwell?"

Tim watched Jake piecing it all together in his mind. "It does fit. Ha! That's why those yearbooks are missing. I knew he was hiding something. How did you work all that out?"

"It doesn't matter, but listen, because this is important." Tim placed his arms around Jacob's neck and they locked eyes. "Rothwell is a dangerous man. He killed Father Hodgson. I have no proof to show you but I know it's true. And he pushed Finn Williams from the bell tower before you came to White Oak. He's going to try to kill you next."

"What?" Jake said with a worried expression, "Why?"

"He doesn't want you swimming for Eton and he doesn't want his past with Tommy dredged up. Plus he knows you're trying to get him sacked over the canings. Not to mention he's just a sick, fucking psychopath."

"How do you know all this?"

"Remember when you held Miranda's hands and you got a glimpse of your future?"

He slowly nodded his head.

"Well, I've seen the future myself and I wasn't fond of a reality you weren't in, so, this is us altering the course of time."

Tim kissed him. If he's fucked things up by telling him, so be it. If he butterflied the nation into the next World War, he doesn't care. It was worth it for that kiss, this conversation, these brief moments together.

"How will Rothwell attempt it?"

"He watches you while you swim. It was him that night when we were together at Ducker."

"I knew all along he was the one watching. I recognized his footfalls."

"He'll drug the water bottle in your locker. Please use sealed Evian from now on, and don't go swimming unless someone else is with you."

He nodded his agreement.

I have to give Jake credit, Tim thought, *because I must sound completely deranged.*

"I believe you, Timmy, and in your superpowers. Thanks for the warning. Now let's go see Eton."

◆ ◆ ◆

Tim climbed into the backseat since Jake was demanding that he perform en route. He wanted to be the only man in the UK that had his own concert violinist accompanying him live as he commuted.

"This is much better than listening to Spotify or a recording..."

Jacob didn't see the black ice on the road.

The Mercedes spun right into oncoming traffic where it was met by a frightfully large commercial lorry. Tim heard the sound of shattering glass and felt it raining down as he saw the ballooning of airbags. The Allegretti was ripped from his hand and he heard the terrible crunch as it splintered into a dozen fragments.

He was bleeding. Tim reached his hand up to his ear and it came away slick and hot. The inside of his mouth tasted like old pennies. He looked at Jake in the driver's seat and saw him slumped against the airbag.

"Jake!" he yelled but got no response.

There was blood everywhere. The interior of the Mercedes spattered with vivid red like a Jackson Pollock. Tim's head was pounding. It wasn't long before he heard the sirens. Perhaps this grand plan to save Jake is all for naught.

Is Destiny just a cruel-hearted bitch?

CHAPTER 20

St. Bart's

Blake Abbot received a call from the hospital when they were halfway to Oxford. "Turn the car around," he ordered. "The boys need us in London."

"Buckle up," Ethan answered as the Rolls Royce accelerated.

Betty was hysterical, even as Abbot attempted to calm her. "I'm sure they'll be fine," he said, holding her, but he wasn't convincing. In truth, they were worried sick.

"Blake," she cried, "I lost his father in a car crash..." Tears streamed down her cheeks. "I can't bury another child. I just can't."

◆ ◆ ◆

Abbot arranged for the boys to be placed together in a private room at St. Bartholomew's. Timothy's injuries were not life-threatening, thank God, but Jacob's prognosis was more dire.

Betty practically sprinted into the room to be at her son's bedside. His head was bandaged, and his face scratched up, but he seemed otherwise whole and well.

"Mum!" he shouted, as they entered the room.

"Timmy, I was so worried!"

Abbot watched them embrace, but he also had an eye trained on Jacob, unconscious and hooked up to several noisy machines. Abbot perused the chart, assessing the damage. Jacob was immobilized, his leg in traction. An IV bag slowly dripped fluid and medication into his forearm. He touched the boy's hand, which was warm and soft.

"They've had to take away a part of my ear, I'll be quite deformed."

"Master Timothy, plastic surgeons can do wonders these days and in the meantime, you must embrace your inner Van Gogh."

"Mr. Abbot," he said solemnly. "I'm afraid I was playing the violin when we had our mishap. The Allegretti was destroyed."

The gentleman sighed. He was playing a rare Stradivarius in a moving automobile. "Well," Abbot managed, "it's insured, of course, but I do think your names will go into the Guinness book for the most costly automobile accident in history."

The surgeon who operated on Jacob entered the room. "Mr. Abbot?"

"Yes, Dr. Bruno. How is he doing?"

The tall doctor looked like he could be an actor in a soap opera. He had dark hair and sparkling green eyes, a stethoscope dangling from his neck. He led Abbot to the back of the room, out of earshot.

"His injuries are substantial. He has suffered three broken ribs, one punctured his left lung which is why he has a chest tube inserted. Jacob's left femur was shattered and will need subsequent surgery when his condition is stabilized, as will his left tibia and fibula. We've reconstructed his knee, or what was left of it. In addition, he has a broken pelvis, which will be quite painful but should completely heal, given enough time."

Abbot watched him sleeping. "And why hasn't he regained consciousness?"

"Both boys sustained concussions, Jacob's much more severe. We've done a CAT scan and his brain function is normal. The body needs time to heal on its own and your lad has been through quite a lot of trauma today. Let's see how he's doing tomorrow, shall we?"

I need to call his father in Bali, Abbot thought.

"I'd like to review his x-rays and have a suggested course of action for his rehabilitation drawn up by a panel of physical therapists and other experts. He will want a plan of attack as soon as he awakens."

Dr. Bruno blinked thoughtfully. "I know he is a competitive athlete. His muscular physique is probably what saved his life."

"Doctor, we are dealing with an extremely determined boy. He has known few disappointments in his young life. My concern is for his mental well-being as much as his physical health."

"One step at a time, Mr. Abbot, but I take your meaning. Where will Mr. Weston find the most hope?"

"In the water," Abbot said in a muted voice. "And as soon as possible."

◆ ◆ ◆

Ethan was waiting in the hall. He looked to have been crying and praying. Bea placed an arm on his shoulder.

"Is he going to make it?"

"Of course," Abbot replied. "The doctor credits his physical condition as one of the reasons he isn't worse off. That speaks highly of you and Coach Lir. Also, that was a sturdy Mercedes."

"Will he be able to swim again?"

"I doubt anything would be able to keep master Jacob out of the pool."

CHAPTER 21

The Old Souls

E than drove Abbot and Bea to a restaurant for a quick meal, then they planned to return to stand vigil until Jacob awakened. Timothy hoped he would regain consciousness before he's pulled away from this universe.

He left his hospital bed to kiss Jake on the forehead. "Wake up, gorgeous boy. I need you."

It's one-thirty in the afternoon when she came storming in. Tim was standing next to Jake's bed, holding his hand.

"Miranda!" He was quite unprepared to see her.

"I know what you did," she exclaimed, giving Jake a darting glance. Her cockney accent was gone, as is the childlike lisp Timothy remembered.

"What do you mean?"

She scowled. "You're far more clever than I gave you credit for. Looks like Jake has sidestepped death after all—by having his boyfriend find a cosmic loophole. You have no fucking idea what you've done."

Tim blinked. "Where's that cute English lass I remember so fondly?"

"We don't have time for games and subterfuge. How much longer will you be in this alternate?"

"About two more hours," he admitted. There was no profit in lying to her.

"Do me a favor and climb into bed and keep your mouth shut until you are back where you belong."

"What exactly are you?"

"I'm a historian. A Time Mender. One of the cunning folk. Holy hell, I should smother him in his sleep and attempt to put this matter back to rights."

Timothy realized that she was serious. "Please Miranda, don't do that! I need him. You said yourself that he's a special soul."

She touched Jake's arm and closed her eyes. "How far back did you travel?"

"Slightly over a year."

She slapped her forehead. "You are going to be hilariously, galactically lost when you return. All those months will be a gap in your memory, not to mention the things you've outright changed inadvertently if this hare-brained scheme happens to work. Your plan is as foolish as a misspelled tattoo and just as lasting. A chunk of your life will be unknown to you and he may still be dead in your world. You know all this, right?"

"I was willing to take that risk and I've already been allowed to have a few more hours with him, so it was worth whatever price I had to pay. No need to make an entire meal out of it," Tim answered.

"Ah, ain't love grand. Come find me when you are pulled back. Ask for my whereabouts at the pub in Greenknoll."

"Why didn't you help him avoid it? You could've warned him."

She crossed her arms defiantly. "As a matter of fact I did warn him and I didn't intervene more directly because I'm not a damned fool. I know the risks. You obviously had help in all this. Who is your accomplice?"

Tim didn't want to tell her, so he just looked away. She roughly grabbed his hand. "I should have known," she said immediately. "Thomas Pe is a sucker for a tragic love story."

"I forced him to help me."

"Please." She held up a hand to silence the boy. "He's

been warned before. He just can't help himself."

Abbot, Bea, and Ethan came back from lunch and Tim watched Miranda's whole expression change.

"Who's this then?" Bea asked.

She clumsily curtsied and said, "I'm Miranda ma'am. Jake is one of my dearest friends."

The accent and the lisp were back. She was a pro. Tim climbed back into bed as Miranda made her way out of the room.

"How are you feeling, Love?" Bea asked her son.

"I have a headache." That wasn't a lie.

Abbot placed a hand on the boy's arm as Ethan entered from the hall.

"What was that gypsy girl doing in here?"

"She came to see how we were feeling," Tim replied.

"Hmm, that pint-sized witch freaks me out."

Ah, Ethan, if you only knew.

Timothy realized that he might be able to help himself out somewhat. He'd let the time-traveling cat out of the bag with Jake, more or less, so he decided to go for broke. Finding a notepad in the drawer near the hospital bed, he hurriedly pens a letter.

If I'm about to lose a year of my life I want him to remember it all for both of us, Tim thought.

He wanted photos and videos. Timothy needed Jake's help to collect an entire year's worth of memories and safeguard them for his return. He needed to keep a daily journal. In short, he wanted a head start in catching up for the lost time.

Another hour passed and Tim's patience was running thin. Then he heard Jake moan.

"He's waking!" Ethan shouted. Timothy sprung up as everyone huddled around the hospital bed.

Jacob blinked his eyes open and looked carefully at each

of his loved ones. "This is exactly why I require a driver."

They laughed.

"I'll get Dr. Bruno," Abbot said.

"Wait," Jake said in a soft voice. "I need to speak to Timmy alone for a moment. Please, everyone."

They dutifully filed out leaving the boys alone. Tears streamed from Tim's face as he pushed the letter into Jake's hand.

"A love note?"

"A plea for help. I'm going to need you desperately."

"Do you think it worked?"

Tim shrugged.

Tears filled Jake's big blue eyes too. "I don't know anyone else who would risk a journey through time, searching to bring me back from beyond the veil. How did you become so brave?"

"It wasn't courage," Tim said. "It was simply that my love for you outweighed my fear. As far as being successful, it's hard to say. The accident wasn't part of the plan, obviously, but at least it's different. Be careful of Miranda, if she comes around. She isn't what she seems."

"How so?"

"Jake, some children seem like old souls because they are."

"Maybe you should have left me in the grave and gone on with your own life," he whispered.

Timothy pulled some loose strands of Jake's long blond hair and smoothed them back into place. "Don't ever let me hear you say such a thing again. You are the most important part of my life."

"What's going to happen to you now?"

Tim squeezed Jake's hand. He's amazed that the boy could so willingly accept this crazy series of events. "Well, right now I'm passed out in the copper bathtub of a nice Asian man fourteen months in the future, and I'm in an alternate universe. So, I honestly don't know, but I'm glad I made the trip to visit you."

He leaned down and kissed the boy on the lips.

"I'm sorry," Jake said, "about the car crash, and disfiguring you."

"Don't be silly. How are you feeling?"

He grimaced. "I'm in tremendous pain, my love. I hope a nurse arrives with my drugs soon."

Tim started to see bright colors leaking into the room which was slowly starting to spin. He struggled to get back to bed. "I think I'm heading home now, Jake."

He felt extremely dizzy. Just before he passed out he heard Jacob's voice. "I'll be seeing ya, Timothy James."

CHAPTER 22

Fire & Air

These boys are driving me to drink, Bea thought.

When she realized how close they came to losing both of them, her heart buckled. Our lives are so fragile. As if we are walking a boundless tightrope, one false step, and all is lost. A part of her wanted to lock the boys up in Brigsley Cottage and throw away the key.

This was a mother's time, the hours when she could sit and watch them sleeping. Her two lads in their hospital beds, and dear Mr. Abbot snoring quietly in a chair at Jacob's side.

He's a fine gentleman, and if he asks for my hand I'll give it gladly. Blake makes me feel like a schoolgirl again, she thought.

Abbot was due to return to New York next week but maybe he'd stay longer since Jacob will need rehab, physical therapy, and lots of TLC. And she was anxious to get a good look at that Oxford house. If her life was to be upended then sooner was better than later.

She took back up her knitting, admiring the dark cashmere scarf she was making for Blake. She'd dropped a stitch which is unlike her. *Damn.* Her best friend Lorraine Marie would tell her to stick to her knitting.

Poor Timmy and his ear, he's always been the most flawlessly beautiful child. She wonders how the accident will affect him in the coming months. She hoped he wouldn't blame Jay.

His hearing won't be affected, thank goodness. He's a child of the air, a Gemini. Gentle and affectionate, but also nervous. Timmy's father used to say, "Everybody needs one good scar. They remind us of where we've been."

Jay, on the other hand, was a true Sagittarius. Unbelievably generous and idealistic, with a wicked sense of humor. Fire and air, these boys were an ideal match. Highly compatible, much like Mr. Abbot and herself. They were born on the exact same day, and no one can understand a Pisces' heart better than another Pisces.

CHAPTER 23

The Ripple

Tim woke up gasping for air.

"Easy now," Pe whispered. "Climb out my boy."

Timothy grasped at the side of the tub, his skin shriveled like a raisin. He felt nauseous and weak. The doctor carefully wrapped him in warm towels as the boy bolted for the toilet to be sick.

"Better out than in."

"Dr. Pe," Tim finally said when his stomach stopped doing flips. "Did it work?"

He shrugged dramatically. "Beats me. Did you see him?"

Tim blinked, remembering. "Yes."

He started putting on his clothes. It could have just been an elaborate dream. An intricate, drug-induced hallucination.

"I don't think it worked," Timothy finally muttered.

Thomas was carefully drying off the device and placing it back in its case. "What brings you to that conclusion?"

"Well, things appear unchanged. You, this house. It's all just the way I left it. Even my clothes are the same."

"Don't blame me, I followed the instructions to the letter. I even chanted for an hour."

"I'm not blaming anyone, it's just I expected more to..."

And just then he absentmindedly touched his ear. It felt different. "Wait a minute!"

He ran into the bathroom and looked in the mirror. Pulling his hair away he could see it. The plastic surgeon did a fine job, but he could see the scar, and feel it. A slight bump. He stared at himself. *I'm older, my hair is longer. I even weigh more.*

Dr. Pe was beaming and dancing about the room. "Still think you didn't go anywhere?"

"Sweet Jesus," Tim said just as his phone began vibrating in his pocket. He read the name of the caller and couldn't believe it.

"Hello?"

"Where the devil are you, Timmy? You need to come home."

He had no words. Tim collapsed down on the floor in a heap and started to sob.
"*Caro?* Are you there?"

"Jake," he yelled. "Oh, Jake. I can't believe it. How are you? Where are you?"

He heard that familiar laughter. "You've gone round the bend, Kiddo. I'm at home and you'd better get your ass back. Some coppers want to speak to you, and Bea is here giving them holy hell. There's been a murder at Oxford."

Some things must truly be inevitable, Tim thought. "Casey Larson," he muttered. "Down by the boathouse."

"What?"

"Isn't the victim Casey?"

"No," he said. "I'm sorry Babe, it's Namika Ito, the violinist. The one you've been competing against in the orchestra. Metro is rounding up all the musicians to ask questions, but they seem especially interested in you."

"I'll call an Uber and come right back."

"An Uber? You drove off in your car this morning."

"My car?"

"The Range Rover. You love that car. What's the matter with you?"

"Do you remember what day it is?"

"It's March fifteenth, the Ides of March, but...oh my

89

God." The realization hit Jake all at once. Tim listened to his breathing. "Then it's all true?" Jacob finally whispered.

Tim looked out the window and there was a gorgeous silver Range Rover parked out front. "Did you do everything I asked you to do?"

"Of course I did. There are probably a thousand pictures on your phone. You're a madman about it. What's the last thing you remember?"

"An hour ago you and I were seventeen, laying in tatters in a room at Saint Bart's Hospital and it was Boxing Day."

"Jesus. Are you okay to drive? Should I have Ethan come get you?"

"No. That would take too long. I'll drive back, but I'm going to need your help. Do you think you can get rid of the policemen for a while?"

"Of course."

"What are you going to tell them?"

He heard Jake giggle. "An elaborate lie, naturally."

CHAPTER 24

Music for the Blind

"You're lying," the boy detective bluntly stated.

Jacob shrugged and poured himself another Macallan M. *This young one is clever*, he thought. *He can't be more than twenty. The older one looks Mediterranean.*

"Why would I lie to the authorities?"

Bea was standing in the corner, her arms crossed and her foot tapping. Jake winked at her. The old guy came up close, trying to invade Jake's personal space. He was wearing one of the ugliest ties Jacob has ever seen.

"Why indeed?"

"Listen, DCI…?"

"Bridges."

"Yes, Detective Bridges, if you're trying to dance with me I must warn you that I always lead."

He involuntarily moved back a pace. "So, you're telling us that he's out playing the violin to blind children?"

"Precisely. Or he could be at an orphanage, he visits several."

Bea placed a finger lightly against her chin. "He might have gone to one of the cancer wards. You should try the Royal Marsden first."

Jacob loved this woman. She could spin a yarn with the best of them.

"And he turns his phone off when he's doing these little charity concerts?"

"Of course," Jake replied. "He hates any distractions when he's performing. I told you I'll give him your card. He'll be only too happy to answer your questions tomorrow."

"Let's talk about you then, Mr. Weston. You seem to be a fit lad."

"Nothing gets past you, Detective. I'm an athlete, a free-style swim champion, but I'm betting you already knew that."

"Ever have any military training?"

"Do you think I'm the killer, DCI?"

"The thought had crossed my mind."

Jacob was seriously considering taking a photo of that hideous tie to show Abbot and Timothy.

"People used to always fear I was suicidal, I'm not sure homicidal is a step in the right direction. Since I'm sure you'll find out anyway, I was taught self-defense by a gentleman in America."

"These were private lessons?"

"Naturally," Jake answered, sipping his scotch.

"What was the name of your instructor?"

"Hansen, but that may not have been his real name. I think he was still Special Ops at the time. My butler arranged it. I was fifteen and my father thought I might get bullied at school."

"Because you're queer?"

"That or the fact that I'm a hopeless smart ass."

Bridges grunts.

"Does this Hansen have a first name?"

"Seth. It's been a few years but he was quite a badass."

The younger cop was watching him, obviously the brains of the outfit. "Are you left-handed, Mr. Weston?"

"I am. I'm in the minority in nearly every conceivable way."

"Okay," Bridges sighed. "Let your boyfriend know we need a word. If we're out in the field, please have him leave a message with Sergeant Eddings at Thames Valley Station."

"Certainly," Jake said, glancing at the antique mantel clock. *If they don't leave soon they might just catch him walking up the drive*, he thought.

The young one stumbled to his feet. He was socially awkward for a cop. "Thank you for the tea, Mrs. Ashlock," he mumbled quietly.

Bea was holding their coats in her arms. "You're wasting your time. My boy has nothing to do with any of this bloody mess."

"We just want to have a chat," Bridges said casually. "Procedure, you know."

Jacob looked directly at Bridges while Bea was opening the door. "He barely knew Miss Ito, she'd only just arrived in England."

"Kid, what did it say about young Mr. Ashlock in her diary?"

The detective glanced up and to the left for a moment, recalling the words from memory. "She wrote that: Timothy is the one true love of my life. The only soul I would deem my equal."

Bridges smiled proudly. "The Kid never forgets a thing, do you? He reads something once and he can quote it chapter and verse. It's quite a gift."

The DCI slaps the young man on the back. Jacob regarded this gawky boy with newfound respect.

"Eidetic?" he asked conspiratorially. The kid nodded shyly. "I imagine that can be both a blessing and a curse."

The slightest smile crept across Skip's face as they left.

CHAPTER 25

Witty Banter

Timothy knocked on the door because for all he knows it isn't the right house, but it is. His mum answered.

"Why on earth are you knocking..." she began, but he embraced her and pecked her cheek. It's then that they see each other. Jake was leaning against the wall, a lopsided grin on his face, and Timothy was awestruck.

He's bigger than before, taller, broader, and blonder, Tim thought.

Jake picks him up off his feet and spins him around.

"What's gotten into you boys? You're acting like you haven't seen each other in ages."

Tim nearly bursts into tears.

"I'm exhausted, so I'll be locking things up for the night," Bea said. "I've got some knitting to do. I'll see you lads at breakfast." She turned and walked out toward the guesthouse where Tim remembered living with Billy.

"She's in the cottage?" he whispered to Jake.

"Of course. It's all just the way we planned it to be."

"Where's Billy?"

He looks confused for a second. "Redgrave?"

"Yeah."

"He lives in a flat with two other blokes near Christ Church."

"Ah, okay. I guess I've got some catching up to do."

"No worries. You should read your journal tonight and we can look through all the photos. You'll be up to speed in no time."

"After," he said, starting to unbutton Jake's trousers. They smile wickedly.

"Why Timothy James, are you making a pass at me?"

He looked up at Jake's grinning face.

"I didn't time travel and save your life just for the witty banter."

They laughed as Jake picked Timothy up and carried him to their room. "I suppose you deserve a proper thank you. Prepare yourself, Mr. Ashlock, for some shock and awe."

When they get to the master suite, Tim watched Jacob pull off his shirt. There's a scar on his side where the chest tube was inserted. Timothy touched it.

"Are you back to normal?"

"What are you asking?"

He stared into those sparkling blue eyes. "Your training. Are you still the greatest swimmer in the world?"

Jacob stretched his arms wide above his head. "*Caro*, I never was." Pulling down his boxer briefs he displayed a small tattoo of the Olympic rings on his pelvis just below his waistline. "I'm not as fast as I once was, but I will be. And I'm fast enough, you'll see. I got the rings tattooed as an incentive."

"Was the rehab difficult?"

"I was punting through the pain. You helped me every step of the way. We discovered yoga."

"I don't remember any of it," Timothy said, squinting. "But I'm glad I was supportive. It must have been excruciating," He carefully traced each of Jake's scars with his finger.

"Certainly it was, it's a constant battle trying to get back my lung capacity. I have to be ready in case Chadwick challenges me to another underwater duel."

"How do you keep going then, when it hurts? What's the trick?"

Jake bit his neck playfully. "The trick, Timothy James, is not minding that it hurts."

He pulled Tim's sweater off and tossed it on the floor. "Time travel is such an odd thing. I've had more sex with you than you've had with me now."

"Only you would distill the intricacies of physics to that level," Tim said, shedding the remainder of his clothes. "I was there. I just can't remember the details."

"What if you could? What if there was a way to get back those lost memories?"

"I've been told that once you overwrite them they are irretrievable."

"Ah, yes," Jake nodded. "The Matthias Krage lecture. He may not know everything on the subject, or he may not be telling us all he knows."

Tim stared. "You know about Dr. Krage?"

"Of course. We just attended that lecture together. Fascinating subject matter." Jake started to kiss him again. "But enough of the foreplay, Timmy."

◆ ◆ ◆

They lay in bed, tangled, sweaty, satisfied. Timothy had missed him so much. The familiarity of his skin, his voice, and his scent. He was burdened by lust and loneliness for more than a year, only finding brief moments of relief from friends, or worse, strangers.

He played with Jacob's long blond hair. "I should go say goodnight to Mr. Abbot. Will he be in the cottage reading or watching a film with Mum?"

Jake wrinkled his brow. "Abbot's in New York, Babe."

"What? That's not right. Mum and him..."

Jake held him gently, trying to be sympathetic. "I thought so too, but after I was settled into my physical therapy regimen he went back to Manhattan to nurse my father. I'm

afraid he and your mum had quite a row about the whole matter. Abbot has an overdeveloped sense of duty to my family. I
think he managed to break Bea's heart."

"No," Tim said flatly. "They are meant to be together,
just like us. They even have the same birthday! I'm not going to
be responsible for ruining their lives. What time is it?"

Jake looked at the bedside clock. "It's nine at night here,
that's four in the afternoon in New York."

"Perfect. It's tea time. Let's call that old lunatic."

CHAPTER 26

Tea Time

Blake Abbot had just poured himself a cup of tea when that horrible little woman came rushing into his pantry. "What do you think you're doing?"

He was holding a teacup to his mouth mid-sip, but then placed it down on its saucer. "Isn't it obvious, madam? I'm scuba diving."

"Don't be insolent with me. Paul is in pain, he's asking for another pill."

"He had his medication twenty minutes ago. Why don't you read to him, take his mind off the pain and let the drugs take effect unless you intend to overdose him on sedatives and pain medication."

"How dare you insinuate…" but thankfully Abbot's phone began ringing.

"If you'll excuse me, I must take this call." Joanne stormed away in a huff.

"Hello?"

"Mr. Abbot."

"Why master Timothy, this is an unexpected delight. How are you and Jacob faring?"

He sipped the tea.

"We are well. I'm slightly out of sorts but I'm trying desperately to put things back in order."

He's a resourceful boy, the butler thought.

"I'm sure you'll succeed. And how is Mrs. Ashlock?"

"She's quite lonely."

Abbot sighed. "I'm sure she understands..."

"Excuse me for interrupting, sir, but I don't. You love my mother, do you not?"

"Timothy, have you been drinking?"

"Not yet, but I intend to start soon. Now don't change the subject. Do you want to die alone, a sour and unloved old gentleman?"

Timothy was starting to get on Abbot's nerves. These matters were hashed out months and months ago.

"You are aware of my feelings for your mother, but as I've explained to you both, I have a commitment here. Jacob's father is quite unwell and I intend to see him through this illness."

Timothy couldn't hold back his frustration. "Have you hired a full-time nurse yet?"

"I was just examining several applications for his new caregiver."

"Is there a young, quite lovely woman named Karen in the mix?"

How bizarre, Abbot thought. *He's mentioning the exact person I was considering.*

"How can you possibly know such a thing?"

"Trust me, Abbot, she's the right person for the job. Hire her and come out to England for a visit. We need to see you right away."

His mind wandered to that outrageous smoking jacket Betty bought for him Christmas before last. "Timothy, nothing would please me more, but I fear your mother may no longer desire my company."

"Leave her to me. We will expect you in a week. Good-bye, Abbot."

And the cheeky boy hung up.

CHAPTER 27

Del Gesù

Timothy was sitting up in bed, reading his journal. It's unmistakably his handwriting. He's in all the pictures, and he can't remember a blessed thing. "This is incredibly maddening. It feels like I'm trying to recall a word that's on the tip of my tongue, but can't. I look at these photos and they're like forgotten dreams. Everything seems perched on the edge of my memory, ever so slightly out of reach."

Jake sat on the far side of the bed, massaging Timothy's feet. "So, they get married in Paris after I die? Abbot just up and quits his job?"

Jake was as curious about the year Tim spent without him as Timothy is about the current timeline, a year he can't recall.

"That isn't the best part," Tim said. "Abbot called your stepmother an ignorant, mean-spirited little cunt."

That had Jake in stitches. "Oh, that is rich. And you killed the headmaster? With my Harold?"

He looked up from the journal. "I assure you it was in self-defense. He almost murdered us both."

"How many bullets?"

"Fifteen," Tim replied. "The Glock heats up when you fire it quickly."

Jacob couldn't stop laughing. "I thought you told me you could never shoot anyone."

"I believe I said I didn't think I could ever shoot anyone. It ends up being incredibly easy when you're in the proper situation and mood. Speaking of which, where is the current Rothwell? Was he caught? Did he go to prison for beating White Oak boys?"

Jake moved to the window and looked out on the foggy English night. "As it happens, he's dead here too."

"Is he? How?"

"A terrible accident," Jake said, moving to the fireplace and poking at the embers. "I only know what I saw on the news, but there was a gas leak."

"He died from asphyxiation?"

Jake continued to stare into the hearth. "No, no. There was a massive explosion. All of White Gables was destroyed in the fireball. They think one of his cigars may have ignited it."

"Jesus. What about Kitty?"

"Lucky for her she was visiting relatives in North Carolina at the time."

"That is lucky. So Rothwell was alone."

"Hmm?" Jake asked, adding another log.

"I say, Rothwell was alone in the cottage when it went up?"

"Oh. No, I believe that the chemistry professor was with him, Wayne Kendal. Tragic."

Timothy watched Jake's face as he casually looked back and winked.

◆ ◆ ◆

Scrolling through the photos on his phone he could see that they transfered to Eton. It looked like they enjoyed themselves there. There was a picture with Jake, Billy, and him at commencement in their robes. Tim is glad Billy was still a part of their lives. At least that hadn't changed. He saw that they went to New York for Jake's eighteenth birthday. Ethan looked overjoyed. Tim had always wanted to go to America. He started to cry.

"What?" Jake asked.

Timothy attempted to pull himself together because he was being such a ninny. "Did we have fun in New York?"

"Yeah, we did, but we were only there for two days, and it was in the middle of the term. Don't worry, we'll go back. I can dazzle you with all your favorite spots again."

Tim kept searching through the pictures and then he saw it. He gasped.

"Finally. I've been waiting for you to get to the Christmas photos."

"Is it? My God!"

He shrugged. "You picked it out. A Guarneri. Who knew there were three great families of luthiers working in Italy in the seventeenth and eighteenth centuries? It took us months to get the acquisition sorted out. You say you can hear a stronger and more brilliant sound, especially in the darker..."

"A Del Gesù!"

Jake smiled and moved toward the wardrobe where he took out the same Bam France shockproof, airtight case. "You should send flowers to our insurance company." He giggled. "Happy Christmas once again, Timmy."

His fingerprint unlocked the case and he picked up the instrument. It was even more splendid than the Allegretti.

"You know who else used to play one of these?" Jacob asked.

"Paganini," Tim whispered reverently.

"Oh, so that you can remember."

"I'd know that in any timeline." He can't help himself so he just starts playing a mournful adagietto that he'd composed when the world was still broken. Jake sat cross-legged on the floor watching and listening. When he finished Jacob simply stared at him.

"I've never heard you play that piece before. Who composed it? You?"

"Yes," Tim admitted. "A sadder version of me."

"What's it called?"

"Weston."

"You must have been a total wreck without me around."

"I made do."

"Did you now? With whom?"

Tim put the violin back in its case and Jake immediately started to tickle him.

"Who were you with Timothy James? I demand to know."

"None of your business. You were dead at the time."

"That's no excuse for cheating."

He was so much bigger and stronger. Timothy was simply no match for him, and Jake relentlessly poked at his sides.

"Uncle!" Tim yelled. "Uncle!"

They lay back on the bed, panting, both of them staring at the ceiling. "It certainly was a beautiful bit of music."

"Hmm," Timothy mumbled. "Well, beauty is in the ear of the beholder."

Jake laughed and touched his face. "You're wittier than the old you."

"The new me has been to the gates of hell and back. So what am I supposed to say to those detectives tomorrow? I can't tell them I was busy time traveling in a copper bathtub when poor Namika was killed."

"I guess you'll just have to lie."

Tim sighed. "I'm a terrible liar."

"They will never believe the truth, and that young detective has a touch of Conan Doyle about him. He's way too clever, he even caught me fibbing."

"Was he an awkward, gangly lad named Skip Loge?"

Jake wrinkled his face. "Don't tell me you've met him."

"A week ago in my mirror universe. My goose is royally cooked."

"You could always confess to it. I killed her because she was a better violinist than me. And by the way, she wasn't."

"Be serious, Jake. And how do you know she wasn't better than me? You've never heard her play."

"I don't have to--I've heard you play."

"You're sweet, but honestly, what am I going to do?"

Jacob grinned. "I have an idea. Hand me my phone."

CHAPTER 28

House Calls

"**M**y gut tells me one of these goddamn musicians is guilty and Timothy Ashlock is our prime candidate. He was the golden boy and then this Ito girl showed up and knocked him off his throne."

Loge and Eddings were walking beside him as they made their way to the grand Edwardian house. "You're wrong, DCI."

The fucking Kid, Bridges thought. They stop in the middle of the street and he turned around and stared at him. "How the hell would you know, Skippy? You've never even met this tosser."

"I waited for him last night. Silver Range Rover shows up about a half-hour after we left. Eight-fifteen, Ashlock gets out, knocks on his own front door."

"What?" Bridges said.

"Maybe he forgot his keys, but guess what else he forgot?"

"Don't tell me. No violin?"

Eddings scoffed. "The lad is guilty as sin."

The Kid went on with the report. "I hear music about ninety minutes later. It was foggy, so I got right next to the house without being seen. The bedroom window was ajar. Ashlock has real talent."

"Judas Priest," Bridges yells, "I don't care how talented he is. He killed this girl and we've got the Japanese embassy, not to mention half of Oxford and her pain-in-the-arse parents jumping up and down on us. So please, Boy Genius, tell me why this toff is innocent."

"Chief," he said as if he's talking to a four-year-old. "Miss Ito's head was turned completely around. A clean break. Unlike what we see in the movies, that is almost impossible to do. Even if we concede that this is a military maneuver, we're talking about a Green Beret or Navy Seal, not a skinny violinist."

"Well, we've watched all the CCTV footage from the Sheldonian around the time of Ito's death. I saw a hell of a lot of students, tourists, and musicians coming and going but I didn't see any Navy Seals."

"We didn't see Timothy Ashlock either," Eddings mumbled.

The trio started to make their way up the High. "So, what's your theory, Boy Genius?"

"Oh, I don't have one, Chief, and please stop calling me that."

"Jesus H. So, what about Weston? He's had some martial arts training and he's lied to us already. Is he big and strong enough? "

The Kid shrugged and pushed his glasses up. "Jacob Weston is at least within the realm of possibility, except that he's left-handed. Did you know that only ten percent of the population are southpaws, but they make up nearly fifty percent of the world's elite athletes? Particularly in boxing, baseball and tennis."

Eddings and Bridges stared at the Kid.

◆ ◆ ◆

The mother answered the door. She hates policemen, that seemed apparent. "Nice to see you again, Mrs. Ashlock,"

Carl said. "This is Constable Eddings, and you've met Detective Loge, may we come in?"

"Gentlemen," she replied, opening the door. "Please. May I bring you some tea? The doctor is almost finished with her examination."

"Doctor? Is someone ill?" Eddings asked.

"My son. He has had dizzy spells ever since the accident."

"Sure he has," Bridges muttered as the Weston boy came down the stairs.

"DCI Bridges. I see you've brought the brains," looking toward the Kid, "and the brawn," he motioned to Eddings. "What will your function be today?"

"I'll be running the show, Mr. Weston, and if you interfere I just might handcuff you to the banister."

He grinned. "That's the best offer I've had all day."

"Where is he?"

He motioned ahead, "Right up here."

Everyone proceeded into the master suite where a woman in a white lab coat was ministering to the boy. "Hello," she said when the group walked in.

"Doctor?"

"That's right. You can call me Dr. Kay."

"I'm afraid we'll be needing your bona fides."

She gave the team a sidelong glance and turned back to Timothy. "You can take ibuprofen if the headaches return. I'm prescribing a mild diuretic just to be on the safe side. You need to rest, Timmy. Don't let these wankers push too hard."

"Where is it you practice medicine, Doctor?" Loge asked politely.

She had long gray hair tied straight back and wore only a touch of makeup. The no-nonsense type. "Why right here, naturally. University of Oxford Medical Sciences Division. I'm Dr. K.L. Matthews, head of the Nuffield Department of Clinical Neurosciences. Now that I've shown you mine, why don't you show me yours."

Weston and Ashlock were already chuckling. "I'm DCI Bridges from Scotland Yard, this is Detective Sergeant Eddings from the Thames Valley Police and Special Agent Loge."

"Well, I want you boys to take it easy on my patient. He had a traumatic brain injury and has recurring bouts of dizziness and memory loss."

"His injury was more than a year ago," Bridges said sarcastically.

"What's your point?"

"He's a top-level student at Magdalen College and a concert violinist…"

"Yes," the doctor replied, "and today he can't remember the names of his tutors or what he had for breakfast."

The Kid chimed in, "Is it anterograde amnesia?"

The doctor looked impressed. "Why, yes. Partial anterograde. He's an interesting case. I've been watching these boys for months. The brain is a mysterious organ."

"Well, I've got a dead girl that I have to ship back to Japan tomorrow, so take an aspirin Timmy because we need some answers."

"I'll do my best."

The doctor checked her watch and turned to look at Weston. "I'm late for a lecture. Call me if his condition changes."

"Will do, Doc. Thanks again."

And they kissed each other on the cheek.

CHAPTER 29

The Outsiders

"Timothy, do you remember anything from last Tuesday?" Skip asked.

"I don't know. This whole week has been a blur."

"Do you remember Namika Ito?"

"Of course. She and I were friends."

He looks healthy enough, Loge thought. His hair was black and shiny and his complexion was perfect.

Bridges took the iPad from Eddings and shoved it right under Timothy's nose. "Look at your friend now."

He instinctively turned away and tightly shut his eyes. "Bloody hell."

Weston lunged across and held his hand out for the device. He stared at the images for a good long time. "Do you know what the symbol means?"

"Not yet," Detective Loge answered. "What are your impressions?"

He handed the iPad back to Eddings. "I think it's interesting that the killer used an extremely sharp knife to carve a symbol into Miss Ito's flesh, yet killed her by breaking her neck. Which do you think came first?"

Skip looked toward Bridges who shrugged his consent. "We believe the symbol was carved post-mortem."

"I agree," Jacob said. "And it must be of great importance to the assailant."

Skip turned his attention back to Timothy. "Were you playing the violin for blind children yesterday?"

He looked at his boyfriend. "I'm sorry, I don't remember."

Bridges groaned.

He's hiding something, Skip thought. *Or he knows more than he's willing to tell us.*

"You and Namika were competing for the soloist violin position."

He met the detective's gaze. "Not exactly."

Bridges was pacing the room impatiently. "What's that supposed to mean?"

Timothy looked at each of the men. "I withdrew my name from the competition."

"Why?"

"She deserved the opportunity to shine."

"Bullshit," Bridges yelled, giving him a look that could shatter glass. "You were jealous and furious that someone could waltz in and replace you."

"No," he stated evenly. "Namika's mother is...demanding. I'm glad she won. She wanted it far more than I did."

"Is that why you let her have it?" Skip asked.

"No, I suppose I felt like we had something in common. We are both outsiders."

Bridges scowled. "What are you blathering on about? You're the most entitled little Englishman I've ever laid eyes on. You look like you walked right out of Dickens."

He cringed. "Then I am the pauper in *The Prince and the Pauper*. I've never felt like I fit in here." He looked at Jake. "I still don't."

"Was she a better musician?" Bridges asked.

Timothy blinked. "Perhaps, technically. There are aesthetics involved in judging musical performances. It's subtle, and quite subjective, especially with the violin, Carl. I didn't kill her though, I liked her, and I respected her talent."

"Did you know she was in love with you?"

"I had an inkling. But it was just a crush, she'd only been in England for a month."

"Have you ever had any military training?"

Both of the boys giggled. "No."

"I've got one last question," Bridges said, folding his arms. "We've just met, right?"

"Is that your question?"

"No, this is: How did you know my first name?"

He sat up in bed blinking at the policemen as Weston moved closer. "We do our homework around here too, *Carl*."

The DCI wasn't happy. "I know you toffs are being evasive and I don't appreciate being fed horseshit when an innocent girl has been murdered. If the two of you care about Oxford and your friends, then you should give us something helpful."

He turned his back on them and stared out the window. "Listen, Bridges," Timothy began, and the DCI spun back around. "Do you know a forensic pathologist named Dr. Leta Kelly?"

Bridges put his hand through his thick, unruly hair. "I've never met her, but I know her reputation. She's a rockstar over at Cambridge. The best in the field."

"You need to call her into this case. She can help you."

Loge and Bridges exchanged looks. It's not a bad suggestion. "It wouldn't hurt to ask, I guess."

"Oh, and Carl," Timothy continued, "put on a decent sport coat when you meet her."

CHAPTER 30

Theta

The call came in on March twenty-first, six days after the first girl was killed. They found her in the underbrush at Christ Church Meadow. This was certainly not what DS Leon Eddings signed up for.

"I've been on the college beat for ten years and I've seen some bad things," he muttered to detective Loge. "No place on earth is crime-free but I'm used to dealing with Oxford's number one offense—stolen bicycles, not serial killers."

Loge tried to look sympathetic.

"Who was she?" Bridges asked. He was in a particularly foul mood.

"We don't know yet, sir."

A whole team from London was combing the site. The college's security had done its best with the local police to tape it off and keep curious bystanders at bay. It was a term break so there weren't the usual amount of people around.

"Her throat is slit?"

"I don't think so," Loge said.

"I can see the wound," Bridges argued, pointing. She was face down in the brush. Her skin was milky white.

"I believe she was garroted," Loge stated.

"What? Like in the Mafia? With piano wire?"

"The practice goes back a lot further than that. In

Spain..."

"Shut up, Kid. Did they run her prints?"

"Yep. If she's a student we should know soon."

"Why does he take their clothes?" Eddings wondered.

"Souvenirs," Bridges said.

Loge was frowning. "This killer takes everything. Clothes, jewelry, wallets, backpacks, whatever, and then leaves his mark. It's expressing dominance. Power."

"Is it sexual?"

"Uncertain. Miss Ito showed no sign of sexual assault."

"You still haven't told me what the symbol is, Genius," Bridges crouched down, careful not to touch anything even though he was wearing latex gloves.

"That's because there isn't an exact match in any of the databases. But if you're asking my opinion..."

"Please."

"It's a stylized version of the Greek letter *Theta*."

"Christ and His apostles," Bridges shouted. "Please don't tell me we're dealing with some secret fucking Oxford society bullshit."

This man desperately needed some caffeine.

Skip pushed his dark unwashed hair out of his eyes. "There are over 150 officially recognized student societies at Oxford, and dozens of unofficial ones."

Eddings whistled. The Kid truly did know everything.

"In ancient times *Theta*, the eighth letter of the Greek alphabet, symbolizes death."

Bridges stared at him. "That seems rather on the nose, don't you think?"

Loge shrugged and his phone beeped. He started reading a text, while the DCI glared at the scene.

"Isn't school out of session? It's the twenty-first of March," he asked Eddings.

"Yes, DCI. The Hilary term ended on March fourteenth. The Trinity term doesn't begin until April twenty-sixth."

"So what is she doing here?"

Loge looked up from his phone. "She's a philosophy student at Merton."

Eddings, who knew Oxford well, points at the castle-like structure just across the meadow.

"Philosophy?" Bridges scoffed. "Worthless. Her parents must be rich."

"She lives just off Sheep Street," Loge continued.

"What's the girl's name?"

"Samantha Milford."

CHAPTER 31

The Card Sharp

"I'm all in," Jacob said, pushing a large stack of chips to the center of the table. Redgrave and Cotton grumbled.

"I'm out."

"Me too. Fold."

He gave them all a lopsided grin. "Well, Chadwick, that just leaves you and me."

Peter looked at his cards again and took a swallow of scotch. "You're bluffing."

Jacob gazed at his boyfriend and licked his lips.

Timothy didn't play poker, and he didn't know Jake was a card sharp, but it was hardly surprising. His chef taught him to play cards when he was still a child. The game was a weekly occurrence at Brigsley Manor, and Tim was glad to see a familiar face or two, but he didn't have a clue who some of these lads were. He sat near the buffet table while they played.

"Then why don't you call me?"

"Fold," he muttered, throwing his cards down. "That strategy will stop working fast in this game, Weston. What did you have?"

Jake smiled and shuffled the deck.

"The rich get richer," Cotton stated.

"Ah well, it's just a game," Billy said, taking another sip of scotch and standing.

"Lord Redgrave, you're turning into a philosopher," Jake teased.

Billy was at the sideboard making himself a sandwich as Timothy leaned in toward him, placing a hand on his shoulder. He knew that what he did to save Jacob had direct ramifications on Redgrave too.

Billy looked back fondly at his friend. "You don't usually hang around here on poker night."

"I just wanted to see what the fuss was about." Tim reached to make himself a plate of food. "How have you been? Honestly."

"I'm terrific, mate. Classes were hard but I'm still in the mix."

"Yeah," Jake called out from where he was eavesdropping. "Who is she, Redgrave?"

"Who is who?" he asked innocently, the color starting to rise in his ruddy cheeks.

Jake poured himself more of the 1926 Macallan that he'd opened for the evening. "You seem unusually relaxed lately, Milord. Confident, happy, some might even say carefree, which is quite out of character. You're obviously getting laid."

The players hooted and howled, while poor Billy's face turned crimson.

"Pay him no mind," Tim whispered. "We just want you to be happy."

He smiled and Timothy remembered an entire year of a friendship that Billy would never know. That bond was never forged in the current timeline, but regardless, Timothy did realize how special Billy Redgrave was, the quality of his friendship and loyalty.

"As a matter of fact, I am seeing a lovely young lady from Pembroke, which is why I haven't been mucking about with you lot."

He sat back down at the felted table and the game resumed. Jake had that playful glint in his eye that suggested that he wasn't finished winding Billy up.

"We should go on a double date."

"Please just deal the cards."

"It would be fun. I'll take us out to the Ledbury or Aqua Shard, whichever you prefer."

Billy glanced at Timothy seeking assistance. "I don't believe she's ready to meet you yet, but that's a kind offer."

Matthew Colton looked annoyed.

"Are we playing poker or discussing Lord Redgrave's love life?"

Jake dealt the cards. "Both, now keep your shorts on Matt because this is getting interesting."

Two brawny lads that Timothy hadn't met were headed up the stairs to go outside and smoke. He poured himself another glass of wine as Billy concentrated on his cards.

Jake plowed on. "You know, mate, I'm glad you've found a girl, honestly I am, and I'm not one to rain on your parade, but some people have taken a fancy to me just to get at my family's money."

Timothy raised his eyebrows at the observation.

"Oh, not you, Ashlock," Jake said quickly. "Don't get your Calvins in a twist. I'm speaking of boys long before you entered the picture..."

Timothy sighed. "Mr. Weston, I believe you're drunk."

Jacob touched his chest. "You may be right," he admitted. "I'm celebrating this evening, but back to the topic at hand — Redgrave, are you worried your young lady is merely chasing a title?"

"Oh, she probably is," Billy stated matter-of-factly. "That's fine by me. I'm going to be the earl one day whether I like it or not. If my future wife is fond of all that rubbish and wants to play lords and ladies, then my life will be that much easier."

There was a knock at the door.

"Would you mind, *Caro*?" Jacob asked Timothy.

He ran upstairs and was shocked to find Casey Larson standing at the threshold. He smiled broadly when he saw

Timothy.

"Sorry, I'm late. They're stopping every pedestrian and bicyclist at the intersection and checking school IDs. It's turning into Stalingrad out there."

Tim hadn't uttered a word, he just kept staring at the hunky rower, remembering dancing with him at a pub in another universe—that Casey was a wonderful dancer.

"So Timmy, how are you?" He hugged Ashlock tight.

"Umm," he answered, still mesmerized, "I'm okay."

"Bet you're happy Hilary is finally over— I know I am. Exams nearly killed me at Corpus. Heard you lads are going down under for some big International swim meet. Can I tag along?"

"Umm."

He headed down the stairs and everyone yelled his name. Timothy was relieved that Casey was alive but he couldn't stop picturing him naked. He walked downstairs to join them.

Casey was tossing down a wad of bills and Jake was passing him chips. "Have you lads heard the news?"

"If it's about Man United I don't want to know," Ethan said.

He looked hard at Jake. "Have you taken away all their phones again?"

"Rules are rules. We're here to drink, play poker and behave like gentlemen, not stare at tiny glass screens."

"What's the news?" Cotton asked, stretching and yawning.

"They found another one. A Merton girl. Nude and stone-cold in the meadow."

The players went running for the drawer where Jake had stowed the phones.

"My girlfriend is at Merton," one of the lads said.

"Was the victim a musician?" Timothy asked tentatively.

"No idea."

Cotton started reading from the online version of the *Cherwell*, Oxford's student newspaper. "Samantha Milford, nineteen, a philosophy undergrad at Merton is the second Oxford student to be slain in a fortnight..."

Timothy felt the blood draining from his head. Billy and Jake were dumbstruck.

"What say we call it a night, boys," Jake shouted, standing up and moving toward Timothy.

"But I just got here," Casey whined.

"Have a drink, Larson, this game is over."

CHAPTER 32

Help Arrives

"If there was some sort of mass hysteria it's the fault of the press," Skip stated. "Every idiot with a smartphone and two thumbs had become a reporter and the worst part of it is this poor girl's parents are going to find out they lost their child by reading about it on Twitter."

"It's a fucked-up world," Carl replied. He had sent two uniforms to inform her parents but they lived way down in Dorchester and the internet was instantaneous.

"All the other news outlets picked it up from the *Cherwell*, Chief. The BBC is asking for a statement."

"Tell them to sod off!"

"But they never do, do they?" she called out. Carl spun around in time to watch the lovely woman making a beeline for him. "Detective Chief Inspector Bridges?" she asked, her hand outstretched.

"Yes," he managed to say. "Carl Bridges."

They shook.

"I'm Dr. Leta Kelly from Cambridge. I've come to help."

"That's the best news I've heard all week. I have both bodies downstairs. You have two ME Assistants standing by that will help you in any way you require."

"Both bodies? I thought the first girl was shipped back to Japan."

"I've managed to hold up that paperwork until you

could take a look. Her parents are furious."

She was glancing at the police files. "Well, that was thoughtful of you, Carl. I guess I'll start with Miss Ito. You'll be able to release her body tomorrow."

"Thanks, Doc."

The Kid walked up and seemed excited. He bobbed his head awkwardly at Dr. Kelly. "What do you have, Skipper?"

"A connection between the two victims."

Bridges cheered. "This Kid is like a Yorkie with a chew toy when he starts digging into something," he told the room. "Let's hear it."

Skip pushed up his glasses and Dr. Kelly waited so she could hear what the young detective had to say.

"Miss Milford attended Bentley Wood High School in Stanmore Harrow."

"Posh," Leta commented.

"Every year the girls join forces with a local boy's school to put on a Christmas Pageant. White Oak Academy."

"Um-hmm," Bridges grunted.

"Before he attended Eton, Timothy Ashlock went to White Oak. He performed *A Christmas Carol* with Samantha Milford."

"Yes!" Bridges raised his fist in victory. Skip Loge was worth his weight in gold. "Detective, I want you to dig into this girl's life. Online and offline. Find everything that links her to Ashlock, then we're going to drag his ass down here for a nice long chat."

CHAPTER 33

The Proposal

I t was six in the morning when the butler arrived in Oxford-shire, and he didn't want to wake the whole house by knocking so he let himself in. She was standing in the foyer when he unlatched the door.

"I see you've found your way back to Great Britain," she muttered.

"Hello, Betty. You look lovely. How are our boys?"

She walked right up to the gentleman and gave him a peck on the cheek. "They'll be happy to see you, I'm sure."

"And what about you?"

She looked away.

"Did you receive my letters?"

"I did. Thank you. You have lovely penmanship."

"Hmm, but you never wrote back."

She tied an apron around her waist. "I never was much of a letter writer, Blake, but I enjoyed reading yours. Have you eaten? I'm going to start making omelets for the lads in a few minutes."

He put his suitcase to one side. "Please allow me to assist you, madam."

She led him toward the kitchen. "You can make some of your delicious coffee, but if you call me madam again I'm going to throw your belongings into the street."

"Fair enough."

She began cracking eggs and whisking them. "You know when you left I thought I'd be just fine without you."

"I had no doubt," Abbot said, grinding some beans. Jacob had purchased some wonderful Arabica from Costa Rica.

"It turns out I was wrong," she stated plainly.

"What?"

"Blake, I'm an old woman, but when I'm with you I feel young and in love."

They studied one another from across the kitchen's butcher block. "If you're duty-bound to Jay's family then I suppose I'll just have to go to New York and serve out the rest of your sentence by your side."

"Betty, I don't know what to say."

"Well, I hope you haven't moved on and found someone else."

"There's no one else. And as a matter of fact, I have something for you." Abbot reached into his breast pocket and with a slight flourish, he displayed the Cartier four-carat emerald solitaire engagement ring he's been carrying around for the better part of a year. He dropped to one knee.

"Betty Ashlock, will you be my betrothed?"

Tears started coursing down her cheeks. "Get up, get up, you silly, old fool. I'll wear your ring but I'm not marrying you until we are in England to stay."

He knocked twice, as was his custom, and entered the suite carrying a breakfast tray.

"Good morning, Abbot," Jacob said. "You're looking rather spry. How was your trip?"

The boys were grinning. "It was lovely, master Jacob, thank you for asking. master Timothy, you are well, I trust?"

"Never better."

"I bring greetings from your father. He's anxious to see

you."

Jake had always had a complicated relationship with his father. Abbot feared that if they didn't reconcile soon, time would run out for them.

"How is he doing?"

"I'm happy to report the cancer is in remission. On his good days, he can walk about the grounds."

"And my stepmother?"

"Remains a caustic, poisonous woman."

Jacob put an arm around the gentleman.

"I believe I'll be ready for the World Championships in Melbourne. Is he well enough to attend?"

"Perhaps. That's a long journey, but I'm sure he would like to be there."

"I'll speak to Coach Lir, but you should put the plan in motion. My first heat will be on March twenty-fifth."

"As you wish," he said, bowing slightly. Tim was questioning the butler with his eyes, watching each movement expectantly.

"Yes, yes," Abbot finally admitted. "You're a genius, Timothy. I'm in your debt."

He jumped out of bed and embraced the gentleman. "Are you going to be my daddy?"

"Sir," Blake Abbot answered, "you're a grown man and I am merely a servant."

"Come on!"

"What did she say?" Jacob asked.

He straightened the cuffs of his expertly tailored jacket. "She said, yes, but with conditions."

"That sounds like Mum."

"Indeed."

CHAPTER 34

The Butcher

Two dead girls and Timothy was the only person who had a relationship with both. If Jacob didn't know better he'd suspect his boyfriend of foul play. Still, there were more than a hundred people in the orchestra and a percentage of them also attended Merton.

Ethan was driving the boys to London so Coach Lir could put Jake through his paces in the pool. They also needed to work out the logistics of his FINA standings. Timothy went because he didn't want to be alone. It's wise to be near people who can provide a decent alibi should the need arise.

"So what do you think? I'll do whatever you say," Jacob said.

They interlaced their fingers. "Then I think you should make every effort to reconnect with your father. He might say something you need to hear, and life is short."

He was thoughtful for a moment. "We should go, then. The lot of us."

"What? To Australia?" Timothy said, shocked.

"I'll need a cheering section, and frankly I don't want to face my family alone."

Tim laid his head back against Jake's broad shoulders.

"And I'd love to spend part of our break down under where it's warm."

Timothy squeezed him. "You know, I met them, your

125

family," he whispered. "At your funeral."

"Ghastly, aren't they?"

"They were under a lot of stress at the time," he answered diplomatically.

"Timmy, there's no need to make excuses."

Ethan was staring at them in the rearview.

"What?" Jacob asked.

"You lads hear anything more about the murders?"

"The detectives all think Timmy did it."

"Go on!" Ethan said, looking at the skinny boy. "You couldn't harm a fly."

He touched their driver on the shoulder. "I'll be needing you to say something along those lines at the inquest."

"Hmm," Jake calculated, "us leaving the country might be just the thing. If someone else happens to get slaughtered while we're away then you'll be in the clear."

Timothy looked at him solemnly. "I don't want another Oxford student murdered just to exonerate me."

"You know what the papers are calling him, don't you?" Ethan said.

"What?"

"The Butcher of Oxford."

CHAPTER 35

The Warning

A s soon as they finished with him, Billy ran up High Street to Jake's house where Mr. Abbot answered the door.

"Lord Redgrave, the boys are still in London. Were they expecting you?"

"I'm not a lord yet, but I do need to see them. The DCI just grilled me for two hours. He asked a lot of questions about Timmy."

The butler motioned toward the sitting room where tea had been placed. It's almost as if they were waiting for someone. "I hope you were completely forthcoming with them."

"Yes, Mr. Abbot, I was. But they already think he's guilty. It seems they're just trying to build a case against him."

Betty came quietly into the room and poured three cups of tea. "You know he had nothing to do with any of this, don't you?"

"Of course, and that's just what I told them too, but they weren't having it. I think they're going to lock him up."

Abbot grasped her hand. "It may be time for us to engage a barrister."

Billy knew in his heart that his friends had nothing to do with these horrible crimes, but his stomach twisted into knots with worry. He texted her repeatedly. *Don't leave your room unless you must, and don't go anywhere alone!*

If a madman was killing Oxford women, the next Earl of Rockhold didn't want his first real girlfriend exposed to any danger. Both the dead girls were friends with Timmy, and that might just be a coincidence, but it was alarming.

Billy decided to ask her to come to Scotland for the break. It would be freezing but his family did have what amounted to a castle. She'd be cold, but she'd be safe.

CHAPTER 36

The Gathering

The Chief Constable of the Thames Valley Police had called a mandatory meeting that would almost certainly turn into a cluster fuck. Bridges and Skip represented the Major Investigation Team from the Yard, which was a sore spot for some of the law enforcement personnel gathered. There wasn't any love lost between Metro and various other police agencies in the UK. Some of them felt like stepchildren because Metro was tasked with protecting the Royal Family.

Oxford had eighty-three neighborhoods, all of them terrified. There were thirty-nine colleges and six Permanent Private Halls of religious foundation. Each of these was an autonomous, self-governing corporation so naturally, they'd all sent senior members of their boards which included titles like master, warden, president, dean, regent, on and on. Titles upon titles.

The DCI shook a lot of sweaty hands and looked into a bunch of worried faces.

The meeting was held in the large dining hall of Christ Church. Glancing around the familiar paneled room, Carl Bridges couldn't help but think that the deans were attempting to summon some magical intervention to solve their dilemma.

Chief Constable Henry Wells made some opening remarks and then handed the proceedings swiftly over. Carl

Bridges was underdressed for the occasion. Detectives wore suits not uniforms on the job, but his wardrobe didn't compare to the Savile Row finery that stood before him. At least Bridges could take comfort in the knowledge that he was allowed to carry a concealed weapon.

He cleared his throat and moved to the front of the assembly. "Gentlemen and ladies. The first thing I want you all to know is that every available resource has been allocated to this case, and I can assure you that the person or persons responsible for these evil deeds will be caught and brought to justice post haste."

There was an audible sigh from the room.

"Detective Chief Inspector..."

The first interruption of the evening.

These old academics just can't help themselves, he thought. *No one enjoys the sound of their own voice more than a former teacher.* He turned to see a portly gentleman who had the air of a diplomat or MP.

"Yes, sir?"

"Are you quite certain these murders are related?"

"We are. Both were female undergrad students, and although we have not made this information public, the killer leaves a signature. A symbol which he carves into the flesh of his victims. That signature is identical on both young women."

"And what is this symbol?" Someone asked from the back.

"We would rather not give specifics at this time, although we speculate that it may have its roots in the Greek alphabet."

"Do you have any suspects?" Another voice from the shadows.

Bridges had already lost control of the meeting and he could sense it would soon devolve into a free-for-all with random questions being thrown out rapid-fire.

He held up a hand to quench it. "Let's save all our questions for later, shall we? The Yard is attempting to connect the two victims with mutual acquaintances. One of the girls had only been at Oxford for forty days so the list of people she came into contact with is manageable."

Bridges turned toward Skip, who was preoccupied with his laptop. He was too much of a nerd to be bothered by a crowd of worried academics.

"Mr. Loge will give you the current profile of our killer. I'd ask you to keep this information private for the time being."

Fat chance of that, Bridges thought to himself.

"I'd remind you that this profile is constantly developing as we acquire new leads. Mr. Loge?"

Skip pushed up his glasses as he stood. He noticed a few of the deans and regents folding their arms, signaling a subtle resistance to being lectured by someone young enough to be a fresher.

"He's a white male, twenty to fifty-five years old. He's patient, meticulous. He blends in easily with the population at Oxford. He may be a graduate student, a professor, or even an educated day laborer. He knows Oxford well. We believe he has a military background or training. He is in excellent physical shape. Currently, we do not know how he is choosing his victims."

One of the decrepit old deans shuffled forward. "Rather broad strokes, wouldn't you say, young man?"

Skip merely stared at the gentleman until he looked away.

"It rules out most of the people in this room," Bridges said lightly, but no one found that amusing.

"There are two primary British military schools that funnel boys into Oxford. The Duke of York's, and Welbeck, but there are dozens of schools that have some form of elective military training. We believe the killer would have been an accomplished cadet or even been in the formal military before moving on to Oxfordshire. Our unsub didn't acquire his skills by reading murder mysteries in the Bodleian Library. He's been trained."

The President of Merton College stepped forward. "But DCI, do you have any actual suspects or is this all just conjecture?"

"Sir, we have linked one boy to both girls..."

The crowd immediately started to rumble.

"Is he in custody?"

"What's his name?"

"Which college?"

Carl Bridges felt like discharging his pistol through the stained glass. "Everyone, please calm down," he yelled. "We have not gathered enough evidence to make an arrest..."

"Surely you can hold this boy for questioning..."

"This is outrageous!"

The detectives looked toward Hank Wells, the Chief Constable, who nervously wiped the sweat from his bald pate and shrugged. It looked like the academic mob was going to get their pound of flesh sooner rather than later.

CHAPTER 37

The Early Birds

They arrived at precisely four AM pounding at the front door, with a fair amount of shouting thrown in for good measure. Jacob glanced out the window near his bed and there were half a dozen police cars with their light bars flashing on the street.

He roused Timothy.

"It's showtime."

Timothy looked terrified. "How many of them came for me?"

Jacob grinned. "Do you remember the end of *Butch Cassidy*?"

As they were getting dressed Jacob distinctly heard Abbot unlatching the front door. The boys walked casually downstairs where Bea was already crying and wringing her hands.

DCI Bridges stood next to five uniformed coppers. "Good morning, gentlemen."

"It's early for these theatrics, isn't it Carl?" Jacob asked.

"Well, the early bird and all that..."

Jake turned toward Abbot. "Is the paperwork all in order?"

"It appears to be. They cannot search the house but they can take Mr. Ashlock in for questioning. Timothy, please say absolutely nothing to them until your representation arrives."

He put his hand on the butler's shoulder. "I understand. Please take care of Mum until they let me out."

"Is he being charged with a crime?"

"Not at this time, but we do have some questions that need his attention."

"Exactly how long can they hold me without making a charge?"

The boys locked eyes. "Because you're a murder suspect, they can hold you for up to ninety-six hours."

"Jake..." he began. He was pale and starting to panic. Jacob remembered how claustrophobic he was.

"Don't worry— you won't even be spending the night down there." They hugged each other tightly.

"Okay lovebirds," Bridges said. "Break it up. Time for Timmy to see his new home."

"You bastard," Bea shouted. Abbot had his arm firmly around her or she'd probably have taken a swing at them.

"Say nothing," Jake commanded as they led Tim away.

CHAPTER 38

The Barrister Knight

Timothy Ashlock was scared out of his wits. The fear clung to him like a pair of wet socks.

Of course, that's just what they want me to be, he thought. *Weak and afraid. Compliant. But holy hell this is truly a nightmare scenario.*

He was cavity searched, and they did a thorough job of it. They wanted to be certain he didn't have any concealed drugs or weapons. It was just another way to humiliate him.

He was sitting in a dingy holding cell at Thames Valley Station with two other blokes. They were just lads who got into some mischief the previous night. One of them was passed out on the floor. The other was scruffy, but wearing a pair of Crockett & Jones loafers so Timothy assumed he was okay.

"What did you do, mate?" the conscious one asked.

"They are under the impression that I'm the Butcher of Oxford."

Scruffy's eyes widened. "Blimey."

"I'm not, by the way."

"You don't look like you could harm a fly."

Christ Almighty, Tim thought.

◆ ◆ ◆

At six in the morning Bridges stopped by the holding cell.

"Are you ready to answer some questions, Mr. Ashlock?"

He looked up from the floor. "Has my barrister arrived?"

"Not yet."

"Then I must decline. I'm sorry."

◆ ◆ ◆

At eight AM Skip Loge showed up. He had kindly brought hot tea and looked rather embarrassed to be a party to Timothy's current situation. His cellmates had been either released or shuffled elsewhere.

"How are you doing?" Skip asked, pulling a chair near the bars of the cage and sitting.

"I'm incarcerated."

"Yes, that's unfortunate."

"You know that I'm innocent."

He shrugged. "At the moment that is the minority opinion."

"So what should I do, Detective Loge?"

Skip stirred his tea. "If you want my advice, I'd sit calmly and wait..."

Tim gave him a questioning look.

"It probably won't be long before another corpse turns up."

◆ ◆ ◆

At nine o'clock there was a commotion within the station as cops began scurrying around. Constable Eddings came and unlocked the door.

"He's here," he announced.

"He?"

"Sir John. Come along."

Who in God's name is Sir John?

A jolly fellow with a gray beard and kind face came barrelling down the hallway with his arms outstretched.

"Timothy," he called. "My God, have they been keeping you in that dirty little cell all morning? There will be hell to pay!" he shouted out to the nearby uniforms.

He took Tim in his arms and embraced him. "What have you told them?"

"Absolutely nothing," Tim whispered back.

"That's my boy! I'm Sir John Colistra and I'll be representing you in this mad charade."

"I'm glad to meet you," Tim said, laughing at the sight of his barrister. Sir John was wearing a dark suit complete with a cape. It was nine AM on a Thursday and he looked like he just waltzed out of the Vienna Opera House on opening night.

He led Timothy to a small conference room. "I'll need a few minutes alone with my client if you please. Turn off all your listening devices or I'll have your hides." Sir John announced in a raised voice to no one in particular.

When they were finally alone and the door was shut his demeanor shifted. "Mr. Ashlock," he said evenly.

"Sir?"

"Being a suspect in a double murder is nothing to trifle with. You knew both these girls. I'm sorry, that must be terribly distressing."

He was watching and studying, carefully making a determination. Timothy knew he wouldn't just ask him outright if he was guilty, but the job would be easier if he was innocent.

"Yes, it is. Are you actually a Knight?"

He chuckled. "Why of course I am. I'm Knight Commander of the Most Excellent Order of the British Empire—which is a mouthful. The Queen herself tapped my shoulder. Not too bad for a boy from Hackney."

"Mum and I are also from Hackney!"

"Yes, I know, my boy," he said, looking at him through bushy eyebrows. "I've done my homework on you."

"What did you do to deserve to be knighted?"

"Hmm? Oh, that. The usual. I was gallant in the face of insurmountable odds." Timothy watched him thumb through a thick file produced from his briefcase. The lawyer glanced up and smiled. "Blake Abbot and I went to school together. I believe he's quite in love with your mum."

"You truly do know everything about us."

He reached over and touched Timothy's hand. "I think you might, like me, still have one or two secrets."

Tim felt himself blush. *If he only knew.*

"Let's get this ridiculous Q & A done and have ourselves a proper breakfast."

They moved into the larger conference room where Bridges, Skip and several other important-looking uniformed men were seated.

"We're ready for you, gentlemen," Sir John said impatiently.

Bridges coughed. "Yes, Mr. Ashlock, we're extremely sorry to detain you but the seriousness of these crimes demanded that we take quick action."

"Your apology is not accepted, DCI. The way my client has been treated this morning speaks to an appalling miscarriage of our esteemed judicial system."

"Be that as it may," Bridges continued, directing his gaze toward the boy. "We do have some questions of a rather personal nature to ask you."

Tim looked at each of his accusers in turn. *They're not a bad lot*, he thought. *Just a bunch of blokes trying to do their jobs and catch a killer. I'd be on their side if I wasn't sitting on the hot seat.*

"I'm happy to cooperate."

"Were you romantically involved with either or both of these young women?"

"I'm in a committed romantic relationship with a young gentleman."

"That doesn't answer my question, Mr. Ashlock," Bridges growled.

Sir John leaned forward. "We concede that Mr. Ashlock had personal and professional ties with both the victims. He is quite distraught at the loss of his friends."

"I'm sure," Bridges said with only a hint of sarcasm. "Were you aware that both of these girls had romantic feelings toward you?"

He shrugged.

Sir John jumped in. "If Mr. Ashlock dispatched every boy and girl that took a fancy to him, we would be knee-deep in dead undergraduates by now."

Skip chuckled and Bridges elbowed him.

"Let's move on to more practical matters. When did you meet Namika Ito?"

"When she was introduced to the Oxford University Orchestra."

Bridges consulted his notes. "That was on February twenty-second."

"That sounds right."

"And where were you on March fifteenth?"

"Umm," he stammered. "I'm not sure, exactly."

"My client suffers from chronic memory loss due to head trauma from an automobile accident. We have an affidavit from his neurologist," John offered the paper which no one took. It sat unread in the center of the conference table.

"Maybe a day or two here as a guest of Thames Valley will jog your memory," Bridges replied, smiling.

Timothy looked toward his lawyer who squeezed his shoulder. "I believe I was visiting an acquaintance that afternoon."

"Where?"

"Stow-on-the-Wold."

Timothy did not want to sit in a cell for four days.

"Did you drive yourself?"

"Yes."

"And who was it you were visiting?"

He bit his lip. "Dr. Thomas Pe, a professor of Asian Studies at St. Antony's College."

"I thought you were studying music theory at Magdalen..."

"I am. Dr. Pe is an acquaintance and a fascinating gentleman. My interests go beyond music, Detective."

"Hmm," Bridges said. "Please write down his address." He gave Timothy a pen and flipped over the paper from Dr. Matthews. "Detective Loge, please check CCTV traffic cams between Oxford and Stow-on-the-Wold for the day in question. If Mr. Ashlock is telling the truth we should have some nice photographs of his travels."

"And Miss Milford?" Bridges asked.

"I wasn't even aware Samantha was at Oxford."

"She lived three blocks away from you."

"So do a thousand other students."

"You knew her when you were at White Oak Academy?"

"Yes," he admitted. "We were in a Christmas pageant together."

"And you were romantic with her?"

"Not really. I was seventeen, we were bored. We kissed backstage. Nothing more."

"Well," Bridges continued, "she told several of the other girls in the production that she was madly in love with you, and that her intention was to bed you."

Timothy leaned forward. "She was a silly and flirtatious girl, not to speak ill of the dead."

"And why do you think she set her sights on you?"

Tim went silent.

"Well?"

"Some people find me rather easy on the eyes," he said, embarrassed. "But I think there was more to it for Samantha. Like some others, she wanted to possess what was unavailable.

I had the added appeal of being just out of reach. Off the market. I ignored her, and she found that irresistible. The funny thing is, had she achieved her goal I believe she would have found me to be somewhat boring."

"Mr. Weston doesn't seem to find you boring," the detective countered.

"Well, Mr. Weston and I have more to talk about."

Bridges took a slip of paper out of a file. It was protected in a plastic sleeve. "Did you write this note to Miss Milford?"

Tim looked down at his handwriting while Sir John leaned in. "Say nothing," he commanded in a hushed tone.

Timothy continued to stare at the note.

"Mr. Ashlock?"

Sir John abruptly stood and flipped back his cape. "You're going to have to hire a handwriting analyst for that answer, DCI, which will be a waste of time and money."

"I see," Bridges said, leaning back in his chair and smoothing his wild mane of hair. "You know, Timmy, innocent people usually don't so quickly hire lawyers."

"Then they are morons. Must you be a prat in every universe, Carl?"

"What's that supposed to mean?"

Timothy's thoughts raced back to having sex with Samantha in another time, in another world. He had managed to erase that indiscretion, among others.

"You're the only person who knew both girls..." Bridges said. "The deans all want your head on a pike."

Sir John laughed. It was a hearty, deep resonant guffaw. Timothy wondered if his advocate was as confident as he seemed. "Detectives, I hate police work. We have a staff that does all the scraping and digging for us. Phone records, social media postings, appointments, diaries—all tedious, very tedious, but oh so necessary, don't you agree? If only you boys were more thorough in your duties..." he dramatically paused. "Then poor sods like me wouldn't have to do all the heavy lifting."

He paraded behind Bridges who turned around to watch him.

"Your point?"

"Oliver Raymond Morgan," the barrister answered with an ostentatious wave of his arm. "He played Ebenezer Scrooge in that Christmas pageant at White Oak Academy, the lead opposite poor Miss Milford who acted as his love interest, Belle."

Bridges stared at Skip who was tapping away on his laptop. "And what of Miss Ito?"

Sir John sat beside Timothy putting his arm around the back of his chair. "Not to malign another bright Oxford lad, but Ollie gives campus tours to freshers. He spent several hours giving Namika Ito a private walk around the city of dreaming spires."

He then produced an eight-by-ten glossy photograph of Oliver with his shirt off. He tossed the image across the table in Bridges' direction. "I'm sure you'll immediately notice that Mr. Morgan is a powerful lad, roughly twice the size of my client and with considerable military training from his youth…"

"Loge!" Bridges yelled, scowling at his colleague.

"Morgan's father was a Colonel in the…"

"Enough," Bridges said, holding up his hand.

Sir John smiled proudly. "I took the liberty of speaking to the magistrate, what do you say we allow Mr. Ashlock go about his business today?"

"Fine," Bridges answered, disgusted. "We'll be in touch."

"Thank you, DCI, and good luck in finding the culprit of these nasty crimes. I'm sure we'll all sleep better when you've finished your work here."

CHAPTER 39

The Old Spies

J acob ran to him as soon as he walked through the door. "Did they make you wear stripes or one of those hideous orange jumpsuits?"

He rolled those beautiful hazel-green eyes. "Thankfully, I wasn't in long enough to warrant a wardrobe change."

"Did you have time to get a prison tattoo?" he joked.

Bea pushed Jacob out of the way. "Enough of your silliness, Jay. My poor dear boy." She hugged the stuffing out of her son.

Abbot was shaking hands with the jovial man in the cape that followed Tim into the sitting room. "I do appreciate your prompt attention to this, John," he stated.

"I hope that means the slate is wiped clean from that unpleasantness in the eighties, Blake."

"Almost," the butler answered. "When the scoundrel is caught and my boys are in the clear."

Abbott opened a chilled bottle of the 2009 Cristal and poured everyone a glass.

"You drive a hard bargain, old chum."

Abbot raised a glass. "Sir John Colistra, the finest barrister in the United Kingdom."

Everyone clinked their champagne flutes together and cheered.

"How did you manage it so quickly?" Bea asked.

Timothy looked bashfully at his family. "I'm afraid Sir John implicated Oliver Morgan to get me off the hook. That seemed rather harsh..."

"Ah," he said, pouring himself more Cristal. "I wouldn't worry too much on that count. Mr. Morgan has a solid enough alibi over at Exeter, at least for one of the incidents, but I wasn't going to mention that to those dullards from Scotland Yard. I love a good mystery, don't you? I'm sure the actual murderer is the person we least suspect."

Colistra was a sly old fox. It was clear to everyone that Abbot and he had a long shared history together.

Jacob turned toward him and couldn't help but smirk. The man was wearing a goddamned cape. "You and Abbot seem to know one another quite well."

"We do," John replied. "We met as shell boys our first week at Harrow. Decades and decades ago..."

Abbot looked decidedly uncomfortable with the subject at hand.

"Odd that he's never mentioned you..."

The two old gents exchanged glances.

"That is strange, especially since I almost married his sister, Rachel."

"Is that a fact?" Bea was suddenly interested in the conversation.

"John, please..." Abbot began.

"Well, I can't believe you never told these lads about us being recruited into MI6..."

"What?!"

Abbot groaned as everyone in the room stared in his direction. "I left all that rubbish in the past when I moved to America..."

Jacob led the barrister by the elbow and walked him toward the window. "You must tell me everything."

John looked back at Abbot who was giving him a rather menacing stare. "I'd love to, my boy, but your butler can be

THE BUTCHER OF OXFORD

quite lethal. If he doesn't want that chapter of his life exposed I'm afraid we'll have to respect his wishes."

Abbot closed his eyes. "Thank you, John. I think it's best if we let sleeping dogs lie."

Jacob found this all difficult to fathom. He knew that Abbot had a military background but he had pointedly refused to speak about his service. He'd known this man for his entire life, and yet seemingly not at all. Of course, the butler did have an array of unusual talents. Picking locks, for instance.

"Sir," he appealed to his mentor and friend. "I must insist..."

"Master Jacob," Abbot said forcefully. "I had an agreement with your grandfather regarding these matters. Trust me when I tell you that Sir John here is famous for his exaggerations, which is why the law is such a natural fit for him..."

"He's saying I'm a good liar."

A wry smile crossed Abbot's face. "Exactly. In any case, I did my bit for Queen and country long ago, and yes, it was in the area of intelligence..."

"Your butler was the best damn spy I've ever met," Sir John said plainly. "If it wasn't for him I'd be dead three times over."

CHAPTER 40

Swedish Roots

No one worked harder or wanted it more than Jacob Weston, but the car crash had changed things permanently. Coach Lir and Ethan watched him cutting through the water next to Matthew Colton. He was matching him stroke for stroke.

"Amazing," Lir commented. "He didn't lose any of his technique. The bones mended and he carried on just as before. The only difference is his speed."

"How do you account for the loss?" Ethan asked.

"I can't," the coach said flatly. "My theory is that the decreased lung capacity is slowing him down. His blood is getting less oxygen, so his muscles can't perform at peak efficiency. It all cascades down to lost seconds."

They watched his perfect flip turn.

"Maybe if he trains harder…"

"That's bollocks. No one trains harder, and I'm not just blowing smoke. He's come further than I would have believed possible. He's fast…"

They watch him fall behind the other lad as Ethan glanced down at the stopwatch. "Just not fast enough."

The coaches compared times.

"What are you going to do about the championships? They are only days away."

Lir shrugged. "What do you think I should do?"

"He might surprise us all," Ethan said with optimism. "He always seems to have an ace up his sleeve."

"He'll get crushed at the World's," the coach said evenly.

"His father wants to see him swim. It might be the last chance he gets to watch his son compete."

"I know," the coach muttered. "So we all cart ourselves to stinking Australia to watch the poor lad lose a race in front of his dying father? That hardly seems right."

Jake climbed out of the pool and grabbed a towel. "You two discussing the World Championships?"

"None of your fucking business," Lir shouted back.

Cotton sat on a starting block shaking the water from his ears. "You nearly caught me at the 100-meter mark."

Jake flipped him the bird. "And I was holding back. I had plenty left in the tank."

Matt grabbed a towel. "You are such a cheeky bastard."

"I'm attempting to lure you into a false sense of security..." Jake said teasing.

Matthew leaned into Lir. "I feel ready."

"Coach," Jake said, "all due respect, but we're going to Australia, and we're taking Cotton with us. It's right in the middle of the break between terms and my father has committed to coming to watch. If I can take third place or better I'll qualify for the Olympic Trials."

"Yeah," Matt said. "You take third and I'll take first and we'll both go to the Olympics. I'll be the lead swimmer for Team GB, and you'll be one of the arrogant Americans."

That's when the idea came to him. "Coach Lir," Ethan said. "I need a minute."

"Fine. You two toffs go get your rubdowns."

The boys headed into the locker room playfully horsing around.

◆ ◆ ◆

Lir looked over at his assistant. "So what's the epiphany?

147

You look like the cat that swallowed the canary."

"What if Jake doesn't swim for the Americans?" Ethan took out his laptop and was feverishly looking up splits for all the European countries.

"Huh?"

"Coach, he has dual citizenship. He was born in Sweden."

A smile slowly crossed Lir's weathered face as Ethan showed him the Swedish Swimming Federation freestyle times.

"This is the first that I've heard of it. Let's go talk to Wonderboy."

The coaches went into the locker room where both boys were face-down on massage tables being worked over by their trainers.

"Weston, you little fuck!" Lir yelled.

"Jesus," he said, flinching. "You scared me."

"Is it true?"

"Is what true, Coach? I'm trying to get a massage here."

Ethan chimed in. "You were born in Sweden, right Jake?"

"Yeah, it's a really funny story about my Swedish bloodline..."

"Tell it to us later," Lir said, slapping Jake's bare ass. "You'll swim for our fair-haired northern brothers. You don't have a snowball's chance in Hell of winning an Olympic medal, but your times just might get you a spot on Team Sweden."

"Hmm," Jake said. "One thing."

"What?"

"My father will never go for it."

Lir was pacing around the humid locker room. "Why the hell not?"

"Because he's a red-blooded American asshole. He's a stinking Republican. If I swim for Sweden he'll think I'm a traitor."

Lir and Ethan sighed.

"Can't you just do what you want? You're eighteen now," Ethan asked.

The head coach was slamming locker doors. "Daddy pays the bills."

"It's not about the money," Jake replied, sitting up and wrapping a towel around himself. "Thanks, Ian." The massage therapist nodded and packed his things.

"I bought into this Olympic dream when I was twelve and had just lost my mother. Swimming is, literally, the only thing I have in common with my father."

Lir looked hard at Jake. "You'd better call him right now because the only way I see you getting to the Games is under a Swedish flag."

CHAPTER 41

Oxford Town Hall

Metro had taken over the Old Library and several other rooms at Oxford Town Hall. The place, like so much of the neighborhood, was an opulent Victorian monstrosity, but it had modern amenities and was perfectly located to be the headquarters for the investigation.

Interview rooms had been set up and constables were methodically calling in more than a hundred musicians, tutors, gardeners, and professors for preliminary interviews. It was a colossal waste of time and manpower but to the City Council and the universities, it at least appeared that Scotland Yard was hard at work.

"Kid!" Bridges yelled.

He walked over to the makeshift office where he was consulting with Dr. Kelly. "You rang, DCI?"

"What did you think of the interview with Morgan?"

They looked up expectantly.

"Great interview, Chief—he's not our guy."

"Why the hell not?" Bridges asked, and Skip could tell he was starting to get steamed.

"Well, for one thing, I thought he was going to piss his pants when you showed him the photos."

"Maybe you were seeing his remorse," Dr. Kelly offered.

Skip flashed her a condescending glance. "Doctor, you're a great forensic pathologist but..."

"You see, Carl," she said, shifting in her seat to make eye contact with Bridges. "We need an expert to look over the tapes of all these interviews."

"Oh for the love of..." Bridges grumbled. "I hate shrinks."

Leta shook her head. "Skip, don't you think a psychotherapist could help with the evaluations and profiling?"

He pushed up his glasses. "Absolutely. Someone who has dealt with psychopaths and sociopaths in particular..."

Leta Kelly immediately lunged for her handbag to find her cellphone. "I know just the person for the job. Carl, you're going to have to okay this. She's a colleague from Cambridge."

"Fine, fine," Bridges said, waving a hand in the air. "The more the merrier. I've already got forty people on the payroll for this case, what's one shrink more going to hurt?"

She began texting. "She's slightly unorthodox, but I'm sure she'll fit in."

Bridges looked at Loge as they wondered what Leta Kelly's idea of unorthodox will be.

Eddings and two other uniformed cops came into the cubicle. "You've taken over Town Hall?"

"Parts of it," Bridges said. "Temporarily."

"Listen Chief, we did the footwork on the gay violinist."

"Finally. What's the word?"

Eddings took out several time-stamped images. "CCTV on March fifteenth. Looks like he went exactly where he told us."

"But?"

"He lied about the meeting. The house he sent us to is owned by a nice Italian family. They've had the mortgage for twenty years, and they've never seen nor heard of Timothy Ashlock or Dr. Thomas Pe."

"That's interesting," Bridges said. "Kid, what was the lowdown on this doctor?"

He sniffed. "There is no Dr. Pe in Asian Studies at St. Antony's or anywhere else at Oxford. I searched the directories for all forty-five colleges in every department. There was a Thomas Pe at Balliol College as a student."

"Was there?"

"Yes, in 1880. I doubt he's involved."

Bridges stood and stretched. "Thanks for the pictures, Eddings. I'll keep you boys in the loop."

The uniforms left and Skip watched Bridges putting the kettle on for tea. "It doesn't fit," he murmured to himself.

"What doesn't?" Leta asked.

"Ashlock's alibi. Weston and he are too clever for this lame maneuver. They would never lie about something that they knew damn well we would catch. It can only mean one thing."

Detective Loge started laughing. "Timothy Ashlock is telling the truth."

CHAPTER 42

The Bombshell

"**S**o how are you feeling?"

Jake turned the speakerphone on and set his iPhone down. He could hear his father's labored breathing.

"Why is that always the first question everyone asks a dying man? I feel like shit. But I'm a Weston so I'll die when I'm good and ready."

Jacob was holding a yoga tree pose. "That's the spirit. Are you still planning on flying down for the meet?"

His father coughed. "I wouldn't miss it. You're going to be an Olympian. The first Weston to win a medal."

"Well, that's the plan. This is just the World Aquatics Championships though. It's to qualify me to compete in the Olympic Trials. I'm still three steps away."

"One goal at a time, eh? That's the way to take it all."

Jacob peered out the window at the storm clouds gathering in the west and he moved into the warrior pose. "Yeah, about that—Since my injury, I'm not exactly the swimmer I once was. Coach Lir thinks I might have a better chance of getting in if I swim for Team Sweden…"

Dead silence on the line.

"Sir?"

"Absolutely not. You're swimming for Team USA. Do

you hear me?"

He's so predictable.

Jacob moves into a seated forward bend pose.

"Well Pop, would you rather have me swim for America or actually be in the Olympics?"

Paul went on another coughing jag. "I demand both. I'm a Weston and so are you. We aren't settling for anything less."

Bloody Hell, Jake thought. *This conversation couldn't have gone much worse.*

"Listen, when we are all in Melbourne I have two important people I want you to meet," his father said.

"Okay, who?"

"Son, this may come as a bit of a shock, but I'll be introducing you to your brother and sister."

He laid back on the yoga mat with a thud and stared silently at the ceiling while his father blathered on.

"...a woman I met long ago. It's important for me that you all get along. I knew this day would come and of course, it won't be easy."

Jake was starting to cry. In a moment he knew he'd be out of control, so he interrupted his father's explanation long enough to deliver one remark— "You're a fucking monster," he shouted and hung up.

CHAPTER 43

The Night Climbers

E ver since time-traveling the world Timothy returned to felt slightly out of synch. He ransacked the place looking for it and couldn't find it anywhere. They will leave for Australia soon and he's completely out of sorts.

What pained him most is the thought of his mum and Abbot not making the return trip to England. They will go back to America with Jacob's parents and God only knows when they'll be back in the UK. It's all so strange. Timothy's mum will know more about Manhattan than he does.

He wandered into the master bathroom and saw Jake dressed in black from head to toe. He's even smeared dark makeup on his face.

"Are you pulling a heist tonight?"

"Funny," Jake said. "Secret Society meeting. Can't tell you anything more."

"Hmm," Tim said, still watching.

"What have you been looking for all evening? Abbot will not be pleased when he sees the state of disrepair."

"My Fender. I thought I'd go down to the Hatter and play a set."

Jake blinked. "You've lost me, Babe."

"My guitar? It's usually in the broom closet of the cottage, but I've searched every cupboard and pantry on this whole estate. There are fifty-three of them, by the way."

"Timothy," he said, pulling a dark cap over his blond mop of hair. "I don't believe you own a guitar, and I've certainly never seen you play one."

"Whoa," Tim said, wandering into the bedroom and sitting down on the edge of the bed. "I took it up after..."
Jake grinned at him with his blackened face.

"Guess you had a lot of spare time with me out of the picture."

"I was pretty good."

Jacob put on black leather gloves. "A problem easily solved. We will go on eBay and purchase the best guitar we can find. I'm curious to see if you can still play it."

"I am too."

There was a knock at the door.

"That's for me," Jake said, but Timothy sprinted down the stairs to answer the call and found Casey and another boy also dressed in black. Larson had a dark rope coiled and slung over a shoulder.

"All right, Timmy?" Casey said, coming in for a hug.

"The chimney sweeps are here for you," he shouted up to Jake.

"Who might you be?" Tim asked the stranger.

"Timothy Ashlock meet Adam Harper," Casey replied. "Adam is the president of our society."

He was feeling a wee bit concerned. "You know if Loge and Bridges are staking out this house they will throw you lot in the Tower of London just for being dressed like that."

"Fair point," Jake said, bounding down the stairs. "We should sneak out the back way past the cottage, lads."

"Hold on," Tim said, waving. "What the hell is all this, Weston?"

"Uh-oh, he's serious. He never calls me by my last name."

"I give you permission to divulge," Harper said.

Jake wrapped his arms around the two boys adorned

in black and laughed. "Timmy, dear boy, we are The Night Climbers of Oxford. A radical group of ruffians that climb to the rooftops of our esteemed colleges where we muse on social justice, protests, anarchy..."

"And there's a fair amount of drinking and tomfoolery," Harper added.

"We are infiltrating and conquering Christ Church at midnight where we will together, as a pack, howl at the moon."

"Sounds dangerous," Tim said, looking into Jake's blue eyes.

"Ah, Timmy. I love you and your many phobias. We have loads of sturdy climbing gear, besides which, it's not like we're trying to summit K2. These old colleges are child's play to scale."

"I can't imagine how a group like this could get authorization..."

"Which is why it's a Secret Society, Ashlock. Are you feeling quite well? Besides, the lions don't ask permission from the sheep."

He takes out his violin since he has no guitar to play. There's a whole folio of original music that he apparently composed but has never heard or seen before. Perhaps he will try to tackle some of that while Jake is out.

"Please don't die. I'm not going back in time to save you again."

"What did he say?" Casey asked.

"I'm not saving you again either, Mr. Larson. Even if it was unintentional."

"He's only joshing," Jake said, pushing them toward the kitchen. The trio sneak out the back door and into moonlight and mist.

CHAPTER 44

The Shrink

She wheeled herself in and immediately started barking orders. Dr. Elsie Courtemarche.

"Elsie!" Leta called out when she saw the bright scarf.

"Leta. Give us a kiss and tell me why I've been pulled away from my research."

Dr. Kelly bent down and kissed her smooth cheek. She smelled like rose petals. "You've got a new chair, I see."

She patted the side of her futuristic Scewo Bro electric wheelchair. "State of the art, smart tech. This thing can even go up a flight of stairs. The old one gave up the ghost months ago. I feel like Patrick Stewart, you know, apart from being a fat black woman."

"With hair," Leta mentioned and they laughed together. Dr. Kelly introduced her. "Elsie's writing a book on all the serial killers of Europe," She told the boys.

"Fascinating," Skip said, while Carl only grunted.

Elsie wheeled right up to his desk. "You don't put much stock in the esteemed science of psychoanalysis, do you?"

"That's an understatement."

"Well, bite me," she yelled, turning her chair toward Skip. "America got all the fun serial killers, but we have a few interesting cases."

"Elsie has interviewed them all," Leta explained.

Skip moved closer to her. "Have you noticed many commonalities?"

"Hmm. Most of the pathology has already been documented, but generally speaking, they're quite a self-absorbed lot. Arrogant, obviously troubled, and whip-smart in most cases. So, show me what you've got with this Oxford psycho."

◆ ◆ ◆

Elsie demanded a real office with a window so Leta found her one. She spent two hours reading the reports and looking through the evidence, then she called everyone in for a meeting.

"Your shrink is a piece of work," Carl said as they made their way down the hall.

"I told you she was unorthodox."

"So am I working for her now?"

"Does it matter if she solves the case?"

He grumbled.

"I think we're all working for her," Skip said softly.

◆ ◆ ◆

Leta knocked on the door.

"Enter," she bellowed and they shuffled in.

"Okay Doc," Carl said sitting on the couch opposite Elsie's desk. "What brilliant insights do you have on our guy?"

"Well, Detective Chief, you haven't given me much to work with here. The first two murders were only six days apart, so he's overdue."

"He's going to kill again?"

"Probably," she answered. "Either he will or he won't. If he doesn't, then you don't have a problem anymore."

Skip chuckled.

"Oh brother," Carl said under his breath.

"How many hours of interviews have you completed?"

Skip looks up, "More than 120 and counting."

"Well, I'm not sifting through all that shit. Make me a highlight reel, Detective Loge. Just the guys who are true candidates. You folks don't know what questions to ask, so we'll have to bring the good ones back in so I can have a crack at them myself."

"We used the standard…" Skip began, but the shrink was already shaking her head.

"Do you have any sense of him, Else?" Leta asked.

She shrugged. "If I had to guess I'd say *Loaded God Complex*. Your boy thinks he has the power to wield life and death, which is why he marks them. He's methodical. Dangerous. The Asian girl's head was turned all the way around like an owl. You don't see that every day."

"Her spinal cord was snapped cleanly at C3."

"Well, we will certainly require more security around here," Elsie said, glancing around.

"What? Why?" Carl asked.

"Because Oxford is a small town and we are probably being watched. He's likely across the street in a pub laughing at us as we speak. He knows we're poking around. If we get too close to him he will come after us, and in case you haven't noticed, I'm not that fast a sprinter. This has a military feel, don't you agree? We'd just be considered collateral damage in his warped little mind."

That insight took all the oxygen out of the room. Skip looked nervously out the window.

"Eddings is bringing Ashlock back in today. Apparently, he has plans to leave the country during the break," Carl said.

"The gay violinist?" Elsie asked.

"Yeah."

"Perfect. Have the boyfriend come too, I want to talk to both of them."

"Oh, this is going to be good," Carl said, cracking his knuckles.

CHAPTER 45

First Impressions

She carefully watched the two boys through the one-way mirror. The big blond one looked right at the glass and winked.

"He can't see us, can he?" Leta asked.

"Of course not, he's just playing around. There are too many cop shows on Netflix."

He leaned over and whispered something to the pale violinist and they giggled like schoolgirls. *Pompous little shits,* Elsie thought. She continued to watch their body language together.

"Okay, you're right, Skip. The skinny one is innocent."

Bridges scoffed. "Is that your professional evaluation?"

"It is. That boy couldn't step on a spider without apologizing. The only way he commits an act of violence is in self-defense, and I doubt those girls were threatening the boy. It seems like they were both crushing on him. And it doesn't take a genius to see that these boys are gorgeous. They'd make a fortune in gay porn."

"I can't believe I'm paying good money for this," Bridges mumbled.

"Okay, kids. Let's get this party started. Pay attention, Carl, this is the way we play ball in the big leagues."

◆ ◆ ◆

161

She wheeled herself into the room and watched their reactions. Dr. Elsie made a distinct first impression on most interviewees.

"Hello boys, I'm Dr. Courtemarche."

"Doctor?" Tim asked.

"She's a shrink," Jake answered, rolling his eyes.

Elsie already had him pegged. *This is too easy*, she thought.

She glanced down at the file she brought along. "You're Timothy?" she asked, motioning toward him.

"Yes, ma'am."

"Did you murder Namika and Samantha?"

He held her gaze. "No. I didn't." He reached over and took Jake's hand.

"That's good enough for me. Please wait in the other room."

"What?"

"Bridges and Loge have some questions regarding your alibis and whereabouts, but they aren't pertinent. Please leave so I can chat up your lover."

The boys exchanged confused looks as Timothy wandered out.

"Alone at last," Jake muttered.

CHAPTER 46

The Odd Duck

S *he's different from Jane or any of the other therapists I've come in contact with*, Jake thought. *I can't put my finger on it. Honestly, I wonder if the wheelchair isn't some elaborate ruse. I'm half expecting her to stand up and walk around the room. The pattern of her dress and her style of hair suggest her heritage.*

"You're from Jamaica?"

"Originally yes. From Port Royal. Have you been, Jacob?"

"Never. And please call me Jake."

"You should visit—it's lovely."

"What should I call you?"

She gave him a toothy grin. "What's the matter with Doctor?"

"Well, don't you want to establish rapport?"

She glanced down at her bright green nail polish. "I thought our exchange about my birthplace was accomplishing that, but if you prefer, my first name is Elsie."

"Elsie," Jake repeats. "Is the gang all behind the one-way mirror watching our tête-à-tête?"

"Hmm," she said, giving the mirror a fleeting look. "I would assume Carl has got the popcorn made by now."

"It's interesting, isn't it, that the term one-way mirror and the term two-way mirror mean the same thing," Jake commented.

She looked at him quizzically. "You're rather an odd

duck, aren't you?"

"Doc, you're not the first one to make that diagnosis. Aren't you going to ask me if I'm the killer?"

She scribbled some brief notes down just to make him curious. "Would you admit it if you were?"

"Of course not."

"Then no," she answered flatly. "I know your type, by the way."

"Really?" he said, quirking a brow. "Do tell."

"You think psychoanalysis is a waste of time. You're not alone in that opinion around here. But you believe all shrinks get into the trade just so they can work out their own problems."

He whistled. "Elsie, that happens to be precisely what I think."

"Well let me tell you something, asshole," she said, lasering through the boy with her eyes. "I'm a crippled, overweight, black, lesbian alone in the world—so, yes, I've got a few fucking issues to sort."

Jake smiled at her and said, "Good God, you're a breath of fresh air."

"Thank you. So, you boys are planning a trip?"

"Yes. The FINA World Championships in Melbourne, Australia. I'm trying to make it into the Olympics."

"Lofty ambition," she replied, quickly jotting another note.

"You should come with us!" Jake suggested, only halfjoking. "My father is meeting us there and he's completely insane. He'd be a wonderful case study for you, and he's dying of bone cancer."

"Sounds delightful, but I don't work in the private sector anymore, and I have a full plate with these pesky murders."

"I know it's last minute, but you could think of it as a vacation. I'd pay you handsomely."

She leaned in toward the boy. "I want a million dollars."

He burst into laughter. *What fuckery is this?*

"Elsie, what in the world would you do with a million dollars?"

"I'd help people," she admitted in all seriousness. "I want to open a group of homeless shelters across the UK where psych interns can get practical field experience and the many people with mental health issues can find help and relief. You'd be amazed how eating a hot meal and having a roof over your head can improve a crazy person's outlook on life, not to mention just getting people back on their meds and into some group therapy. It's a win-win."

He stared at her.

"So, why do you hate your father?"

Here we go, Jake thought. *Right to the heart of the matter.*

"Hmm. Because he's a dickhead. He cheated on my mother repeatedly. I just found out that I have adult bastard half-brothers and half-sisters that I've never met. He lies constantly. He's selfish and he only cares how things appear publicly, not how they are. He believes he's the center of the universe, and I swear to God he thinks he's too rich to die. And no matter how hard I try, I never seem to be able to please him."

Jake can't believe he gave voice to those thoughts. She reached out and touched his hand lightly.

"I suppose he truly deserves a fatal dose of cancer then, huh?" she said in a whisper.

"Wow," he mumbled back. *This woman is a trip.*

"End all this nonsense!" Sir John came crashing into the room. "This interview is over. I can't believe I wasn't informed..."

"John," she shouted, "stop being an idiot!"

"Elsie?" he finally noticed her. "What are you doing here? I thought you were off writing a book."

She held open her hands. "Duty calls."

"These are my clients, Dr. Courtemarche. I can't have

interviews taking place when I am not present. My boy, don't utter another word."

"Sir John," Jacob said, evenly. "Please go away and let us finish our chat. Could you have all the recording devices turned off in the next room?"

"Of course, Mr. Weston. Immediately."

He stormed out confused but with a sense of duty.

"You know him, I take it."

Elsie nodded. "John and I go way back. He's a fine barrister."

"So I've heard. He must have left the house quickly. He forgot his cape."

She gave Jake a sly grin.

"So do I make the check out to you, or do we set up some kind of foundation?"

"What?"

"The million dollars, Elsie. Let's start helping people."

Her eyes suddenly went misty. "Just like that?"

"Just like that. Listen, I'll have my man Abbot set all the wheels in motion."

"But...you mustn't...it's, well, it's a breach..."

Jacob Weston had managed to flummox the great therapist with philanthropy.

"If word gets out people will think you're bribing me."

"I don't care."

"Neither do I," she whispered. "Are you sure? Don't you want to see a business plan or a mission statement? You hardly know me."

"Ah, I think I know you well enough."

She kept looking at him, sizing him up, analyzing. "Do you think spending a pile of your dad's money to help the homeless will heal some of the anger and pain you feel towards him?"

"I hope so."

She nodded. "Do you want some free advice from a world-renowned shrink?"

"Absolutely."

She held his hand. "When you see your father this week in Australia, kiss him farewell and tell him you love him."

That wasn't what he expected her to say. "But I don't love him."

"It doesn't matter. It's what he needs to hear."

Jacob pulled his hand away.

"What about what I fucking need to hear?" he shouted, raising his voice to a woman in a wheelchair.

"Try not being such a selfish prick, Jake. That isn't the path you want to tread. You don't want to become him, do you?"

"Selfish?!" he screamed. He's incredulous and starting to hyperventilate over it. "I'm giving you a million dollars..."

"Listen to me," she yelled back. "Let the old fuck die with a smile on his face and the healing process will begin for you. Trust me on this."

The room went still and Jacob swears he can almost hear her heartbeat.

"So, what are we going to call our charity? The Weston Shelter?" she asked.

"No way. My goddamn last name is plastered on enough buildings in this world. Let's name it after you."

She shook her head. "Thanks, but no thanks. It's too inside baseball if I'm running something that has my name on the wall."

Jake grinned. "Let's name it after Timothy then. The Ashlock Shelter for the Homeless. And let's keep the name a secret for now."

CHAPTER 47

The Women of Oxford

One murdered fresher was terrible enough, but when the second girl turned up dead the movement began. They named it simply, Women of Oxford, an unofficial society with the mandate of empowering female students and preventing them from becoming victims of the Butcher. It spread like wildfire throughout the colleges.

The women quickly mobilized under their unofficial leader, Missy Mikulicky, an overweight, suspicious girl with a bobbed haircut and a sharp tongue. Lisa Simone and Madelyn Drepa became her two closest lieutenants, and together the girls worked out the broad strokes of what would become the society's mission statement.

Makeshift memorials quickly sprung up at Merton and All Souls, the colleges of the two victims.

Many of the women in the student orchestra immediately signed up as a show of solidarity. Maddy and Leigh began organizing a march through the streets, while other girls were planning candlelight vigils and speeches.

"Do you think these women will make a difference?" Skip asked Elsie one afternoon while watching several Keble girls putting up posters for the march.

"You mean like scare the killer underground?"

He nodded.

"Not likely. If anything this kind of attention will egg

him on to more flamboyant behavior. We're dealing with someone who enjoys the attention and thinks he's smarter than everyone else."

"Sounds like you're describing Jacob Weston."

"That profile fits a lot of Oxford toffs," she countered.

Skip had been reading Oxfess religiously and many of the posts were about the Butcher. "The women have announced that they will not stand idly by while their sisters are brutally raped and murdered in the streets of Oxford."

"There was never any indication of sexual assault," Leta replied. "And we certainly never mentioned any theories publicly."

"The women are exaggerating what are already heinous crimes," Skip said. "Do you think we should have a conversation with their organizers?"

"Absolutely not," Bridges stated. "They will use whatever we tell them to add fuel to the fire. Let's just focus on catching this person and then these girls can move on to fight for other social injustices."

"They are scared," Elsie said. "So they want to do something to make themselves feel more in control. It's a natural response."

"But what are they doing?"

Skip looked up several of the published documents from their meetings. "They are enlisting a policy whereby women are never walking alone. They are also handing out plastic whistles to everyone who joins their cause. You want to know something else that's interesting about this association?"

"What?"

"No men allowed."

Leta laughed. "Turning the tables on all the private boy's clubs that thrive around these old tombs. A pure sisterhood."

Bridges shook his head. "It's only a matter of time before the back-stabbing and in-fighting begins. I'll bet you five quid they will tear themselves apart before we catch this guy."

"That's a bet," Elsie said.

CHAPTER 48

Jet Setting

"**I** appreciate this more than you'll ever know," Cotton said, hugging him as they entered the private jet.

Jake scoffed. "As you can see, my friend, there are loads of empty seats. I'm glad you're coming with us."

"But we're swimming against one another."

Jacob pulled a face. "I'm only swimming against the bloody clock."

Coach Lir and Ethan went to the back of the plane where they could strategize and worry over the International meet and their two contenders.

Bea and Abbot were unusually quiet. She looked out to the horizon and sighed. The sky was that mean shade of gunmetal gray that she had known forever. "I suppose this is the last I'll be seeing of England for a while."

"There, there, Betty," Abbot said, taking her hand. "You might take a fancy to Manhattan."

"And what about Jay's family? Will I take a fancy to them as well?"

Abbot looks down at his perfectly shined shoes. "Oh, I'm sure you'll despise most of them."

David Commons, the head steward, greets each traveler with a kind word and a dimpled grin. "This is going to be great fun, isn't it? I haven't been to Australia for ages. Janice will be so jealous."

"Where is she?" Jake asked.

"Maternity leave. I guess she wanted to have another baby before that biological clock stopped ticking."

"Speaking of which, how is your family doing?"

He smiled proudly. "Lori and the kids are all great. She sends her love."

Timothy, Matthew, and Jacob take over the center of the plane where a bottle of Salon Blanc de Blancs Vintage Brut is already chilled. "This is a special bottle," Jacob stated, popping the cork.

Tim just shook his head.

"What?"

"Every bottle you have in your cellar is special."

They all toasted as the plane took off.

"That's true enough," Jake admitted. "But this is the tête de cuvée."

"The one constant in the universe," Cotton stated, refilling his glass. "If you drink with Jake Weston he will never serve you a bottle of plonk."

◆ ◆ ◆

Several hours into the flight everyone had settled into their routines. Bea was knitting another scarf, this one multicolored. Matthew and Timothy were watching the latest Marvel film together, while Ethan and Coach Lir were drinking and watching past performance videos of various swimmers.

Jacob motioned for Abbot who followed him to the front of the cabin.

"Master Jacob?"

"I'd like the truth, Mr. Abbot."

"On which topic?" the butler asked politely.

"My mysterious brother and sister. You've known the whole time?"

"At first I only suspected, but yes, obviously I knew. Your father would have to get up pretty early in the morning to keep an expensive secret like that from my prying eyes."

"Then why didn't you tell me?"

The gentleman placed his hands on the boy's broad shoulders. "Because you were twelve years old when they resurfaced."

"And later?"

"By the time you were thirteen you were grieving the loss of your mother and you had the added issue of needing to come out to every person you've ever said hello to—a process that apparently has no end date."

"So sue me. I'm out and proud."

"Precisely, and I didn't want your siblings trying to take that away from you or make you feel bad about yourself."

"And would they have?"

"I'm sure they will attempt to even now. However, you are somewhat better equipped to deal with that nonsense these days."

David walked past with heated washcloths, and Jacob took him by the arm. "And you, my old chum, you knew about my hidden relations as well?"

"Umm."

"Yes, of course, he knew," the butler said, swatting away Jacob's hand. "Your father has made several trips to Kentucky in the last three years and has also taken those creatures on lavish vacations."

"You should have told me," he said, feeling betrayed by his lifelong friends.

David leaned toward Jake. "We were informed quite early that we'd be dismissed if we mentioned anything about Kentucky or the Harmers."

Jacob folded his arms across his chest. "Harmers, huh? This is all so disturbing. I can't believe I missed something this big."

"It wasn't my place to tell you, I'll mention this though,

Janice has always wanted to slip you the info on the sly."

Jake laughed. "I'm just upset that I've been deprived of knowing them for all these years."

"You are lucky for that."

"Why?"

"Your brother is a brute, and your sister is a bitter, conniving, pixie. Everything good in you came from your mother...your compassion, your kindness, and generosity. Your constant willingness to seek out the best parts of everyone. Those are from Janett, and unfortunately, your brother and sister were not blessed enough to have her blood or her influence. They are your father's children through and through."

"And what did I get from my father?"

Abbot and David grinned. "Your temper, your gambling instinct, and your aggression. You are a blend of them, the yin and yang. The perfect mix," Abbot stated.

"Jake," David said, "you wouldn't want to hang out with them. They're vile. You get to know people fairly well when you travel for hours and hours trapped on a plane. Take my word for it, you've missed nothing."

"Suzannah is calculating and mean— she reminds me quite a lot of Joanne. And your brother is only interested in fast cars and busty Instagram influencers."

"Frankly, I always thought that they would contact you, particularly your sister. They're obsessed with you."

This gave Jacob pause.

They sat down while David went off to attend to the others.

"Sir, why now? Why do you think he wants us all to meet? It's about the money, isn't it?"

"Yes. The three things your father cares about are himself, his money, and the Weston name. This summit is about all of those.

The bastards have his blood, but no name. Joanne and her idiot son have the Weston name but no blood. You are the only one who has both. It's anyone's guess what your father has in mind, but you need to watch your back. The Harmer's, Joanne, all of these greedy people circling like buzzards, would be a lot better off if you were dead."

CHAPTER 49

Headmasters & Gypsies

"How did they die?"

The headmaster glanced up from his paperwork. "The house exploded."

"Were you on campus?"

"No, I had an apartment in Greenknoll back then, but I heard the explosion. It took several hours for the fire department to contain the blaze."

"Faulty gas main?"

"That's what the investigators told us."

TJ Fulton was their English professor and a confidant of Weston's. His wife, Jane, was a counselor at the time and had filed a rather interesting report on the boy.

"Your wife wrote that Weston was unbalanced. A risk to himself and others."

Fulton frowned. "Jane wasn't my wife at the time, and the truth is that Jake and she never saw eye to eye. I wouldn't take that evaluation too seriously."

"I'd like to speak to her."

"Yes, well, as I mentioned, she'll be back in town next week when school resumes. She's visiting her mother in Geneva."

"You were named interim headmaster right after the fire?"

"Yes." He gazed out the window toward the church. "The Board of Directors only just made my position permanent."

"Congratulations," Skip said and Fulton smiled.

"Mr. Weston had quite a fixation on suicide as a teen..."

"Jacob has a curious mind, and he's still a teen."

"Yes but now he's also an adult. Many of the boys who attended White Oak Academy mention encounters with ghosts."

Fulton nervously drummed his fingers on the desktop. "Active imaginations are a healthy thing, Detective."

"So you've never personally seen a ghost here?"

"Of course not."

"You were Timothy and Jacob's English professor, is that right?"

"I had that privilege."

"I understand that you encouraged Weston's talent as a writer."

"He's a boy with many gifts."

"He was working on a novel..."

The headmaster touched his mustache. "Aren't we all?"

"The title of Jacob's book is *Brilliant Flames*, is that correct?"

"That sounds familiar. Book titles often change in the process of writing the manuscript."

"What was the subject of his book?"

"I believe it was a fictional thriller based loosely on a man named Thomas Sweatt."

"Sweatt was a serial arsonist who set more than three hundred fires in the United States," the detective cited.

"Ah, so you've heard of him. I don't believe Jacob ever finished writing that novel."

❖ ❖ ❖

Skip walked down into the nearby village to get lunch and do some thinking. The pub at Greenknoll was quiet, so he sat in a booth and looked over his notes while eating an extremely dull spinach salad.

"You've been asking lots of questions about my friends."

He looked up and a girl not more than eleven years old was staring. Her hair was braided and she was wearing a Pink Floyd tee-shirt that was too large.

"Hi," he said, but she just stood there watching.

"Which friends are you speaking of?"

She quickly sat down beside him. "Jake and Timmy of course. You're some kind of policeman?"

"That's right."

"You seem rather young," she said, and he grinned at the irony.

"What's your name?"

"Miranda."

Skip ate a bit more salad and took another sip of sparkling water. "Miranda what?"

She smiled. "Just Miranda."

"There's some trouble where Jake and Timmy go to school, and I'm trying to sort it out."

"And what's your name?"

"Skip Loge."

She smiled innocently. "Take my hand, Skip Loge."

He wondered what kind of a game this was, but she thrust her hand emphatically toward him so he grasped it. She closed her eyes.

"What are you doing?"

She let him go and met his gaze. "Just getting the lay of the land. I'm going to tell you a secret Skip Loge and it will help you catch this murderer."

"What?"

"You're busy looking in all the wrong places. The person who did these things isn't altogether human. You need to broaden your mind."

"Is this some kind of prank?"

"Everyone at Oxford is in danger. Does it leave a mark in the flesh of its victims?"

There's no way this little girl could know that fact. Skip wondered where she was getting her information.

"Okay, Just Miranda. Yeah, the killer carves a stylized Greek letter into the flesh of the victim shortly after death."

"Hmm, and is this creature quite strong?"

She was hitting close to the target so he'd gotten more interested. "Yes, the murderer is an extremely powerful man."

"You've got a real problem on your hands, but you're a smart cookie, you should go to the library and do some research."

"And what field of study should I be looking into?"

She laughed at him. The sound was light and delicate, like a wind chime. "Oh, legendary creatures. Folklore, mythology, fairy tales, you get the gist. You can return the favor by sending Timmy my way when you see him."

She got up and started to leave.

"Are you telling me there's a monster roaming around the colleges of Oxford? Some sort of Jekyll & Hyde?"

"Don't be silly, Skip Loge. You don't believe in monsters, do you?"

CHAPTER 50

The Send

Suzannah and Paul Harmer were excited that he agreed to come. Weston collected the children at the ranch in Kentucky and together they flew aboard his private jet to Orlando, Florida.

More than sixty-thousand Christians had gathered as a part of the new Jesus Movement known as The Send, a modern-day revival of pastors and evangelists coming together, attempting to inspire a new generation with some very old ideas.

They arrived at the Camping World Stadium where various stages, booths, and multi-colored tents were erected for the weekend.

"It's like a circus for the Lord," Paul beamed.

He's got the circus part right, Paul Weston thought.

"Who's this guy again?"

"Leroy Sanford," Suzannah told her father. "The greatest faith healer to walk the earth since Christ Himself."

"Right," he said as they made their way toward the encampment. Paul Weston was nobody's fool, but a drowning man will grasp at anything floating past him and none of the traditional medical treatments had stalled his cancer for a single day. He'd tried Chinese herbal medicine including rhino's horn and various other endangered animal extracts. Acupuncture, Manuka honey, Turmeric and other magical spices, shark cartilage, massage, and aromatherapy. Maybe it was time to give God a chance, but Weston suspected his affliction wasn't all that high on the Almighty's To-Do list.

"This way Papa," Paulie said, grasping the old man's hand. They made their way past snake-handlers frightening the faithful with their poisonous reptiles, while others babbled loudly in tongues. Some healers offered psychic surgery pulling what looked like chicken gizzards from their sickly patients. Paul grinned as they passed a stall where a preacher claims he can heal those burdened with homosexuality.

A swimming pool had been set up where make-shift baptisms took place every hour on the hour, and business was booming. There was lots of singing and shouting and booth upon booth of zealots hawking their religious paraphernalia. In Florida, there are hundreds of ways to make a few bucks off Jesus.

Weston knew his healing would come at a price too. The truth was that he would sign away any amount of money to have ten more years of life. He was ushered into a white tent where everything had been pre-arranged by Suzannah.

Leroy Sanford was an imposing figure. He weighed in at over three hundred pounds and had silky white hair down to his shoulders with a matching goatee. He was wearing a three-piece suit, also white, which made him look even more enormous, and a bit like Colonel Sanders.

He came charging toward Weston like a freight train. "Do you believe, brother?" he shouted at the top of his lungs.

Paul wasn't quite sure how to respond to the bellowing man so he simply nodded.

"I can take this cancer from you," he whispered seductively. "All you need is a small grain of faith."

"I believe," he said, and for an instant he actually did.

Sanford placed one gigantic hand on Paul Weston's head and cried out, demanding God to remove the tumors from his servant. "Let the demon cancer be gone!" he yelled, raising his right hand above Paul's head. "In the name of Jesus Christ!"

Weston stared wide-eyed as the performance continued. Dozens upon dozens of people yelled, "Hallelujah!" The lights flickered and from somewhere in the back of the tent the sound of thunder boomed.

The whole process took less than fifteen minutes. Weston's Platinum American Express card was charged an obscene amount and the trio made their way slowly back to his plane.

"Do you feel healed?"

"Don't be a moron. I'm just covering all my bases."

The siblings looked at one another nervously. "We don't want to lose you, Papa," Suzannah said meekly. Weston knew she was worried they'd be left in the cold when he died.

He turned to the Harmer children, looking at them sternly. "I want to make sure you understand why I'm having you come to Australia."

"He's our brother," Suzannah said.

Weston sighed. "Jacob is more clever than the two of you morons combined," he stated matter-of-factly. "So don't try to outfox him because it can't be done. Stick to the script and it will be a lovely family outing."

CHAPTER 51

Missy

A half dozen girls had gathered in an alcove at Pembroke for their brainstorming meeting. Together they stood and recited their pledge: "We, the women of Oxford will no longer be oppressed, fearful, or objectified. We band together in this blessed sisterhood to claim our rightful place as leaders. We demand equality for women in every college, and justice for our fallen sisters. So say we all."

Missy skipped over reading the minutes from the previous meeting and proceeded into the current agenda. "The memorials at both colleges must be maintained daily," she chided. "We need to show them we are serious and that we are never going away. We can't forget our sisters Namika and Samantha. We are petitioning the colleges for permanent memorial statues to honor the victims of the Butcher."

Lisa Simone took off her thick glasses. "Many of us will be leaving over break, but our work here needs to be tended to by the women that stay."

Missy turned her attention to Madelyn. "We hear you are spending some time away from us, have you prepared everything for the march? It's scheduled for the week Trinity starts."

Madelyn nodded. "The candles are on order. I've let the presidents know what the route will be. We have volunteers putting up fliers all over town."

"Well, we all hope you have a nice vacation," she said sarcastically.

"I'm going to Scotland, not leaving the planet. I'll have my laptop and can still work on the cause remotely."

Leigh nodded. "Give her a break, Missy."

She scowled. "Our priority is to the eleven-thousand women who are students at Oxford, not to mention female support and staff. We have a chance, right now, to make a difference, but we need to be in their faces."

CHAPTER 52

The Race

The FINA World Championships was an annual competition that featured swimming, water polo, and diving over six days. The boys arrive forty-eight hours before the first qualifying heat for Freestyle Swimming.

Jacob's father and his entourage would arrive the next morning. The original plan was to have everyone stay in suites at the Hotel Windsor, an ancient Victorian relic that was elegant, sophisticated and reminded Jake too much of Oxford.

Abbot got off the phone. "I've moved you to the Pan Pacific. Your suite has a view of the Yarra and the entire Port. Are you quite sure about this?"

"Positive, and thank you. I don't want to see my family until after the first round is over. I can't deal with the distraction."

"Understood."

Lir came over. "You boys get some rest. I've spoken with the American coaches. We're going to meet at the arena at six o'clock tomorrow morning and figure out all the logistics. Ethan will fetch you at five-thirty, so don't keep him waiting."

"He'll be ready, Coach," Timothy promised.

◆ ◆ ◆

Their new hotel was sleek and modern. The panoramic suite had floor-to-ceiling windows that looked out over Port Phillip Bay and the entire Melbourne skyline.

"This is more like it!" Jake said, bouncing on the king-size bed.

"I agree. This is posh."

"Let's call room service and order a feast. I don't want to leave this suite until it's time to swim."

He'd already changed into one of the thick hotel robes. "Whatever you want, your majesty."

He hugged Tim tight. "I'm glad you're here. I'm positive this ordeal with my family is going to be hideous. If my siblings are anything like my father and stepmother then they are mean-spirited and cruel. We have to stay strong, Timmy."

He remembered Jake's family from the funeral. They were unpleasant. "I don't know how Mum's going to survive living under the same roof as those people in New York."

"I hope Bea wrestles Joanne to the ground."

They started laughing.

"Mum has a temper, she can only be pushed so far."

Jake went to the window while Tim pulled out his phone to take a photo. They were finally making memories he could keep.

"It's strange, you know. They've known about me for years and years. Lurking around my social media, or whatever, and they've never once made contact."

"Maybe they weren't allowed."

Jake rubbed at the blond stubble on his cheek. "I would have broken that commandment. I'd have made a Herculean effort. I was so lonely growing up, it would have been nice to have a brother and sister."

"Well, now you do."

"Ha! But now I have you, and Ethan. Cotton, Billy, Casey, and all my other friends. I don't need greedy siblings scratching at the door."

He'd padded into the massive bathroom and turned on the tap for the tub. "Hey," he called out. "Let's take a bath!"

"Okay," Tim answered, removing his clothes and leaving them in a pile by the door. "That sounds relaxing."

Jake was rummaging around in his duffel until he found what he was looking for.

"Is that nail polish?"

"Yes," he grinned. "We have to do each other's toenails. Divine decadence."

"Mr. Weston," Timothy said, "you've finally gone round the twist."

CHAPTER 53

Corpus

His phone started ringing at three AM He fumbled at the nightstand and checked the caller ID: Owen Forrestal. That could only mean that Scotland Yard was getting impatient.

"Forrestal, are you still in London?"

"No sir, I'm coming to pick you up. I'm in a van, fifteen minutes from your hotel..."

They had worked a couple of homicides together in the past. Owen was old school, by the book, a Yardy for life. Bridges was surprised he wanted to pound the pavement of Oxford ferreting out a serial killer.

"You've been reassigned to my unit?"

"Yes, Chief. I'm glad to pitch in."

"I'm getting dressed now. Where are we headed?"

"Corpus Christi College. Student housing within the College's walls, a place called Kwee Court. The bodies are still warm."

Bridges put him on speakerphone and splashed his face with cold water, running a comb through his unruly hair. "Bodies? Plural?"

"Afraid so, DCI. Two freshers. Both eighteen."

"Our guy is upping his game." Bridges texted the Kid and ordered him to assemble the team and meet at Corpus.

"We need the building secured, no one in or out. Where were the bodies found?"

"Second-floor shower room."

"It needs to be sealed off as well and a guard placed until we arrive."

"Already done. I'm nearing your building, and guess what?"

"What?"

"That American detective, the boy genius, is sitting on your front stoop."

"Kid!" he yelled, opening the outer lobby door.

"Hiya' Bridges," he stood and brushed off his corduroys.

"How did you get here so quickly?"

He smiled timidly. "My hotel is only a block away."

"Right, and how is it you knew about these new murders before I did?"

"Yeah," he stammered. "Well, I monitor the Thames Valley Police radio with a scanner in my room. I heard it come across, and figured we would be heading over there this morning."

Forrestal pulled up in an unmarked black van.

"I didn't want to wake you, so I waited."

Bridges put a gloved hand on Loge's shoulder as they climbed in. "Good work. Try to get one step ahead of our guy and I'll buy you a vegan dinner."

It was still technically night when they pulled into the college yard, but even at that early hour news traveled fast. Corpus was lit up like Piccadilly Circus.

"Christ," Bridges muttered. "This is going to be a shit

show. I thought everyone was supposed to be on break."

Forrestal cleared his throat. "We better catch this guy before all the entitled children return for classes or there's going to be a panic. The Yard is already hearing from dozens of Chancellors and Deans. Frankly, they're worried there will be a mass exodus from Oxford."

Skip was looking at his iPad. "Forensics is already here and is taking samples and searching for trace evidence. All the showers and taps were turned on so the assumption is…"

Carl shook his head. "The water washed away anything relevant. What about cameras?"

"No cameras in the showers, but it doesn't matter since apparently, the whole security system is down at Corpus," Forrestal said soberly.

"What? Disabled by our guy?"

"No Chief, they were updating their system, installing a new one over the break. It will be operational in two weeks."

"Outstanding," he muttered, sarcastically. "Any other good news?"

A nervous old woman was sitting in the hall in a thin floral robe. She was hysterically crying. *Must be the matron*, Skip thought. Leta had arrived and was trying to console her as Bridges approached the women.

"This is DCI Bridges," Leta said, introducing him. "Martha here is the matron."

The woman grabbed his hand. "Nothing like this has ever happened at our college," she cried. "My poor, poor girls. I've been here for twenty-two years and I've never seen the like." She stared up at Carl Bridges with red-rimmed eyes. "Please DCI, you catch this murderous bastard."

"I'll do my best," he pledged, turning to Dr. Kelly. "Have we got statements from all the people in the house?"

She straightened his necktie. "Patience, old boy. Forrestal and Eddings will be organizing interviews. The constables have roused everyone out of bed. So far, it looks like no one saw anything unusual."

"I'm not surprised," he said, surveying the scene. "We had better catch a break soon. Where's our shrink?"

"On her way. It's four in the morning."

"Have you determined the cause of death yet?"

"Preliminary, yes. You're not going to believe it," Leta whispered.

"Try me," he grumbled as the Kid rushed up to them.

"Bridges," he said excitedly, "these girls were electrocuted!"

CHAPTER 54

4:08:40

A debate raged between the American coaches and Coach Lir over which race Jacob would have the most competitive edge in. The 400 Meter Freestyle had always been his best event, but because of his decreased lung capacity, Lir felt that he would do better in the 200 Meters.

The Americans watched tapes of all his 400s and were duly impressed. It made no difference to Jacob because either way he was sure to win. He always felt a kind of magical glow in the water and he knew that despite the setbacks and the injuries, he would shine here, in this arena. He'd capture the magic of Australia like a jar full of fireflies.

Coach Rader was a legend in the swimming world. An Olympian in Atlanta in 1996 although he never medaled. He was a giant, boisterous, happy man who looked like a big, blond lumberjack.

"Jakey-boy," he shouted, slapping him on the back, "do well here and it's on to the Olympic Trials. How do you feel?"

"Never better, Coach," Jake said truthfully. His upbeat attitude was infectious, despite Lir and Ethan standing near the diving boards looking worried. Jake saluted them.

The 400 was a crowded event. Forty-nine swimmers would compete in seven heats. Jake's race came up before he had a chance to be nervous about the crowd, the pool, or his family. He had never studied other swimmers because he'd always competed solely against the clock, so this group of international athletes meant nothing to him. His strategy was just to swim fast and kick some ass.

Cotton would be swimming the 800 meters. This was a decision Lir made on the plane after he determined the field was too strong in the 400. If Jacob thought about that long enough it might worry him, but it is what it is.

He was wearing a blue Fastskin suit and a stars and stripes swim cap that Coach Rader gave him for luck. Bea had given him the rainbow pride scarf that she finished knitting on the plane; it was the perfect accessory for a partially naked swimmer. He adjusted his EarPods and turned up Timothy's rendition of the Bach Chaconne in D Minor. Jacob Weston leaned back in his folding chair, finally settling in, just waiting for the race to be called.

But he sensed it when they arrived. His father has managed to acquire seats directly behind the FINA judges, front and center. He glanced over and saw Timothy seated next to his dad, which was strange enough, but on his father's right sat two young people. A boy and a girl in their late teens with dark hair and sullen, brooding faces. Jake's brother and sister.

He didn't see Abbot or Bea anywhere nearby. *I hope they managed to find decent seats*, he thought. Oddly, his stepmother and her son were also MIA. *Curious.*

◆ ◆ ◆

Ethan touched his shoulder and it was time. Almost seven years in the pool had led to this moment, this race. He shook out his wrists and adjusted his goggles, then proudly draped the scarf around his neck. Jacob Weston was ready.

Reaching down into the water he splashed his face, beginning to focus on the task at hand. His fastest time was 3:41 which should be enough, but that was before the accident. He'd take anything close to that and be a happy camper.

The starting gun fired and Jake realized the truth as

soon as he entered the water. He will have no speed today. He'll set no records. The water hated him and Jacob Weston was going to lose. Each stroke felt like he was pulling himself through a vat of maple syrup. His lungs burned and every muscle fiber ached. Lir was right. He wasn't ready for this, not by a long shot.

It was pure agony. The distance seemed endless, the clock ticking ever onward and the other boys were all much too fast. Anger welled up and he felt his heart hardening into stone.

When it was all said and done he came in 40th place with a time of 4:08:40. Climbing out of the water he looked over to his father who would not meet his gaze. Timmy was close to tears, and his brother and sister—well, they were hysterically laughing.

◆ ◆ ◆

Escape.

Jake needed to be somewhere else. He brushed past everyone and stormed into the locker room to change. People were talking to him, Ethan, Lir, the Americans. He couldn't understand any of them, all he heard was a dull humming against his eardrums.

During the confusion, Jake looked to the far side of the vast changing room and saw Matthew Colton. They locked eyes and he drew near. Jake didn't want to distract him, he knew Cotton was mentally preparing for his race, and watching Jacob have a meltdown wouldn't do him any favors.

Matthew didn't say a word, he simply hugged him. Perhaps better than anyone Jake knew, Cotton could understand what he's feeling. He released his friend and they stared at one another, then the swimmer turned around and went back to his preparations.

◆ ◆ ◆

Jacob managed to find a back door out of the venue. His phone was blowing up and he could only guess what the texts said. He ignored them all. Instead, he ran toward the taxi queue and was surprised by who was waiting there.

"Going somewhere?" Abbot asked.

"Sir, don't try to stop me."

"Oh, I wouldn't dream of it."

"Did you expect me to accept defeat with grace and humility?"

"That would have been refreshing."

"Well, I'm afraid I must disappoint again. It's what we losers do best," Jake fumed.

"Hmm, I assume you are going to a pub somewhere to marinate your bruised ego."

This was exactly the conversation that Jacob was desperate to avoid. "Something along those lines," he muttered under his breath.

"And what should I tell master Timothy? You've abandoned him to fend for himself amid those horrid people."

He looked at this kind, old soul. "Mr. Abbot, I believe I'll just take a long walk. I need a few moments alone."

"Your father expects you for dinner at seven o'clock. The Vue De Monde restaurant in the Rialto Towers. Please call your boyfriend as soon as you are able."

"Thank you, I will."

Blake Abbot looked at the boy who had become a man. "Whatever else transpires this evening, I want you to know that you have made me very proud," he said. "Never forget our secret, Jake. When the world is in tatters we remain, first and foremost, gentlemen."

CHAPTER 55

Hot Water

"Electrocuted?" Bridges said. "Seriously?"

Leta Kelly patted Loge on the back. "That's my finding as well. The electrical current on wet skin is several times greater than the current on dry skin. There's a good amount of burned tissue with both these girls. Certainly, enough amperage traveled through them to stop their hearts."

Skip was drawing a diagram on his notepad. He bent down to examine the drain.

"Christ," Bridges said. "This looks ten times more—sexual."

Leta met his gaze. "Yes, the flutes make it bizarre. I won't know until after I autopsy the girls whether they were inserted pre or post mortem. Or if the act was voluntary or forced."

Bridges lowered his voice, "You don't think they voluntarily used…"

Dr. Kelly stopped him. "You'd be surprised at the assortment of foreign objects that people insert into their bodies. I'll have an answer for you at the lab."

"Where's the bloody shrink? This case seems to be venturing into her territory now. I want Courtemarche to see this tableau before we move the bodies."

Skip approached the DCI and motioned toward the tiled floor. "I think I know how he did it."

"Shoot," Bridges said.

"The killer arrived well before the girls and placed something inside the drain, probably a towel, to block it. He then reattached the metal cover and bolted it. After fifteen minutes with the taps running there would be several inches of standing water in this tiled area."

"I get it," Bridges said. "Anyone taking a shower would be sloshing around in a bog."

"Precisely. Then it would be just a matter of bringing a frayed electrical extension cord about twelve feet from that outlet," Skip pointed to a wall socket that exhibited scorch marks.

"And dropping the exposed live wire into the water. The wiring in this building is ancient and not well grounded. This event blew out every master fuse on all three floors. That was at 2:15 AM according to the matron. Power wasn't restored by the maintenance crew until 3:05, giving the killer plenty of time to carve the symbols and do whatever else was done here this evening, then escape into the night."

"So," Bridges continued, "he then removes the towel, bolts the drain, carves his Greek symbol into their foreheads, and does his thing with the flutes. Then he turns on all the faucets, takes the electrical cord and whatever other gear he's brought along, and just walks out the back door?"

"Everything he needed could easily have fit into a small duffle. It wouldn't have looked out of place, even at that hour."

Carl Bridges massaged a pinched nerve in his neck. "It's plausible. Good work, Kid."

◆ ◆ ◆

Elsie arrived at six o'clock.

"You took your sweet time, Doc," Bridges said.

She wheeled around the area taking in the entire scene. "Don't give me any grief, Carl. I'm not one of your flunkies that's at your beck and call twenty-four-seven. These dead girls aren't going anywhere."

"Actually, they have an appointment with Dr. Kelly in her lab."

Elsie pulled her Jamaican print shawl close around her shoulders and looked over to the doctor. "Ah, sorry Leta, I didn't mean to hold you up."

"It's no problem, Else."

"I assume you've photographed this six ways to Sunday?" she asked Skip.

"Yes."

"Well, then cover these poor girls up and get them out of here," Elsie commanded. "I've seen enough."

Forrestal and Eddings stood to the side as the MEs and several orderlies placed the girls into black plastic body bags, zipping them closed and loading them onto stretchers.

"What have you got, gentlemen?" Bridges asked.

Owen approached him carrying a laptop. "I've got statements from everyone who was in the house, Chief. About a dozen residents and staff members were in the building."

"Send everything to the Kid and copy me and the doctors on it all. Who were they?"

Owen bent down to tie a shoelace. "Twin sisters. Sheri and Terri Muller. Both medical students and members of the Oxford Student Orchestra. They were flautists."

"Why were they still at Oxford during the break?"

Eddings wiped his brow. "I knew these girls. They grew up here, from working-class folk. They weren't rich."

Forrestal nodded. "The DS is correct. They both had jobs as librarian assistants during the break. Books need to get restocked, shelved, and organized before every term. That's one of the reasons the breaks are so long."

"And the big question..." Bridges began.

Skip jumped into the conversation. "I've looked through their Instagram and other social media. They were close friends with Timothy Ashlock, Douglas Turner, Casey Larson, and several other gentlemen we've questioned."

"We believe these girls were targeted, don't we?"

"That seems likely," Skip replied.

"So how did the killer know they'd be taking a shower together at two in the morning?"

Forrestal checked his notes. "Several students mentioned that the girls would often shower after a late night on the town. They preferred privacy and there was a greater likelihood of hot water being available at night."

"Hmm," Bridges said. "That seems like information not a lot of people would be privy to."

"I'm hungry," Elsie announced, wheeling her way toward the men. "Detective Loge, I'd like you to escort me to breakfast."

"What? No way, I need him here."

"Carl, the boy genius has to eat too, and I'd like someone with a loaded firearm by my side. Surely you can spare him for an hour or two."

Skip shrugged and packed his things. "I'm starving."

Carl gave Leta a pleading look. "I can't give you anything else until after I've done my examinations. I could use a couple of hours."

"Let's meet back at my office at noon," Elsie said. "I'll give you an update of this psycho for your profile then. He's taken things to the next level."

CHAPTER 56

The Vue De Monde

"**I**'m on my way back to our hotel," Jacob said into his iPhone. He was jogging beside the harbor and was nearly out of breath. "Will you meet me there?"

"I'm already waiting for you. Listen, about the..." but he was interrupted mid-sentence.

"Don't tell me what I already know, Timothy James. I'm fine, or at least I will be. The last thing I need is your pity."

Tim sighed into the phone. "Are we still having dinner with your relatives tonight?"

Jake laughed, stopping his run to look up at the sky. "Timmy, *Caro*, we can't deprive my blessed family the opportunity to kick me while I'm down, now can we?"

"Mum thinks we should just blow it off and go to a crappy Aussie pub to get blind drunk on cheap beer."

"Ah, Bea," Jake said. "You can take the girl out of Hackney..."

"She just loves you, P.S. your siblings are truly revolting. I can't believe you're related to them. Suzannah and Paul won't even say my name out loud."

"What? You're kidding. What do they call you then?"

Timothy stared out the huge windows of their room and spotted Jacob far below, a solitary blond boy on his cellphone staring across the expanse of water. "The one time they

200

referred to me was to complain to your father. I believe the phrase was, 'do we have to sit with the faggot boyfriend?'"

"*Mon Dieu*, I'm sorry. We've all been called things we can never forget."

He touched the tinted glass with his fingertips. "It doesn't matter, but can you please be your old self tonight and give them a real dose of gay wit and sarcasm? They need to be dropped down a peg."

"Well, now I'm kinda looking forward to the festivities," Jake said, stretching out his hamstrings.

"I can see you," Tim mumbled.

Jake squinted up at the sleek, high-rise hotel in the distance. "You've always been able to see me."

The boys entered the elegant Vue De Monde restaurant and immediately headed for the Lui bar. It was late summer in Melbourne so they were wearing light Tom Ford suits. Jacob was in blue and Timothy in black.

"When will they arrive?"

"My father is always at least twenty minutes late. He thinks it makes him seem important."

"Hmm," Timothy said. "Makes me think he can't read a clock face."

Jake ordered two special macadamia martinis and they sat and admired the stunning view from the Rialto Towers. The restaurant with its dark walls and subdued lighting made a fine place to observe the sunset and city lights.

They touched glasses.

"I'm going to speak to the maître d and find out who our waiters will be tonight," Jacob said, excusing himself.

Off to plan some mischief, Timothy thought. *Excellent.*

The Harmers arrived just as Jacob was returning. Paulie wore a cowboy hat and a sweater that looked two sizes too small. He was obviously a gym bunny and a juicer. Suzannah was wearing acid wash skinny jeans and a puckered gauze blouse.

Jacob threw open his arms as soon as they entered. "Brother! Sister!" he shouted loud enough for nearby patrons to take notice. "We meet at long last."

They accepted his embrace stiffly. Timothy smiled and wondered how this extroverted, benevolent brother routine was going to play out.

"You're much bigger than you look in your pictures," Paulie said, mentally comparing their measurements.

"Am I?"

The Harmers completely ignored Timothy's existence, as had become their new custom.

"You remember my faggot boyfriend, don't you?" Jake said, grabbing Tim's hand and making him blush. "You were all seated together at my extremely pathetic athletic performance."

"Yes," Suzannah finally said, smacking her chewing gum. "Hello again."

Paulie frowned at the gay couple. "You seem in awfully good spirits considering how badly you lost."

"Well, win some, lose some," Jacob said gaily, clapping his steroid-infused half-brother on the back. "I'm still handsome, rich, and in love. And at least my swimming gave you and Suzie-Q here a good laugh."

Paul and Joanne Weston arrive and survey the group. "Son," Weston said as if he's testing to see if the word still applies.

"Father," Jacob responded. Joanne was smirking like a nun. "Evil stepmother," Jacob continued. "Where is Denny tonight?"

"He had other plans."

"Lucky him. And, where are my coaches? Not to mention Bea and Abbot?"

His father scoffed dramatically. "Don't be absurd, Jacob.

We aren't inviting the servants to dinner, it's bad enough we have one of their offspring at the table."

"He's talking about you, Timothy James. Well, if you can have your bastards then I can have my boyfriends."

Paul motioned to everyone like he was directing traffic. "Let's just sit down, shall we? I need some gin."

They were directed to one of the premier window tables. Jake smiled as he turned toward Suzannah, "Are you wearing jeans in a Michelin starred restaurant?"

She glanced down at her legs, quickly crossing them. "These are very expensive. They're Gucci."

"Of course they are, honey, and acid wash was all the rage in 1987— are you also chewing gum?"

She self-consciously spit it into a cocktail napkin and deposited it into an ashtray, and that's when Jake smiled.

As they were settling the maître d leaned towards Timothy, hardly noticing the others, "Is the table to your liking, Mr. Ashlock?"

Timothy winked at Jake. "Yes, thank you. It's lovely."

"Very good, sir. I've told the chef you're back. He's very excited."

"So where are Ethan and Lir?"

"Ethan Polley was hired to be your driver, and I fired Coach Lir after your disgraceful performance today."

Jacob winced. "Of course you did."

Weston ordered a Bordeaux-style wine grown in Matakana, New Zealand from the sommelier, while waiters flocked around pouring sparkling water. Each one greeted Timothy by name, asking if everything was up to par.

"They all seem to know you," Suzannah mentioned.

"Yes, this is my favorite restaurant when I'm in town," Timothy answered cooly.

Joanne looked skeptical. "Well if you're such an expert on the place, what should we order?"

He nodded thoughtfully at the mean little harpy. "Jacob and I are going to share the chef's ten-course tasting menu, which you should try if you're feeling adventurous."

The Harmer's looked like they'd strayed off the trail and were abandoned in the forest. "If you ask nicely, maybe Timmy can persuade Chef Bennett to make you a nice burger or a grilled cheese," Jacob said to his siblings, patting Suzannah's hand.

"Do you know why you lost today, brother?"

"Hmm, that's a tough one. Perhaps it's because the other lads were faster swimmers..."

"Maybe it's because you are a homosexual," she said as if the word itself turned her stomach. Jake started laughing so hard, he nearly spat wine all over her.

"She has a valid point," Paulie said dumbly. He was still wearing his cowboy hat at the table. "This entire country was founded by criminals and perverts, it makes my skin crawl."

Jacob looked at his father, incredulous. "You've got to be kidding me with these two mouth-breathers." He raised his wine glass, "To sodomites and fops," he toasted, but only Timothy would touch his glass.

He turned his attention toward his sister. "Suzie, there are lots and lots of gay athletes, homo Olympians, and queer gold medalists. Why, if you took the gay out of the Olympics no man would ever win another medal in figure skating. I think Adam Rippon won for best makeup in 2018," he joked.

Timothy squeezed Jake's thigh under the table appreciatively. "Dear brother and sister, you should know that love has no gender, no religion, no bias."

"We'll have to agree to disagree," Suzannah replied sharply.

"We can blame your loss today on bad coaching," his father said. "Nothing more. It will hardly tarnish the Weston name. Next time you'll win."

"Except that there isn't going to be a next time. I'm quitting all this nonsense in the pool."

His father looked out the window and was silent as a tombstone. Now they truly will have nothing in common but the past.

"There is a group at Oxford called, The Octopus Club. It's a sort of underwater hockey game that started in the fifties. It's developed into a game called, *Octopush*."

"Doesn't sound like something that gets awarded gold medals," Paul grumbled.

"There's more to life."

Suzannah blinked. "Maybe if you found Jesus…"

"I didn't even know He was missing," Jake quipped.

"My sister and I are going to be opening a conversion therapy camp to help cure people like you, God willing."

"Are you?" Jacob said, turning like a cobra toward his brother. "How wonderful! Just what the hillbillies need, another pray away the gay camp to torture adolescents and incite more suicides. Praise God! And who's money will be funding this endeavor?" Jake asked, looking directly at his parents.

"Some of the money is coming from churches," Suzannah replied.

"Oh, don't tell me, congregations like Westboro Baptist?" Jake's tone was rising steadily.

"That's a great one," Paulie nodded. "They're down in Kansas."

"What's their stance on spray tans and steroids, brah?"

"Settle down, son," Weston said, trying to lower the volume. "I know you're still upset about the swim meet."

"I'm upset because I can vividly remember being the gayest kid at Heavenly Hills Christian Camp."

"We didn't fly halfway around the world to get insulted by this faggot loser, Papa," Paulie whined.

Tasmanian sea urchins with caviar arrived, along with a tray of oysters. Timothy and Jake dug in immediately. These ridiculous people have not spoiled their appetites.

"That's an interesting question," Jake said, feeding Timothy a Moonlight Flat Clair de Lune. "What the fuck are you two doing in Australia?"

Suzannah smiled smoothly, delivering the line she's

been rehearsing. "Daddy wanted the whole family together for once, and we've been looking forward to it."

"Bullshit," Jacob said.

Timothy leaned in. "This is going far better than I imagined."

Jacob wiped his mouth on a linen napkin and stood abruptly. "If they bring the mud crab, don't eat it all before I return," he warned. "Excuse me, Father. I need to place an important call."

"What do you think you're doing interrupting our dinner?" Joanne hissed.

Jacob looked closely at his biter, bat-faced stepmother. "I'm calling for reinforcements, naturally."

While he was away from the table Paul Weston directed his sickly attention to Timothy.

"Whatever you might imagine your relationship with Jacob to be, you are just my son's latest indiscretion, and trust me on this point, you will not be his last. We Westons have insatiable desires. When Jacob finally discards you and ends this tawdry affair, I can assure you that the family will retake possession of that pretty violin."

Paul looked down at his food, he barely touched a bite. Timothy held back the sudden urge to break something.

"You are my boyfriend's father and I respect that, so I will not speak my mind. You have me at a disadvantage."

"Nonsense," Weston said, coughing. "We're all adults and free-thinkers here, and I'm interested in your honest opinion, Mr. Ashlock."

"Well, you're a billionaire and I'm just a poor musician, but I don't think you know your son half as well as you think you do. Jake and I are soulmates."

"Is that right?"

"It is," Timothy had lost his patience with the Weston clan. "There is also the matter of my having been made a vice-president of the JP Weston Corporation, perhaps you aren't aware of that development. Also, I'd be willing to wager that

THE BUTCHER OF OXFORD

Jake will still be holding my hand when we attend your funeral."

"How rude!" Joanne shouted. "Paul, why must we eat with this gold-digger?"

Timothy chuckled and muttered, "That's the pot calling the kettle."

"You should remember that your mother is now one of our servants," Joanne seethed. "And I can assure you that we will demand more respect from her than you are displaying tonight."

"Good luck with that," Timothy said, sipping his wine and looking away.

Jacob returned and Timothy gave him a portion of mud crab. "What did I miss?"

"Absolutely nothing," he whispered, "but I'm glad you're back."

The waiters next brought a steaming plate of Australian marron curry. "Those are crawdads where we come from," Paulie crinkled up his nose, disgusted. "And only poor people eat them."

"A type of crayfish, yes," Jacob remarked. "The Aussies call them Yabbies, and they are considered a luxury product here. Would you like to try one?"

"Pass," Paulie said.

"I'm sure your macaroni and cheese is lovely, but you two should try to expand your horizons."

"Fuck you."

Jacob smiled slyly. "Now, now, brother. Our blessed Lord and Saviour is listening."

Matthew Colton entered the restaurant wearing his GB Team sport coat and a Magdalen College tie. "At last!" Jacob said with glee.

"All right then, Weston?" he asked. "Luckily I was already on Collins Street, what's the emergency?"

"I'm about to murder my entire family," Jacob whispered. "I desperately need you to stay my hand."

Timothy signaled to one of his waiter friends and another place setting and chair magically appeared at their table.

"May I introduce Matthew Colton, Great Britain's finest young swimmer, who finished the 800 in first place today."

Jacob kissed him on both cheeks. "Well done, mate."

Everyone at the Weston table greeted him cordially.

"Looking very patriotic," Timothy said, eliciting a smile.

"I haven't had to pay for a single drink since I put this blazer on," Cotton announced. "I may never take it off."

While everyone was shaking his hand, Jacob reached across the table and discreetly placed something into his pocket. "You're in time for the cured kangaroo."

He sat happily, grabbing some cutlery. "When in Rome."

Paul Weston regarded their guest coolly, "So, will you be going to the Olympics, Mr. Colton?"

"That's the hope, sir."

"Good for you."

"It's nice to finally meet a winner," Suzannah said.

Jacob winked at his dear friend.

"Before his car crash Jake used to kick my ass in the pool," Matthew explained. "That's how we met. The Eton Trials."

"And since that day he's never stopped flirting with me," Jacob told the table.

"Jake please," Tim scolded.

Cotton flushed with embarrassment. He bashfully looked to Jacob's father. "That isn't entirely accurate..." he began, but Paul simply waved it off. He was more than accustomed to Jacob's outrageous remarks.

Flinders Island lamb with sweetbreads arrived next. "How are you enjoying the meal so far, Mr. Ashlock?" a waiter asked.

"Delicious. Please send our compliments to Shannon. He's a genius."

Cotton laughed. "Who the devil is Shannon?"

"The chef and Timmy go way back," Jacob explained.

◆ ◆ ◆

After chocolate espresso soufflé, and traditional Australian biscuits with tea the boys get up to leave.

"I think it's time we found that pub Mum was talking about."

"You are so right, Mr. Ashlock," Jacob said, turning to bow to his siblings. "I can't tell you how memorable this encounter has been."

"We'll see you again soon, brother," Suzannah said.

He blinked and gave his most charming smile, "Not if I see you first."

Matthew shook Mr. Weston's hand, thanking him for dinner.

The maître d and several others crowd around to bid Timothy farewell. Suzannah managed to catch one of the waiters by the sleeve, "I'd like to have a cappuccino now if it isn't too much to ask."

The boys looked at her and laughed.

"You'll have to excuse us. We, deviants, are going to find a gay bar in Melbourne to be with our tribe," he said, holding Cotton around one shoulder and Timmy around the other.

"Just a minute," Paul interrupted. "I need to have a private conversation with you, father to son. We should find the time."

"It will have to be later tonight. We are leaving Melbourne early tomorrow."

Weston stared at him. He barely recognized the striking man his boy had become. "Very well. Meet me at the Windsor in two hours, and try to remain coherent."

They began to make their way out. "And Jacob," Weston said, "leave your *soulmate* at the bar."

CHAPTER 57

Freakshows

They were just sitting down to breakfast at Vaults & Garden, Elsie's favorite eatery in Oxford. "I didn't think to ask, but you do carry a gun, don't you?"

"Yes."

"And you know how to use it?"

There were a total of six people sharing the room at that hour. "Of course. Are you expecting me to need it during breakfast?"

"One never knows." She aligned her chair to the table. "So, I'm anxious to get your take on this morning's carnage. What do the twin murders say about our killer?"

Skip opened his laptop. "It's a new wrinkle, and not just because of the sexual element. A trap was set. It took planning and patience. A double homicide is tremendously risky, so he's taking greater chances. It shows an escalation."

Elsie sipped her coffee. "I agree. But what does it say about his emotional state? What's he feeling?"

"Anger. Carving the symbol on their foreheads is also an intensification. It reminded me of the seven P's carved onto Dante's forehead before he entered Purgatory."

"Your mind is amazing, Skip. You should think about going on Jeopardy! I'm sure with that vault of information between your ears you would make more money than Ken Jennings and James Holzhauer put together."

She watched carefully as the boy genius cringed. "The last thing I would want to do is take my freakshow and put it on display for the world to mock. I'm not a dancing bear, Elsie."

He was devouring the vegetarian Oxford while Elsie was tucking into her avocado toast. "You see, dear boy, you do care what other people think of you. If you can worry about an unseen TV audience of strangers mocking, how much more are you concerned about people that know you?"

"Are you analyzing me, Doctor?"

She laughed casually. "Occupational habit. I'm afraid I do it to everyone. But you and I are friends and I just want you to be the best possible version of yourself. Do you have contact lenses?"

He nodded. "They're itchy."

"You'll get used to them. When we've finished breakfast we are visiting Reign Vintage. It's a shop on Cowley. You need a new look, Mr. Loge. It's time for a makeover."

CHAPTER 58

Addendum

Jacob arrived at the Royal Suite in the Hotel Windsor only slightly worse for wear. He was managing to toe a fine line between tipsy and sloppy with his current state of inebriation, but as he noticed on more than one occasion, a certain amount of drunkenness is essential in any serious conversation with his father.

The nurse escorted him through the formal sitting room complete with a marble fireplace to the master suite where his father was already in bed, an IV administering medication into his forearm. The old man looked as though this trip abroad was taking a toll.

"There you are," Paul said, glancing up from his newspaper.

His nurse Karen excused herself and closed the door silently behind her, leaving the two men to their own devices. The large suite had become unbearably hot to Jacob and his feet felt as wobbly as a three-legged dog on a sailboat.

"Where have Joanne and Denny run off to?"

"I don't know," Weston said. "I've asked them to make themselves scarce so we could be alone."

"How ominous," Jacob muttered. He removed his coat and rolled up his sleeves, trying to find relief from the heavy air in the room. He glanced at the ornate marble surroundings. "This room looks like England."

"Well, don't you love it there?"

Jacob opened the glass doors to the terrace, allowing the summer wind to ruffle the sheer drapes. "I do, but this hotel smells like Queen Victoria's musty corset."

He squinted at the IV bag trying to make out the typed name of his father's medication.

"It seems we've both been putting on a brave front this evening, eh son?"

"Well, we never let them see us sweat, do we?"

"Never," his father agreed. "You know, I went and saw a faith healer in Florida with your brother and sister."

Jacob laughed. "So I suppose all this medication is rather superfluous, correct?"

His father gave him a dubious stare. "I won't know until my next scan, but one can always hope," he sighed. "So, how did you feel about the meet?"

Jacob feigned a smile. "If you must know, I'm gutted about it. I wouldn't have dragged you all this way if I thought I was going to lose."

They stared at one another until Jacob finally heaved himself into a wing chair across from the bed, drunk and exhausted. He could feel his father's lecture approaching like a hurricane.

"You're very much like her, you know."

He touched the crocheted afghan laying across his lap and Jacob immediately recognizes that it's one of hers. "That's the real reason I sent you away to school. I couldn't stand you staring at me with her pale blue eyes. In all the ways that mattered, you belonged to your mother."

Jacob considered the man that he feared for so much of his childhood, now a faint shadow of who he once was. His hair, his muscles, even his voice had withered. "That's the nicest thing you've ever said to me."

"Hmph," he scoffed. "Well, you managed to inherit all her weaknesses too. You're stubborn and strong-willed, you have a nasty habit of collecting strays, you don't respect the boundaries of class and position and, just like your mother, you've never been able to hold your tongue."

He aimed to point out character flaws but Jacob wore each of those traits like a badge of honor. "And were you respecting the boundaries of class while you were banging the assistant horse trainer? You managed to spawn two incredibly vile human beings by repeatedly fucking one of your employees!"

Paul laughed at this, which set off a violent coughing jag. "Let that be a lesson to you."

Bloody hell, he knows how spoiled and mean-spirited the Harmer's are, Jacob thought. "I understand now why you wanted me kept away from those bed-wetters for all these years."

"Stop being a snob. Everyone can't be as refined as you are, son. We shouldn't fault them for that."

"Then can we fault them for everything else? The white-trash, homophobic little nazis," Jacob said, suddenly realizing that his father wanted him to see his siblings in all their terrible glory. Paul Weston certainly wasn't going to make excuses for his horrible bastards and God knows he wasn't going to apologize for anything. Jacob had never heard his father say he was sorry. Not once. Ever.

"Exactly what is this clandestine meeting all about? I'm sure you've cooked up some scheme that involves me."

"You're quite perceptive," his father answered.

"So I've been told."

"I've written an addendum to my will that I wanted you to be made aware of."

It always comes down to the money, Jacob thought.

"Now son, this blueprint only goes into effect if you fail to meet the conditions I've prescribed."

"I'm on tenterhooks," Jacob replied, searching the room for a bottle of something, anything, to drink.

"Please don't make light of this discussion. You stand to lose several billion dollars if you don't succeed in this endeavor."

"Very well, father, I'll bite. What do you want from me? A gold medal?"

"A son."

"What?" Jacob said nervously. Even he didn't see that coming.

"For generations, the Weston fortune has passed down to the legitimate firstborn male heir. Your current lifestyle doesn't provide a way to ensure that our name and legacy will endure. So, I've given you until your twenty-fifth birthday. If you fail to produce a true heir by that deadline the estate will be divided three ways."

Jacob felt the throbbing of an epic headache beginning right behind his eyeballs. "The Harmer's, Joanne, and me?"

"I'm afraid so, and God help our house if it should come down to that. I hate to think of the Weston name dying out."

"This estate is my birthright, you can't divide it up like you're carving a turkey."

His father looked back down at his newspaper. "The lawyers say otherwise. Everything comes with a price, Jacob. I'd assumed you knew that from being born into this family."

"And if I should succeed in producing an heir?"

"Then Joanne will receive a small allowance as dictated by our prenup. And your bastard siblings can be compensated in whatever way you deem fit. I'll leave that decision entirely in your hands."

It was all very Machiavellian.

Jacob stood out on the balcony and watched the Australian night unfold. *You have to give the old man credit*, he thought. *He has a way of always getting precisely what he wants.*

"So that's why you were so eager for me to meet them," he whispered.

"I wanted you to have all the facts at your disposal so you could make an informed decision."

It was blackmail, of course, but Paul Weston had done far worse in his life and this was of paramount importance to the dying man. The future of the Weston bloodline.

"I'm going to do just as you ask," Jacob finally announced from the terrace. "I'm going to be a father to a slew of Westons and our name shall live on forever."

Paul smiled, breathing in a sigh of relief and his son smiled right back.

"Wow, I guess I've managed to say something right for once," Jacob laughed, sauntering back to his father's bedside.

"So, you're going to get married and settle down?"

"If that is your wish, father, then that is what I'll do."

He nodded. "I knew you'd come around. You're a true Weston. I'm glad we see eye-to-eye on this. If you make fast work of it I might even be able to hold my grandson before my hourglass runs out of sand." He pulled the colorful afghan up to his chin. "Now what about this Ashlock boy? What are your plans for him?"

"It's just as you described, he's one of the strays that I've collected along the way—but I'm keeping him."

"If you must," Paul said, a soft grin teasing his lips. "The men in the Weston family have always had voracious appetites."

"True." He leaned over and kissed his father softly on each cheek.

We finally see each other, Jacob thought. *Perhaps this is our one moment of clarity together, but I'm capable of a few surprises too.*

He continued to watch Paul Weston with his mother's pale blue eyes. "You've been a wonderful father and I love you. Thank you for traveling all this way to watch me swim."

Paul waited for the punchline, the sarcasm he'd become so accustomed to hearing, but it never arrived.

CHAPTER 59

Suspicious Minds

The young detective walked into the briefing room both self-conscious and transformed. His dark-framed glasses had been discarded in favor of contact lenses. He unconsciously rubbed the back of his neck, missing his long hair. Elsie had brought him to a stylist to have his thick brown curls cut into a taper fade. His new wardrobe was an eclectic mix of vintage layers in contrasting colors.

Carl watched him sit down without comment.

"Go ahead Bridges, let's get all the clever observations and critiques out of the way."

"Kid, you finally look like you fit in around here. It suits you."

"Heavens!" Leta squealed when she laid eyes on him. She grabbed Skip's hands and made him stand and spin. "You look fantastic! How did this happen?"

"Elsie," Skip mumbled.

As if on cue, Dr. Courtemarche wheeled into the room, admiring her handiwork. "He was always a diamond in the rough."

"Maybe now that the boy genius is gorgeous we can get down to catching our killer," Bridges stated, staring at a wall pinned with dozens of suspect bios and photographs. "So, who do we like for this?"

Skip was considering every image, reading the Post-it

notes with clues and other data stuck beside each picture.

"Well, don't all go at once," Bridges barked.

"I'm leaning toward the conductor," Leta said.

"Elsie?" Carl asked.

"Hmm, he's interesting. Certainly, he knew the victims and had access. His background is murky, and he's been intentionally vague during his interviews. I chalk that up to him being a closet case and not wanting us to dig up any of his conquests. He's the kind who might use his position of authority to get favors from the student body. He's a narcissist, and extremely intelligent."

"Loge, who do you like?"

Skip rubbed his eyes. His contacts were already bothering him. "The rower, Casey Larson. He has strong ties to Ashlock and Weston, not to mention many, many people of all persuasions at Oxford."

Carl looked toward Elsie.

"He's a strange bird, no doubt. He likes rough sex with both men and women. Privileged, entitled, and attractive. Only the murder of the twins had any real sexual element, however. His increased need for gratification may have led him down this path."

Skip was consulting his laptop. "Larson is also a medical student at Corpus, and there was a cheating scandal last term where his name was mentioned. Maybe he went on this murderous spree because he knows he's about to get sent down."

"What about the boy the lawyer gave us? Oliver Morgan?"

Skip shook his head. "His alibi checks out for Samantha Milford's murder, and he's been out of England so he couldn't have killed the twins."

"Do we think that more than one boy could be involved in this?"

The DCI turned to look at Elsie.

She moved her wheelchair so she was right up against the wall of suspects. "If you're suggesting a partnership I'd tell you that serial killer teams are extremely rare but not unheard of. They are usually married couples who kill, like Fred and Rosemary West here in the UK. We don't have suspects that fit that pathology."

"What about Weston and Ashlock?"

Skip laughed, but it didn't deter Carl from weaving his web.

"Maybe it's part of some weird thing those two have going on, or it's a factor of some Oxford society ritual. We know for a fact that Weston is a member in at least two secret societies."

Elsie turned her chair in Carl's direction. "You truly are daft, Bridges. I know you want the two of them to be guilty, but it simply isn't them. They're ten thousand miles away right now."

Carl riffled through his papers. "I want to see proof that they are actually in Australia. If it's some Satanic ritual, as everyone seems to think on Twitter, then maybe it's a whole group of boys doing this, so let's not be too quick to take the gay lovebirds off this wall. Maybe other boys are doing the killing while the masterminds are on vacation."

"Unbelievable," Elsie muttered under her breath.

"Carl, after carefully examining the Muller twins I can tell you with some confidence that the flutes were not forcibly inserted."

"Are you telling me that those girls were using musical instruments as sex toys?"

"I'm telling you what I'm telling you. These girls very carefully placed those flutes where you found them, obviously while they were alive."

"Maybe they were forced to do it to themselves," Skip said. "Or to one another."

"That's a possibility and it would bring a torture element into our case," Elsie stated. "Maybe they thought if they did as they were told they wouldn't be killed."

"The Women of Oxford are going to have a field day

with this," Forrestal said.

"I don't want the information leaving this room," Bridges said. "Let's lock this guy up before it gets any more grotesque."

Skip packed up his laptop and started to leave.

"Where do you think you're going?"

"My contacts are bugging the hell out of me, so I'm going to take them out, then I'm going to the library."

CHAPTER 60

Farewells & G'days

An old couple and a young couple sat on the rooftop terrace having breakfast. Everyone but Timothy was accustomed to getting up at the break of dawn. Abbot and Bea to begin their workdays, and Jacob to start his morning workouts.

"It's hard to believe you people are used to getting up at this ghastly hour," Timothy said, rubbing the sleep from his eyes.

The four watched the sunrise shift its colors, spilling like blood across the morning sky. "This has always been my favorite time of day," Bea commented.

"I heartily agree," Abbot said, resting his hand over hers.

"Are you sure you're doing all right, Jay? I'm rather worried."

Jacob smiled at her. "I'm right as rain, Bea, but it's me who should be asking you the question. You're the one who is going to be trapped with my family in New York."

She took a spoonful of strawberries and cream and smiled back. "Don't worry your pretty head about us. Mr. Abbot and I can navigate any storm."

Jacob turned to the gentleman, "I trust an old spy like you will have no trouble acquiring the information we discussed."

Abbot let the espionage comment slide, "Consider it

done. You are expected back on April twenty-fourth, two days before the Trinity term begins. Are you sure you won't be requiring a cook or a driver?"

"Abbot, we can manage. We're trying to escape the crowd, not create a new one. We fended for ourselves when we were boys at White Oak."

"Very well," he said. Timothy looked up at Mr. Abbot expectantly and the former MI6 operative gave him the slightest nod.

"We've purchased airline tickets for Lir, Ethan, and Cotton to get home?" Jacob harped.

"Yes, yes," Abbot continued. "First class on British Airways. They'll be well looked after, I assure you."

Tears began to form in Bea's eyes as she looked at her son.

"Mum?"

She quickly fanned her eyes. "I promised myself I wouldn't blub like an infant. It's just this is the furthest apart we will ever have been."

"Don't worry. We'll all be together again before you can say, Jack Robinson."

She smiled at the reference. She used to say that whenever he was afraid to spend the night away from home.

"We should be off," Jake said, standing. In moments they were all teary-eyed, hugging and kissing each other goodbye. Timothy wondered when he'd see his mum's face again.

The lads boarded the private jet and immediately settled in the back. It was a two-hour flight to get to Byron Bay where Jacob had rented a house for their getaway.

David Commons came by and helped the boys get situated. "Somewhat quieter for this trip, eh guys?"

Jacob gave him a lopsided grin and pulled a sleep mask over his eyes. "Don't wake me until we get there, okay?" He snuggled a blanket across his lap and quickly took off his shoes.

"There's going to be a slight delay before we can leave, not more than a half-hour," he told them.

"Will you be heading home to the states once you've dropped us off?" Timothy asked.

"Yeah, we'll all be going stateside on the other jet with the family. I guess this trip wasn't exactly what you expected?"

Tim winked. "There's still a few weeks to make it memorable."

Jacob fiddled with his music and within minutes he was asleep, drool forming at the edge of his mouth.

When the stranger came onboard, Timothy immediately rushed up to shake his hand. "I can't thank you enough for doing this."

"No worries, mate. Seems a shame to wake him though," he said, laughing in the direction of the conked-out Jacob.

"Trust me, he'll be glad we did."

"Let me then." He snuck over and planted himself across from Jake, grabbing his stockinged foot, "Wakey, wakey, eggs, and bakey!"

He pulled an EarPod out of one ear and said, "Timmy, that's the worst Aussie accent I've ever heard."

"Sorry, mate, had it all my life."

Jake lifted off the mask and looked confused. He wrinkled his brow. "Are you?"

"You can call me Thorpey. It's great to meet you. Took a peek at some of your old races—not too shabby."

"Timmy," he yelled. "It's Ian Thorpe! On our plane!" Jake ripped off the eye mask and wiped the drool from his mouth, then he started to cry. They immediately hugged.

"All my life," Jake began, but he couldn't seem to locate the end of the sentence.

Ian nodded. "Water is our world. You hit a rough patch but it's not over yet. We need to chat."

The two swimmers sat drinking tea and conspiring for

twenty minutes, gossiping like housewives at a Tupperware party. Ian was older and slightly heavier but his smile was every bit as electric as it was during the Olympics. They promised to stay in touch and see each other again. Timothy took a bunch of photos of them clowning and mugging, photos Jake would cherish forever.

After Ian left, David came over with mimosas. "The captain reports we're ready to leave, so buckle up. Next stop, Byron Bay."

Jake fell into his seat, emotionally exhausted. The boys held hands as the jet roared down the runway. "That was dirty pool. How did you manage it?"

"I had some assistance from Abbot. Ian was at the World's doing some commentary for the sports channel and FIMA." Tim pressed his leg against Jake's. "I don't think you should quit swimming just yet, it's the only thing your father and I have ever agreed on."

"Thorpey was telling me about the Gay Games and the Outgames. Both sound pretty interesting and it's a way for me to be active in the community."

"Why are there two different organizations?"

Jake chuckled. "Because the queens who run each of them can't get together and agree on anything. Same reason we have a rainbow flag, our tribe could never settle on just one color." They laughed.

"Anyway, the Gay Olympics is a way for me to continue swimming and irritate my father—so, a win-win. Which reminds me..." Jacob pulled out his phone and started sending a text.

"Who?" Timothy asked.

"Coach Lir and Ethan. I'll have to hire them back at considerable pay increases to train me up for all this."

Jake looked out the window as the morning sun reflected off the Australian coastline. "That was a lovely thing you did for me—bringing me back from the dead and Ian Thorpe. What will you think of next, Timothy James?"

CHAPTER 61

The Bodley

There were five buildings near Broad Street which made up the Bodleian Library at Oxford University. Duke Humfrey's which dates back to the fifteenth century, the Schools Quadrangle from the seventeenth, the famous Radcliffe Camera and Clarendon buildings from the eighteenth, and the most recent New Bodleian which was renamed, surprisingly, the Weston Library.

Scholars at Oxford refer lovingly to the complex as Bodley or *the Bod*. When Detective Loge decided to begin his research he was asked to take the formal declaration required of all new readers, an oral oath that states:

I hereby undertake not to remove from the Library, nor to mark, deface, or injure in any way, any volume, document or other object belonging to it or in its custody; not to bring into the Library, or kindle therein, any fire or flame, and not to smoke in the Library; and I promise to obey all rules of the Library.

One of the younger librarians immediately took an interest in Skip. Troy Bramblett was a scholar of the classics working on his dissertation. He brought another stack of books and set them quietly in front of the detective.

"Here you are, sir."

Skip pushed up his glasses and scanned the titles. "Thank you, and please don't call me sir—you're the scholar."

Bramblett put his hands in his pockets shyly. "So why all

the folklore and mythology?" he asked in a hushed tone. "I was told you were trying to catch the Butcher."

"Oh this," Skip motioned to the dusty tomes. "It's more of a side project. A strange tip I'm following up on. Say, Troy…"

"Yes?" he asked, and Skip noticed that the librarian had impossibly long lashes.

"Did you know the Muller twins?"

Troy sat beside him. "Oh, yes. Everyone who works in Bodley knows every other assistant and librarian. We're a family here. They were sweet, those two, never apart. We all feel awful about what happened."

"I imagine it all must seem like a terrible nightmare."

"How do you manage it?" the librarian wondered. "Your job. There must be images in your mind that are impossible to erase."

Skip nodded. "You're right. I just try to remember that I'm helping. It's a great feeling to catch the bad guys—and I do get to meet a lot of interesting people."

He smiled and Troy blushed then leaned toward the detective. "Old libraries are spooky on the best of days, the stacks are filled with secrets and ghosts. I feel much safer having you here," and he patted Skip on the back.

This makeover seems to be doing wonders, Loge thought. *I owe Elsie a nice dinner.*

His research turned up some possibilities, none of them credible in any realistic way. A Jekyll & Hyde dual personality seemed like an interesting avenue to explore, perhaps the murderer himself was unaware of his actions, but it didn't explain Miranda's warning of the culprit being not entirely human unless she was being metaphorical, which didn't seem to be the case.

There were plenty of texts which mentioned malevolent entities, demons, and witches rampaging through the countryside murdering, raping, and striking fear into the hearts of villagers but Skip couldn't allow his scientific mind to entertain such superstitious tales. This was likely nothing more than a very troubled young soldier with a fixation on female musicians.

He placed his glasses in his breast pocket and looked across the room to where Troy was seated behind a desk. Their eyes met just for an instant and both men looked away, grinning.

CHAPTER 62

Piano Man

Autumn in Byron Bay was spectacular with temps in the mid-20s Celsius and thin crowds since children were back to school. Jacob ran into the warm ocean near Little Wategos Beach, naked as the truth, whooping and hollering as he dived into the waves.

Timothy carefully backed their rented four-by-four campervan into the shade of some wattle trees, happy that they were finally alone together, then wandered along the coastline, occasionally bending down to place something in his pocket.

A short time later Jacob ran up, glistening. "I love this place, Timmy."

He gave the naked lad some cotton sweats. "Here, this is a family beach."

Jacob reluctantly dressed. "What were you doing?"

"Looking for treasure," he replied. "Sea glass." He pulled several smooth, colorful pieces out of his pocket. "When I was a boy, Mum would take Henry and me out to Brighton Beach. I'd spend the whole afternoon collecting."

Jake nodded. "Glass is made from sand."

"Exactly!" Tim agreed. "I always thought that sea glass was sand trying to find its way back home."

◆ ◆ ◆

They were en route to a secluded rental house near Belongil Beach, but Timothy would have been just as content to wander around Eastern Australia camping out of their lovely van.

"I'm never leaving," Jacob declared.

"Hmm," Tim said. "It is charming, but won't you miss me when I'm back at uni?"

"I'll write you exquisite love letters like John Keats to Fanny Brawne."

Timothy consulted the GPS and carefully drove toward their vacation home. "That sounds romantic, but I think you're just running away from your problems."

Jacob stuck his head out the window shaking out his wet hair as they made their way down the highway. "Of course I'm running away, it's one of the primary advantages of being rich. We never have to look our hardships in the eye."

A small dirt road through a grove of eucalyptus trees brought them to the doorstep of their new home. It was a Balinese-inspired cottage with a plunge pool and sun deck as well as an alluring spa.

"I have to admit you've outdone yourself, Mr. Weston," Timothy said, gazing out at the private water garden and exotic botanicals.

"It's perfect," Jacob said, jumping onto one of the outdoor daybeds. "We have almost four weeks to spend here and I plan to get as brown as a coconut before returning to England."

Timothy opened the door and saw that boxes of food had been delivered and placed in the kitchen. "Are we feeding the entire town?"

Jacob laughed. "I intend to do a sizable amount of cooking while we're here. You will be amazed at my culinary skills."

Timothy wandered from room to room spellbound. The air in Australia just felt cleaner, and more hopeful. It was as if the bright afternoon light streaming in through the windows was filled with adventure and wonder.

There was a baby grand piano in the living room and as he made his way around it, he spotted the surprise. A fender guitar and amplifier with a huge red bow attached. Jacob entered the room nearly crowing.

"For me?" Timothy asked, holding it like an infant.

"It took a good deal of work to arrange that and have it sent over before we arrived, I'll have you know."

"I'm sure," Timothy remarked. "I'll bet Abbot was on the phone for an hour." The two boys laughed. "Thank you. This is wonderful."

He began absently plucking at the strings while Jacob was tearing open boxes of food and planning what to put on the grill for their meal. "It's a shame you don't play the piano, we could have a jam session."

Jacob grinned. "I do play the piano."

"What?" Timothy said, disbelieving. "You're joking."

"Of course I can play." He held up two lobster tails. "My mother insisted. She was a fiend about it."

"Prove it," Timothy demanded, still not quite buying in.

Jacob huffed loudly, wiping his hands on a dishtowel, then proceeded to sit down on the bench. He did some quick scales to get a feel for the instrument. "What would you like to hear?"

Timothy just shook his head. "I suppose you read music as well?"

"Yes, of course, I can read music, Ashlock, I'm not a baboon. But I'm better just playing by ear."

"Why didn't you tell me?"

He shrugged.

"Music is your thing and frankly my playing is profoundly mediocre. I had heaps of lessons and a long steady stream of frustrated teachers as a child." He smiled sadly, looking down at his star sapphire ring. "My mother loved music. She would have been so...I don't know," he sighed. "She would have been quite taken by you. Music hath charms."

"Play something."

His fingers lightly brushed the keys and Timothy immediately recognized the opening chords of his original composition.

"That's my song! Dear Lord, did you transpose it for the piano? Remarkable!" Tim exclaimed.

"It's actually MY song, isn't it? *Jacob's Ladder*?"

Timothy turned away. All this time he didn't know or even suspect. What other secrets were hidden within this strange, enchanted boy? Jacob continued to play as Timothy tried to remember all the pianos in the many rooms they had occupied together.

"I'm speechless," he finally said.

"Why Timothy, you can play the violin and swim underwater? How utterly astounding!"

"Don't mock, it's not the same thing."

"Criminy, it's exactly the same thing."

Timothy switched on the amp, plugged in the guitar, and quickly set the treble, bass, middle, and reverb to find the sweet spot. He adjusted the neck-strap until it felt right. "Can you play a blues chord progression in C major?"

"As you wish."

And this was the moment they knew that the things you learn have a way of staying with you. As long as you hold a memory you retain your knowledge and experience.

The hours and hours Timothy spent practicing the guitar were ingrained in his very being, his muscles had kept their memories. He wailed on the guitar and it was so brilliant that it stopped Jacob's playing mid-chord. He stared at his lover, mouth agape like a beached fish.

Timothy's eyes closed and he was smiling, then he noticed he was playing alone. He looked over and saw Jacob staring. "Why did you stop?"

"I'm...I'm just rather awestruck, to be honest. I'm certainly glad I bought you a guitar, though."

He played a few bars of Schubert, absentmindedly.

"How many classical composers were gay?"

"Are you quizzing me?"

"Yes. I'll take gay composers for eight hundred, Alex!"

Timothy laughed. "Well, Schubert undoubtedly was. There's loads of evidence on that count. Also Handel and Tchaikovsky. There's an abundance of musical genius in that gay trio."

"You're nearly as clever as I am," Jake said.

"Mmm, nearly."

"Are you hungry?"

"More tired than peckish."

"Well then, let's grab a blanket and nap on our luxurious patio."

The two slept for hours, tangled together, languid and happy until the sun had gone down and the boys awakened, famished.

◆ ◆ ◆

Jacob cooked fresh vegetables and lobster tails on the patio grill while Timothy watched him work. He dashed pink sea salt and ground pepper on everything.

"The trick is only using the freshest ingredients. There's a community market in town that we must check out on Saturday. It's called the Blue Knob Farmers' Market." He winked as he brushed olive oil on the lobsters, turning them over.

"I think everything tastes better when it's cooked outside," Timothy said. He had lit all the candles around the patio. The stone fountain quietly laughed at them in the still air.

"I agree," Jacob said, filling their plates. He'd made several buttery dipping sauces that Timothy brought to the table.

Jacob opened a 2017 Bindi Chardonnay. "We're only drinking Australian wine while we're here. I want to educate my palate on all the local fare."

They touched glasses. "To absent friends," Timothy said.

Jacob met his gaze, "Here's to swimmin' with bow-legged women."

They laugh and tuck into their al fresco meal. "Next week I will teach you how to make Monsieur Dezo's famous *mousse au chocolat*. I had to beg him for a year to surrender the recipe."

"I do like this side of you, Jake Weston. It reminds me of all those months you were trying to woo me when we met at White Oak."

"Hmm, I remember winning you over in just under a month," Jake replied. "By Paris you were mine."

"Actually, you had me on the first day, the rest was just me playing hard to get."

"Timmy, you're rewriting history, which I've heard is a very dangerous thing for time travelers to do. As I recall on our first few meetings, you denied being attracted to same-sex admirers."

He placed a hand on Jake's collarbone. "I was lying."

"Lying, Mr. Ashlock? You?"

"You're a poker player, I know you're familiar with the concept."

Jacob scoffed. "We call it bluffing. A gentleman never lies." He wiped his mouth with a napkin and stood, looking at his watch. "We must be off."

"But it's late, what about the dishes?" Timothy asked.

"Worry about them later. Now don't dawdle, the sky waits for no man."

"I'm ready," he said, reaching for a hoodie and grabbing a bag of chocolate Hobnobs for the road.

CHAPTER 63

Edgar

H e walked beside her wheelchair as it hummed down the walk. "Here it is," Skip said.

"Spiced Roots?" Elsie asked. "You've brought me to a Caribbean restaurant in Oxford?"

"I'm told it's quite authentic, but you'll have to judge for yourself. I thought you might like a taste of home."

She looked at him softly. "You're something, you know that?"

They found a nice table and ordered two specialty drinks. "These concoctions are called Storm in a Teacup," Skip said, reading the menu. "Bermudian rum, soda, ginger puree, and lime-infused tea."

"I'd forgotten how wonderful rum is," she mentioned taking a long swig. "So what are we celebrating? We haven't caught the murderer yet, so you're obviously in love."

"Please stop being analytical for once."

Elsie placed a hand to her chest in mock offense. "You know I believe Leta and grumpy old Bridges are smitten with one another."

"I know. It must be something in the air."

Elsie perused the selections carefully, "Well, I'd give my kingdom for a middle-aged lesbian with a partiality for the disabled."

"She's out there, Doc. You just have to believe and be ready when she appears."

Elsie ordered the marinated, slow-cooked jerk chicken, extra spicy, while Skip opted for coconut and pumpkin rundown with island veggies.

"So this person you met..."

Skip blushed. "I don't believe I acknowledged meeting anyone."

"Is it a boy or a girl?" she pressed.

He glanced to either side as if someone might be recording the conversation. "If you must know— a boy."

"I thought so. We need to find you some modern frames since you insist on wearing glasses, other than that the makeover seems to be a complete success."

He looked down. "I've been doing a lot of thinking lately."

"About?"

He couldn't bring himself to say it, the speech he practiced in his mind had fled the scene. "Do you think everyone is two people? The person they show to the world, the one everyone sees, and the real them? The hidden identity?"

She reached for his hand. "Every person I've ever met has a secret they are terrified will get out."

He nodded thoughtfully. "Can I tell you mine?"

Elsie took a good hard swallow of her drink. "You can tell me anything, Skip, you know that."

He could feel the heat coming off his skin. He must be seven shades of red. He leaned in close to her, brushing her cheek with his. "I'm wearing ladies' panties," he whispered.

She raised a brow ever so slightly. "Right now?"

He nodded. "Black silk lace."

She took a bite of chicken acting as if they were just discussing the bleak weather or the price of cab fare. "That's very J. Edgar of you, Detective Loge. Are you telling me you might be considering a more complete makeover?"

He exhaled loudly because a weight had been lifted. "I

know it isn't normal."

She shushed him. "Between you and me, I hate that word. There is no such thing as normal. Average is another thing entirely, there's plenty of average in the world—but no one has ever accused you of that."

"So if I want to wear a dress?"

She looked directly at him. "Then we should find a nice frock that goes well with your figure."

"What about makeup?"

"Do you want to wear it?"

He shrugged. "I don't know, Elsie. I'm confused. I just, hmm, I just want to feel pretty."

"That's everyone, kiddo."

"And I'd prefer not to lose my job."

"I hear you. Listen, don't trouble yourself with all the labels. You might be trans, but you might simply be a cross-dresser. We can solve your mystery, I promise you that. It's like I told you a week ago, I just want you to be the best version of yourself."

Skip squeezed her hand. "Thank you. So what about you?"

Elsie mopped up the last remnants of her meal with a slice of bread. "What about me?"

Skip grinned. "What's your terrifying secret?"

Elsie leaned in, crooking a finger toward the young detective and beckoning him closer. "Jake Weston wants to give me a million dollars."

"What? You can't take it, that's a bribe!"

She giggled. "Oh, I'm taking it. It's to start the foundation I've been dreaming about since I was in college."

Skip was genuinely upset by the revelation. "Elsie, you're compromising the case. Jacob Weston is a suspect."

She ordered a cup of Blue Mountain Jamaican coffee. "Oh my Lord, you're as bad as Carl," she sighed. "Those boys are ten thousand miles away and we still have girls being slaughtered. Surely you don't think they're involved."

THE BUTCHER OF OXFORD

"I'm troubled that Timothy Ashlock knew every victim. The key to solving this spree centers on him."

"You think the killer is targeting him? Murdering his friends as a way to hurt him, or possibly implicate him in their deaths?"

"Yes, and it's working. He's grieving the loss of people he loved. He's feeling guilty, and we are implicating him and his boyfriend. Even if he's not the killer, he will always be associated with this scandal. It will follow him forever."

"You may be right, and if you are, then everyone close to Ashlock is in grave danger."

"You need to tell Bridges about the money."

"Why?"

"Because if you don't, then I'll have to. I'm sorry."

She blinked once. "You have a very strict moral compass, Skip. You're an interesting study. So, I'll be keeping your secret, but I'm forced to reveal mine. Seems like I got the fuzzy end of the lollipop."

"This wasn't how I imagined our dinner going."

She smiled. "Don't let it bother you," Elsie said putting on her thick Jamaican accent, "Everyting goin' to be Irie."

CHAPTER 64

The Magician

They ventured to Australia's most easterly point, where it sat perched atop a bald, rocky headland. The Cape Byron Lighthouse.

"It's quite bright," Timothy noted.

"That it is, this is the brightest light on the entire continent. The lighthouse has been in continuous use since 1901," Jacob reported. "But that isn't why we've come."

"Then why are we here?"

"It's a surprise, *Caro*. I'll show you at 12:23."

They sat huddled together on a bench watching the dark Pacific crashing against the coastline. Jake consulted his watch, "It's time. Watch this."

The moon began to rise from the dark water, glowing and huge. Timothy clasped Jacob's hand while they marveled at the sheer beauty.

"This is the waning gibbous phase," Jacob explained. "We missed the full moon by a few days, but luckily we'll be here for the next one."

"It's amazing."

"I owed you a vacation and I needed a reminder of how vast and unimaginably gorgeous this world is."

"You're a magician, Jake. Every day we spend together is a gift."

"Ha! In two weeks the Lyrids meteor shower will be going full strength. We'll have to take our camper somewhere wonderful and remote to watch it."

Timothy nodded. "Whatever you say, Darlin'. I'm entirely in your hands." They watched the moon rise until the lighthouse was surrounded. "May I take a photo of this?"

"If you must," Jake allowed.

"Our friends expect to see our adventures, even if it's just a glimpse."

Jake laid his head back. "Just remember that it isn't about the jazzy filtered photo on your media feed, it's about the memory in your heart and mind."

"Very noble," Timothy answered, snapping another. "But you know, more than one thing can be true at the same time, and this is also about, well..."

"Making our friends jealous?"

Timothy sighed. "Something along those lines."

Jacob laughed. "Let's go home and light a fire. I've got a long day of yoga, tanning, and reading planned for tomorrow."

◆ ◆ ◆

After rather acrobatic sex in the outdoor spa, Timothy pulled himself out of the steamy whirlpool panting. "How close is our nearest neighbor?"

"More than half a mile, shy boy," Jacob answered. "I guess you won't be posting that on your stories feed."

"I think not."

They grabbed robes and lay tangled together on one of the large daybeds, staring up at the unfamiliar sky. "No Big Dipper in this hemisphere," Timothy said, studying the stars.

"True," Jacob agreed, "but they get the Southern Cross as a consolation."

"I'm exhausted."

"Okay, let's find our bedroom."

CHAPTER 65

Nocturnus

He was engulfed in darkness, padding barefoot across the ice-cold concrete while all he could hear was the sound of a ticking clock that slowly turned into dripping water.

He held the gun in front of him even though he wasn't able to see. A lonely violin chord echoed off the tile walls, then he heard the screech of tires and a strange low hissing.

"Don't come any closer!" he yelled into the blackness. He could smell chlorine. Fear gripped him like a kitten in a thunderstorm and he started firing blindly, the gun flashing into the night. He shot again and again until every bullet was spent.

They were laughing. Suzannah reached for the light switch and the fluorescents flickered slowly to life. It's then that he saw Jacob, naked and facedown in the pool.

Blood poured from the wounds until all the water had bloomed red. "A pool of blood," she told her brother.

Timothy dropped the gun, screaming, "No, Jake! Please! No!"

He watched as the blood began to roil and churn, then the snakes slithered out. Hundreds of vipers, coiling, and hissing, slipping out of the water and coming towards him.

Timothy screamed and screamed...

"Wake up!" Jake whispered, shaking him gently.

Timothy was covered in a silky sheen of sweat. He bolted upright, looking quickly around the room and blinking, not recognizing anything.

"Bad dream," Jacob said, hugging him.

"It was so real," he murmured, starting to sob and pulling closer. "Oh Jake, you were dead. It was all my fault. I shot you, my God..." he started to babble and cry all at once.

Jacob ran his fingers through Timothy's hair and said, "I'm right here. I promise I'm not going anywhere."

They cuddled together, slowly falling back toward sleep, their breathing in time, rising and falling until even their heartbeats were synchronized.

This was the truth of love, not fireworks and ecstasy (although those are splendid on occasion), but slow and steady oneness—the rare unity of spirit.

CHAPTER 66

Ambush

B ea knocked twice and entered the massive room. Thick drapes covered the windows making it dark as a cave. The air was stifling.

"Rise and shine," she commanded, pulling back the curtains and opening a window.

"Betty? What the hell are you doing here? Where's Abbot?"

"He's off doing your errands, buying things you don't need, paying your bills, and whatever else is on today's agenda. You have that poor old soul chasing around New York like a bloody squirrel."

Paul Weston frowned at the stout woman picking up things and tidying his room. "Joanne!"

Bea just laughed. "She's not here either. Now your nurse Karen tells me you haven't left this bed in three days. You need to remind your legs what their function is or they'll stop working altogether."

"Are you a physician too?"

"Never mind that, let's get you up. I think we should have tea in the garden, don't you agree?"

She helped him get out of the huge bed as he pulled his robe tightly shut. Paul Weston hated being told what to do and was often as prickly as a rosebush when anyone bossed him around.

"I suppose you aren't going to leave me in peace," he grumbled.

"Fat chance of that. Now shall we walk outside together or should I get your wheelchair?"

"I think I can manage."

He held her arm and they made their way slowly downstairs. Karen smiled at Bea. "Some fresh air will do you a world of good, Mr. W."

He scoffed. "I'm surrounded by experts."

Bea had set the outdoor table with a full English breakfast. The Daily Racing Form sat next to Paul's place setting. "Now isn't this lovely?"

He grumbled, but his tone was softer. "It's kind of you to go to the trouble. This is nice. I guess you were pretty certain you could get me out here."

Bea winked and sat down, pouring herself a cup of tea. Weston just shook his head. "Are we dining together?"

"I'm an old woman and I need a cup of tea. You aren't the Queen, you know. Plus there are a few things we need to discuss."

Paul opened his race form with a crack. He fumbled for his reading glasses in the pocket of his robe. "I've been ambushed. I don't know what Abbot sees in you."

She chuckled. "Are we going to discuss how we choose our mates?"

"Probably not a great idea. You and Joanne truly despise one another, don't you?"

"I won't deny it, but I'll not speak against the woman while she isn't here to defend herself."

Paul looked at his housekeeper over his glasses. "She doesn't extend you the same courtesy, you know."

Bea sipped her tea. "I've heard from our boys. They're having a wonderful time in Australia."

"Are they?"

She watched the elder Weston, looking for some similarity between father and son. Both were stubborn and spoiled, but that might be more from money than from blood.

"There were two more murders at Oxford recently. Twin sisters."

Weston put the paper to one side. "Is that a fact? While the boys were in Australia?"

Bea nodded. "That would put them in the clear, I'd wager."

"That's good news," Weston said. "Not about the poor girls…"

"I agree," Bea replied quickly. "Now Abbot has been talking about the possibility of hiring an assistant butler, more like a footman."

"I don't want any more new people. He had to twist my arm to allow you into the fold."

She sighed. "You're being ridiculous. We are running four households at less than half the cost of what you are spending on the stables with all those horses."

Paul scowled. "Abbot should not be sharing financial information with you."

Bea waved Karen over. "It's time for your medication. I think you'll find there's very little Mr. Abbot doesn't share with me."

CHAPTER 67

Coppertone

They put a blanket on the sand where Jacob had prepared a picnic fit for a king. Timothy donned a floppy hat and a long-sleeved tee-shirt.

"Seriously, Ashlock? This is the wardrobe choice for our outing?"

"Mr. Weston, I'm not an American with whatever strange combination of nationalities and heritages you possess. I'm a full-blooded Englishman, which means I'll go from pasty white to blistering red in about three minutes under the Australian sun."

"I have the solution," Jacob said, pulling out a tube of Coppertone SPF-100 sunscreen. "This will protect you." He took Timothy's shirt off and began rubbing the lotion all over him.

"Coppertone?"

"Yes," Jacob answered, "Do you have a problem with Coppertone?"

Timothy grinned. "No, it's just that I would have expected you to have some rare, expensive sunscreen that can only be bought in a members-only boutique in Cannes."

"You think I'm a snob, Timothy James?"

The boys stared at one another good-naturedly.

"Why, because you shave black truffles onto your porridge in the morning?"

Jake took out a different spray of Coppertone for himself, this one SPF-8. "I'm being serious. My father recently called me a snob. Am I?"

Timothy laid back, closing his eyes, allowing the sun to warm his skin. "I think that question has a built-in trapdoor, Babe. You're not a snob, not in the classic sense. You like what you like because you like it, but you do have expensive taste. If you were a real snob you wouldn't have chosen to spend your life with a poor bloke from Hackney."

"My thoughts exactly. That's a relief."

Timothy cleared his throat. "But you don't suffer fools gladly. You might have been a bit kinder to your brother and sister."

"Hmph. Those two are Philistines."

"Snobbish," Timothy said with finality.

Jacob removed his swimsuit. "I'm going back to Oxford with an all-over tan. Don't attempt to talk me out of it."

Timothy kept his eyes closed. "I can't think of a single person we know who will be surprised by that information."

Jacob inhaled deeply. "You know, when I was a lad, maybe twelve or thirteen I used to spend a lot of time at our country club during the summer. There was a lifeguard there, Dave Phillips. He was always covered in Coppertone, and he'd sometimes share it and rub the pungent cream on my shoulders and back. I was madly in love with him in my barely-into-puberty, awkward way. The smell of this sunscreen is highly erotic to me even now."

Timothy chuckled. "Only you. So, was that your first big summer romance?"

"Hmm?"

"You and the lifeguard? Was he the first?"

Jacob smiled fondly. "Oh God no. He didn't have a clue. He was seventeen. We lived on different planets."

"I didn't even know sunscreen went up to SPF-100," Timothy remarked, stretching.

"I think it's a special British version." Jacob fiddled with his iPhone. "Speaking of first loves, Billy finally posted a picture of him and his mystery woman on Instagram. She's stunning."

Timothy raised his head. "Let me see."

He pulled close to Jacob and then gasped. "That's Maddy Drepa."

"You know her?"

"Very well," Timothy answered. "She's the harpist in our orchestra."

Jacob was enlarging the picture on his screen. It was Billy and Madelyn bundled up on the Scottish highlands, arms around each other. In the background, you could see his family's estate. "Are her eyes violet? That can't be their real color."

Tim nodded. "She's one of the most beautiful girls I've ever met in my life. I'm worried about Billy though. Maddy is the kind of girl..." he sighed. "She likes to have a good time."

Jacob continued to scroll through photos. "Well, she can't be having much of a good time at the Redgrave's."

"Why would you say that?"

"They're in Scotland and it's March. They must be freezing their asses off."

The boys rolled over onto their stomachs. "Did you read anything on Oxfess or the Cherwell?"

Jacob glanced at him through his mop of blond hair. "I did, have you?"

Timothy nodded. "Two more of my friends are dead."

"It's no wonder you're having night terrors."

"I don't understand why anyone would want to hurt the Muller twins. They were as timid as butterflies."

Jacob leaned up on his elbows and took some pears out of a basket, handing one to Timothy. "I can't help but notice a pattern emerging..."

"Me," Timothy whispered. "Even when I'm thousands of miles away I seem to be at the center of the storm. Sir John texted saying Detective Loge wants to see me as soon as we return."

"What do you think we should do?"

Timothy smiled, taking a big bite of the fruit. "Stay in Australia forever, traveling the coast in our campervan."

Jacob winked. "Now who's running away?" He picked up his paperback.

"What's that you're reading?"

Jacob waved the book, slightly embarrassed. "Just a silly gay romance novel."

Timothy examined the cover. "Sometimes I feel like we're characters in a gay romance novel."

"Really?" Jacob asked. "You know, to qualify as a romance it has to have a happily ever after, or at the very least a happily for now."

"Does it? That's silly. What about Romeo and Juliet?"

Jacob shook his head. "Technically not a romance. It's a tragic love story."

"That's utterly absurd."

"Hmm, well, rules are rules. I don't make them up, I just report them. Goodreads librarians are quite adamant."

"I'm not sure I believe in happily ever afters," Timothy replied sadly. "Do you?"

Jacob rubbed more sunscreen onto Timothy's back. "I want to believe. I suppose eventually someone dies. Wouldn't it be nice if the two of us were in our eighties and came back to this very spot in Byron Bay to die peacefully together in our sun loungers?"

"Sign me up for that," Timothy agreed, falling asleep in the warmth.

CHAPTER 68

Bridget

"Where is the goddamned Kid?" the DCI bellowed.

DS Eddings looked up from his files. "Mentioned he was off to the library, Chief."

"He's spending a lot of time there lately, what's he bloody doing?"

Leta Kelly was smearing cream cheese onto bagels. "I'm going to go out on a limb and guess that he's reading."

"Text him and get him back in here. What about the computer girl?"

Leta gave him a bagel. "She's a brilliant statistician and her name is Bridget Lee. You've met her several times."

"Yeah, yeah. Scotland Yard reports she's developing an algorithm that can crunch all the details and clues and spit out the perpetrator."

"It's the future of criminal investigations," Forrestal said, dropping crumbs on his bright green tie.

Elsie came wheeling into the room. "I'm dubious when it comes to trusting computers."

Carl looked over at her. "Well I don't trust shrinks or computers but if this girl can catch the bastard with her laptop then I'll start remembering her name."

"So why was I summoned?" Elsie asked.

"We've got four suspects in custody for questioning. No

one has been charged, but I'd like you to rake the conductor, Julian Adler, over the coals."

"Sounds like fun."

Skip came rushing in.

"Finally!" Carl shouted.

"Sorry Bridges."

"What were you doing in the library? Is our killer a grey-haired librarian?"

Elsie glanced over, raising a brow quizzically. Skip quickly opened up his laptop. "Doubtful, however, the twins worked at the Bodleian. I'm doing my research, following leads."

"Have you sent all your files to the computer girl?"

Skip looked confused. "You mean Bridget?"

The DCI sighed.

"I've copied her on everything. I've also done the digging you asked for on Adler. We've come up with some troubling details."

"Excellent, give that to the doctor so she can better needle him. Now, where are we with forcing those two nancy boys to come back to England?"

Elsie spun her chair around. "You can't legally compel them to return. Weston isn't even British."

Skip agreed. "She's right. We did speak to Sir John, their barrister. He assures us they will be returning before the Trinity term begins on April twenty-sixth."

"I'd like to have someone in custody long before then."

◆ ◆ ◆

Bridget Lee had compiled all her files and was ready to give her initial findings. She placed her MacBook down on the conference table.

Dr. Kelly handed her a cup of tea. "You look like you've been working hard."

"It was a lot of data to input," Bridget said, stretching

and cracking the vertebrae in her neck. "More than eighty potential suspects." She refreshed her lipstick and tucked her brunette hair behind her ears.

Carl walked in with Forrestal and Loge. Elsie was right behind them. "Computer girl," Bridges said.

"DCI."

"You've uncovered our killer, I assume? Now we can go make an arrest?"

She looked down at her computer.

"He's kidding," Leta whispered.

"I can only give you probabilities and percentages based on the evidence you've gathered," Bridget admitted, her fingers expertly clicking over the keyboard. "You lot are the crime solvers."

Skip was looking over her shoulder at the screen. "You take a wide variety of data into account?"

She nodded. "Everything from proximity during the windows of opportunity, to life history, education, social media presence, affiliations, hobbies, known associates and friends, employment history, psychological profiles, phone records, purchases, and bank records, as well as more subtle information."

"Such as?"

"Body language during an interview, breathing rates, vocal modulations."

"All the telltale bits that are right up my alley," Elsie remarked.

"It still boils down to means, motive, and opportunity," Forrestal said, crunching into a bagel.

"Quite right, Owen. My algorithm just quantifies the information and distills it down into a probability. A statistical interpretation."

"A number," Skip told the group.

"Well, I am curious," Bridges remarked. "Where does Timothy Ashlock fall on your scale?"

"Thirty-five," Bridget answered.

"Is that out of a hundred?"

"Correct."

"And Weston? Jacob Weston?"

"Forty-seven."

"Why don't we let Mrs. Lee tell us who's at the top of the list," Leta chimed in.

"Statistically, anyone scoring over seventy would be well worth further investigating. Peter Chadwick scored seventy-three. Matthew Colton was seventy-one. The rower, Casey Larson, scored seventy-five. The two gentlemen who scored the highest were the musician, Douglas Turner at seventy-seven, and the conductor, Julian Adler. He scored eighty-one."

"Ladies and gentlemen we have a winner," Carl announced.

"I'll need an hour to prepare for the psych interviews. It would be helpful if you put our subjects in cold empty rooms and gave them caffeine," Elsie said.

CHAPTER 69

Maestro

Julian Adler was visibly agitated. He'd spent the night in a small, dingy cell and was now hungry, dirty, and exhausted. DS Eddings led him into the interview room.

"When will I be released?"

Eddings shrugged. "Don't know. Maybe after your chat with Dr. Courtemarche."

They watched Adler sitting alone for twenty minutes, then Elsie decided to make her entrance.

"Showtime."

She wheeled into the room wearing a bright green and yellow Jamaican print dress. He stood as she entered.

"Please Maestro," Elsie said cordially. "Sit. I'm sorry they've kept you waiting so long."

"I've spent the night here."

"So I've heard. That must have been unpleasant."

"It was," he complained, brushing at the grey stubble on his cheek.

"I'm sorry for the loss of your musicians. You must be upset by the murders."

He stared at the floor. "It's a tragedy. Those girls were talented, lovely young women. It will be difficult for the orchestra to move on without them."

"Did you know Samantha Milford?"

"No."

"But you met her?" Elsie pressed.

"I don't believe so."

She took out a slip of paper from a file she'd brought along. "Samantha auditioned for the orchestra and you were in attendance."

"Ah, well. Hundreds of young musicians audition for the Oxford University Orchestra. Surely you don't expect me to remember every student I've ever listened to. What instrument did she play?"

"Clarinet." Elsie took out an image of Samantha with the instrument. Adler smiled sadly, pausing.

"I'm sorry, I don't recall her."

Leta, Skip, and Bridges were watching the interview from behind the one-way mirror. "He's lying," Skip said. "He paused too long, and he touched his face. He remembered Miss Milford."

"Hmm," Elsie said, her eyes narrowing. They considered each other from across the table. "I understand you were fighting for the British in the war with Afghanistan."

"It was my honor to serve."

"In the course of your service were you required to take any lives?"

Adler looked down, the muscles in his neck flexing. "We were at war, Doctor."

"Have you ever killed anyone with your bare hands, Maestro?"

He blinked. "I'm not at liberty to disclose the details of my military service and I don't see how it could be relevant to your investigation."

"Well," she mentioned casually, "I'm just trying to establish that you have a history of cold-blooded killing."

He crossed his arms. "That's ridiculous."

"Namika Ito was killed in your concert hall following a rehearsal."

"I'm well aware."

Elsie brought out a photo of Namika Ito's death scene and dropped it on the table in front of the conductor. He looked at it nonplussed.

"Her neck was broken in what can only be described as a combat judo move."

He sighed.

"You've been trained in this method, have you not?"

Julian Adler abruptly stood and Elsie instinctively moved her wheelchair back. "I'm sure you're aware that I've been trained in many methods of hand-to-hand combat."

"Your military superiors report that your demeanor toward prisoners of war was, quote, 'overly zealous and aggressive.'"

"I would take issue with that assessment."

Elsie stared at him. "Please sit down."

He complied.

"Let's chat about more pleasant things. Are you currently in a romantic relationship?"

He laughed. "My personal life is no concern of yours."

She opened the file again, dropping a photo of a young, brunette boy on the table. "Do you recognize this person?"

"Here we go," Carl said, rubbing his hands together.

"I do. He is a talented musician. A pianist. I believe his name is Moretti."

Elsie tapped her fingers against her chair. "I think you know his name quite well. Andre Moretti. We have copies of more than a dozen letters you sent to this young man. Love letters."

The conductor looked away.

"He was fifteen when you took him on as a pupil."

"The boy was a musical prodigy."

"And how would you describe your relationship with Mr. Moretti?"

"Consensual."

"That relationship began when the boy was sixteen?"

He looked angry. "My private life has nothing to do with

the death of these girls! And by the way, Doctor, the age of consent in Italy is fourteen."

She smiled. "It's interesting that you have that fact at your fingertips. But young Mr. Moretti filed a complaint against your advances with the conservatory of music in Florence."

"He tried to extort money from me," Adler explained. "He's a wretched street urchin."

Elsie took another photo out of her file. "He was found dead in a hotel in Cinque Terre. He was strangled, and barely seventeen."

"I didn't know that," Julian said, picking up the photo and examining it.

"Another lie," Skip said. "He definitely knew."

"What do you think?" Carl asked them.

Bridget and Leta nodded.

"Let's charge this bastard with the murders," Bridges said. "One way or another, he surely belongs behind bars."

CHAPTER 70

Meteors

Jacob put the last box of supplies into the campervan. He had loaded it up with all the creature comforts for the trip, including twice the amount of food and wine they would consume in two days. There was a Sony boombox for music, and a double sleeping bag made by The North Face. Timothy saw him put a ten-inch steel Buck knife near the headboard of their sleeping area.

"That's a pretty big knife."

Jacob gave it a quick flip and caught it by the handle smoothly. "Well, I didn't bring a gun to this continent."

The weeks they spent together in Australia had browned his skin like a marshmallow held over a campfire.

"Where are we headed?"

"Nightcap National Park. We want to get away from the coast and closer to the dark, clear sky. Away from civilization, away from our worries and cares."

Timothy chuckled. "We'll be driving for hours if we're trying to escape my worries. I seem to attract them."

"That's nonsense, *Caro*. You're my lucky charm."

Timothy buckled his seatbelt. "And you are my blue-eyed boy."

Driving toward the park Jacob was giddy with excitement. "The Lyrids meteor shower is ancient. Chinese records of the event go back as far as 687 B.C. They described the au-

257

tumn stars as falling like rain."

"But what causes a meteor shower like this?" Timothy asked. He knew Jacob loved the opportunity to show off his knowledge.

"These meteors are debris from the long-period comet Thatcher, which only visits earth every 415 years. That ice ball won't be returning until 2276."

"And meteorites?"

Jacob was closely watching the road as the traffic grew thinner. "Travelers from outer space. Metallic asteroids are mostly iron, but can have a mix of nickel, iridium, palladium, platinum, gold, magnesium, and other precious metals such as osmium, ruthenium, and rhodium."

"I think you made up some of those names."

"I never fib about science, especially concerning things from outer space which can make it through the friction and heat of our atmosphere. I love them. Magical rocks from far, far away."

"This is an adventure," Timothy said wistfully.

"We may also get to see a few meteors from the Eta Aquarids. They enter the atmosphere extremely fast and leave glowing green trains behind them. It's when the earth passes through the field of debris from Halley's Comet."

"Finally something astronomical I've heard of," Timothy said.

"Halley's is coming back in 2061. You and I will watch it together."

◆ ◆ ◆

The boys arrived at their camping spot on Nightcap Ridge, above Minyon Falls with a grand view of the entire primordial rainforest below and an unobstructed view of the sky above.

"Ah," Jacob said, satisfied. "The Byron Bay Hinterlands." He began lighting coals and mesquite for the dinner he was planning to barbecue.

Timothy helped by chopping vegetables and making a salad as well as setting the outdoor table. "You have something special planned for our entrée?"

Jacob gave his boyfriend the patented lopsided grin. "Since you asked, we are having Australian Wagyu steaks from Jack's Creek. It was the winner at the World Steak Challenge in London."

"So, the world's best steak?"

"That's the rumor. We shall see if my grilling skills can rise to the challenge."

He opened a bottle of Penfolds Grange 2014 Shiraz and poured it into crystal glasses. "This is heaven," Timothy sighed. Jacob had blues playing softly in the background.

They watched another spectacular Aussie sunset over the rainforest during their meal. "We're set to have clear skies tonight for the show," Jacob said, tucking into his steak. "Although it might get chilly here on the ridge."

"I'm looking forward to it."

When dinner was over they doused all the lights and fire leaving only a small lantern for illumination. "Our eyes need to adjust to the darkness. I adore places where you can feel the stars and the infinity of the sky. Life, despite everything, is like a dream," Jacob said.

The boys stared heavenward.

The night pressed on but neither boy saw a single meteor. "Are you sure you have your dates correct, Mr. Weston?"

"The Zenithal Hourly Rate or ZHR for the Lyrids is known to be a relatively low number, perhaps ten to twenty meteors per hour."

"Those seem like optimistic figures considering we haven't seen any," Timothy joked. "Did you bring me out for a snipe hunt?"

"Come here."

They bridged the distance between themselves and embraced, then swayed to the music in a lazy imitation of dancing. "I recognize this music," Timothy said.

"I would hope so, these are all classic blues and R&B tunes by their original artists."

They were still looking skyward.

"No," Timothy whispered. "I mean I recognize the order of the songs. This is your playlist from our first Thanksgiving together."

He hugged him close. "I'm astounded that you can recall that."

"I've memorized a lot of song sequences which are more arcane than this charming progression. I know the orders of entire symphonies."

They finally saw dozens of meteors streaking across the sky. Bright fireballs, and glowing green trails. Jacob squeezed him tight. "Here we go."

At Last, sung by Etta James, played while they watched. "I love this song," Timothy stated.

"My lonely days are over," Jacob sang lightly, "and life is like a song."

The meteor shower intensified, making the boys giggle like middle-school children. "I'm so glad we did this," Timothy sighed. "This whole trip is something I'll never forget."

"Behold, iron falling from the sky," Jacob said.

The boys kissed passionately. "We are starstuff, Timmy."

"You never disappoint."

They sat against the van, a blanket wrapped around their shoulders. "I've been doing a lot of thinking about my father's request."

"I wasn't going to offer an opinion," Timothy replied.

"It's not disinheritance, per se. It's more like simple

blackmail. My father is putting me out to stud like one of his prized stallions. I have until I am twenty-five to sire a Weston heir or face losing the lion's share of my fortune."

"Should we be praying for another immaculate conception?"

"Well, I can't imagine myself Tinder-dating Oxford ladies looking for Miss Right with the sole intention of impregnating her. Actually, I've grown rather fond of the idea of a family, not the tosh about my bloodline and all that, but of children knocking about the house."

"That plan would still require a woman," Timothy said, his voice low and tight.

"I'm thinking of two women, my friend. Surrogates. Saints who are willing to bless those of us that can't have babies on our own."

Timothy stared.

"Have I corrupted you, *Caro*? Maybe if you'd never met me you would have settled down with some lovely girl."

"Jacob, we can't control who we fall in love with, but to your broader point—I was always destined to muck about with both genders. When I was sixteen a dear friend told me that I shouldn't limit myself."

Jacob looked over at his boyfriend in the starlight, his face like polished marble. "Well, I won't be able to raise these ankle-biters by myself."

"Won't you have a squadron of nannies, babysitters, and maids?"

He laughed. "Of course, not to mention tutors, but I was thinking more about you."

"What about me?"

Jacob turned and gazed into those hazel-green eyes. "I'm asking for your hand in marriage. Will you make me the happiest person alive and be my husband?"

There was a silence between them as they simply watched one another. "We aren't even twenty yet," he mentioned.

"I'll never marry anyone else. I love you, Timmy." He took off his star sapphire ring and placed it on the boy's finger.

"Your mother gave you that right before she died. I can't accept..."

Jacob grasped his hands. "I want you to have something that is very dear to me."

They deeply kissed.

"Is that a yes?"

"You know it is. I can think of worse things than being married to Jacob Weston," Tim said, starting to both laugh and sob.

"Good. I promised my father I would get married, but I didn't say to whom."

◆ ◆ ◆

Jacob and Timothy were asleep together, naked in the duo sleeping bag. The dawn light was trying to peek through the curtains of the camper when Timothy felt a weight slithering over the bag near his feet.

He opened his eyes and saw the large reddish-brown snake moving at the base of their bed.

"Jake!" he whispered urgently, grasping the boy's arm under the covers. "There's a snake in our camper."

Jacob instantly opened his eyes. "Don't move," he commanded, slowly lifting his head to assess the animal.

"Did you know that twenty-one of the twenty-five most toxic snakes in the world live in Australia?"

"Interesting trivia," Timothy whispered. "Does this one make the list?"

"It does, I'm afraid. It also has a reputation for a nervous and aggressive temperament, from what I've read on the subject. This is my first encounter with a live specimen."

Jacob reached slowly for the knife he placed nearby. "He probably finds our camper quite warm and comfy, but he can also sense the heat coming off our skin, and this animal's eyesight is excellent. Our guest lies between us and the door, which is a problem. He may become bellicose if he feels threatened."

The snake appeared to be watching the couple, while slowly coiling. It hissed.

"We are lucky our visitor is atop the sleeping bag rather than inside with us."

Timothy was all but holding his breath. "So you're saying this is a glass-half-full scenario."

"Precisely."

"What's our plan?"

Jacob was inching his way up to a sitting position. "I'm going to annoy him until he strikes and then I'm going to kill him."

"That sounds like a dangerous and awful idea," Timothy uttered.

"*Caro*, the snake seems to be frozen, getting ready to attack even though we've been perfectly courteous hosts. I'm estimating his length at just under five feet, which means he can almost reach our faces..."

And at that moment the snake lunged toward Timothy. Jacob instantly maneuvered his pillow to block it like a gladiator wielding a shield as the snake opened its dark mouth exposing its fangs and catching on the fabric, while Jake swung the knife up and cleanly sliced off the animal's narrow head. The whole incident happened in the blink of an eye.

The boys jumped up together. "That beast was aiming for me!" Timothy yelled.

"It appeared to be."

"I didn't even have time to scream, but you moved faster than lightning! You saved my life."

Jacob lifted the body of the snake, mentally measuring it. "I suppose we're even then. Timothy, I give you the Coastal Eastern Taipan. The third most venomous land snake in the world. He must have come in through the window."

"Sweet Jesus. I may still faint."

"You should stay right where you are, while I perform a search."

"What are you saying?"

Jacob smiled weakly, holding up a flashlight. "Well, where there's one…"

When he was satisfied that there weren't any other intruders, Jake climbed behind the steering wheel. The boys agreed that their current location above the rainforest had lost its luster.

"Let's go out to breakfast," Timothy suggested.

"Great idea, my love. Next stop is the quaint town of Bangalow."

"If it had bitten one of us, how long would we have had?"

Jake grinned. "Anywhere from thirty minutes to around two hours. Untreated, the mortality rate is one hundred percent. That particular species always delivers a fatal dose of venom."

"Bloody hell. If you had died, DCI Bridges would have locked me up for two hundred years."

"Murder by way of lethal reptile," Jake laughed. "You know Cleopatra famously committed suicide by allowing an Egyptian cobra to bite her boobs."

"Jacob, please…"

As they approached the nearby town he muttered, "Now, a photo of that encounter would have made a great Instagram post."

CHAPTER 71

Scotland

Castle Rockhold sat on the north coast of Scotland near Caithness. It had been in Billy Redgrave's family since it was built in the late sixteenth century.

It was now a national tourist attraction since Lord and Lady Redgrave had been granting public tours for more than two decades. Allowing the public inside was the only way they could afford to maintain the grounds and the structure. Even a fortress was vulnerable to centuries of battering by the elements.

"I hope you aren't finding it too cold here," Billy's mother said to Madelyn during breakfast.

"On the contrary, Lady Redgrave. My family is from Iceland so we've never been afraid of a cold snap." She buttered some toast and nibbled at the corner.

"Maddy's been in this drafty old pile of rocks for weeks and hasn't complained once." Billy was proud of her.

Lord Redgrave was smoking a cigar near the huge marble fireplace. "Miss Drepa, your smile could warm the entire coast of Scotland. We're so happy Billy brought you to visit."

"Sir, I find the highland invigorating, and your family and staff charming. I feel much safer here than back at Oxford where a murderer is still on the prowl."

Billy had just been checking his phone and looking at

social media. "Not anymore! Metro has arrested someone! It looks like it's safe to return for the Trinity term."

Lady Redgrave looked relieved, and Maddy jumped at the news. "Who?" she asked, intrigued.

Billy showed her the headline on the feed. "It's your conductor, Julian Adler."

Madelyn's violet eyes flickered as she moved from the table to look out the leaded windows. "I've been alone with him dozens of times and he was always such a gentleman," she stated. "Why do the police think he's the killer?"

Billy shook his head as his father glanced up from the book he was reading. "Madness that brings someone to take life away from an innocent person is cowardly. Whatever twisted motive this man might have, it will be scant consolation to the families of those poor girls."

"At least you're safe," Billy said, joining Maddy and tightly hugging her. "I don't know what I would have done if..."

She laughed and pecked him on the cheek. "You mustn't worry about me, Love, I'm unstoppable."

Madelyn and Billy walked along the plateau facing the North Sea. She wanted to see the cairns and other prehistoric remains.

"This is an old, old land," she said wistfully.

Billy looked at the standing stones and brochs. "You do have an appreciation for history. I hardly ever come out here."

She smiled, her cheeks flushed in the chilly breeze. "Let me ask you something personal."

"Ask away."

They walked toward the cliff. "You and Timothy Ashlock are good mates, right?"

He nodded. "One of my best. We go back to shell days. I don't know what school would've been like without him."

"Have you ever kissed him?"

He burst out laughing. "Don't be daft."

"I know how the lads are at boarding schools."

He gave her a knowing wink. "I've managed to avoid all that nonsense, and if you want to know the truth, I think Weston and Ashlock are the perfect couple."

"What makes you say that?"

He held her hand as they hiked along the ridge. "Those boys have a love that travels deep, like gold weaving its way through stone. I'm hoping for something along those lines myself someday—just not with another lad."

CHAPTER 72

Employees

Two quick raps on the door and he entered Paul Weston's den without a sound. He poured some strong Kopi Iuwak coffee (the beans imported directly from Vietnam), and placed it on his employer's right side. Weston made a grunting noise that Abbot assumed was meant as thanks.

"Sir, pardon the interruption." Abbot waited for the man to at least acknowledge his existence.

"Yes, Abbot, what is it?" He glanced at the butler then looked back at his computer monitor. Weston didn't feel as sick when he was tracking his finances.

"I'm afraid this conversation needs your full attention, Paul."

"Paul?" he repeated with a teasing sarcasm. "Are we on a first-name basis now, Blake?"

The butler straightened his cuffs and tie. "For this conversation, I'm afraid we must be."

"Sounds quite serious. Are you handing in your resignation?"

Abbot looked surprised. "Actually, yes. How did you guess?"

He looked out the window toward the Long Island Sound. "Weston intuition. It runs in the family," he turned brusquely. "But it doesn't take clairvoyance to see that our ladies hate one another."

"I made a commitment to your father, and I do realize you are unwell."

"So you feel guilty for leaving me on my deathbed?"

"You must be more positive in your outlook. You appear better today, so you may outlive me."

"Dear Blake. Never bullshit a bullshitter. I'm far too rich and smart for that, at least give me some credit."

The butler sat on the leather couch, something he'd never done in his employer's presence. "I do. And I have some advice before I take my leave. Listen. Ask yourself why this horrible little harpy and her brat have clung to you for five years? Use that intuition to see who these people are. Follow the money and notice that it leads directly to the two usurpers under your roof."

"What are you saying?"

"I'm saying that I'm an old man and you are an even older one, but it's not too late for either of us to be happy."

"Maybe I should run away with my nurse," he said, laughing.

"That isn't the worst idea you've had."

They shook hands.

"As I recall your commitment to my father was that you would serve the Weston household until Jacob inherits."

Abbot tilted his head slightly. "Yes."

"Then serve the family by going back to England and watching over my son. He's agreed to find a woman and further the Weston name, and he'll need guidance in such weighty matters."

The butler blinked. "A woman?"

Weston nodded. "And a grandson for me. Perhaps he'll even name him Paul."

Blake Abbot thought that particular scenario was highly unlikely.

"It was never a good idea to have our two fillies under the same roof. For what it's worth, I think Betty is an interesting woman."

"She's quite headstrong," the butler admitted.

Paul looked at him and chuckled. "Where I come from we call that stubborn. My first wife had the same quality, and so does my son."

"Indeed. What will you tell Joanne?"

Paul Weston looked back at his computer. "I'll tell her that I dismissed you and your girlfriend for her sake."

CHAPTER 73

Purple Potatoes

J acob peeled the white sweet potatoes and dropped them into the boiling pot. "You're going to love these."

Timothy was cleaning up the mess. "Are they magical potatoes?"

Jacob considered the silly question. "I believe they are. These are Murasaki grown in Bundaberg, Queensland. White on the outside but with purple flesh, supercharged with vitamins. We'll be having purple potatoes with our grilled lamb this evening."

"That sounds lovely," Timothy said sincerely. He noticed the eggs that Jacob had left out. "Will you be using these eggs?"

"Yes. I'm finally going to teach you to make *Mousse au Chocolat* tonight."

"Ah, the secret recipe," Timothy mumbled. "Does it call for warm eggs?"

"Don't mock, and yes. Extremely fresh, room temperature eggs. I'll have you know that everyone I've ever made that dessert for has fallen madly in love with me."

Timothy snickered. "And how many people have you prepared it for?"

Jacob gave him the lopsided grin as he transferred the softened vegetables out of the water and into a bowl to mash.

"I'll never tell."

He added a heaping amount of butter to the sweet potatoes and noticed Timothy raising an eyebrow. "The French discovered long ago that the answer to nearly every culinary question is butter."

"How will you be grilling the chops?"

"With rosemary and minced garlic, and more butter. It's a very traditional Aussie preparation. Everyone should know how to cook one or two amazing meals. By the way, did you see the latest news from England?"

Timothy sighed. "If you mean about Julian, yes."

Jacob gave him the bowl. "Keep mashing these while I put on the lamb and check the grill. I suppose it's finally safe for us to return home."

Tim looked at him, his hazel eyes searching. "Are you thinking what I'm thinking?"

"I am if you're thinking that doofus Bridges and his team have locked up the wrong person."

"So the killer is still loose?"

Jacob adjusted the fire. "We'll know if another one of your musical girlfriends turns up dead."

"If everyone who loves me is being killed then I'm glad Mum and Abbot are far away from Oxford. I couldn't bear it if something happened to them, or you—perhaps we should just stay here."

"Ashlock, nothing's going to happen to me. I'm looking for murderers under every rock these days."

"I'm going to miss it here," Timothy moaned. "I've gained five pounds from all your cooking. You could have been a chef in another life."

He turned the lamb, drizzling olive oil on the sizzling chops. "I think about it. All the lives we don't choose to live, the paths we never go down, the choices we make or avoid. We are shaped by all the opportunities in our lives, even the ones we miss. Perhaps I'll open a chic restaurant here if I lose my fortune and everything goes tits up."

Timothy hugged him. "That doesn't sound so bad if it's something you love."

"We had a chef at the main house for a while named Matt Stein. My mother was going through a fish craze and the man knew everything there was to know about seafood. He'd fly Copper River Salmon and fresh Kumamoto oysters from his connections up near Alaska and the Puget Sound, so we always had the freshest fare.

The problem was the man was heartless and mean as a scorpion. His default position was to scream at anyone within reach. The yelling became so bad that he eventually damaged his vocal cords.

Anyway, he was a sad and abusive bastard with a very large chip on his shoulder and eventually we dismissed him. But here is my point; you could taste the anger in his cooking. For food to be truly ethereal it must be made with love." Jacob sighed. "And also a good amount of butter."

CHAPTER 74

Home Sweet Home

The Rolls-Royce Phantom Eight was waiting on the wet tarmac. It had been raining in England for days. Ethan ran to meet the boys as they walked down the aircraft stairs.

"All right then, lads?" he asked. They hugged. "Jesus, you're as dark as a pecan," he said, examining Jacob in the fading light.

Timothy was watching the skies begin to clear. "Home sweet home."

The boys rushed into the idling car while Ethan grabbed their luggage. The raindrops scattered across the windshield, shining like diamonds in the twilight.

"It's good of you to hire me back."

Jacob scoffed and waved the gratitude away. "You're indispensable, mate, as is Coach Lir."

Ethan bashfully smiled. "You hear they caught the Butcher? The detectives called me in when they thought you boys had something to do with it. Quite a relief that all that is over, eh?"

"It is," Jacob answered, as they navigated the streets of London. "Have you worked out my training schedule? I want to beat every other queer boy at the Gay Games."

They laughed. "Lir said he's going to make you the fastest nancy boy that ever jumped into a pool."

"I'm counting on it."

Ethan was nervous as they approached Oxfordshire. "I'm not supposed to give away the surprise, but I'm guessing you already know they're waiting for you."

"I'd heard a rumor," Jacob said lightly.

"What are you two on about?"

"Your mum and Abbot are back home in England where they belong."

CHAPTER 75

Ophiuchus

Abbot had fires glowing in each of the three fireplaces at Brigsley Manor. He had strategically placed Jacob's favorite candles in every room and had a CD of the Oxford Student Orchestra performing Bach on the house stereo system.

They opened the door and immediately fell into Bea's waiting arms. "My boys!" she gushed. "Welcome home!"

"Mum!" Timothy squealed in mock surprise.

"And Jay! Why you're as brown as a fieldworker."

He winked. "That's precisely the look I was going for. Did you kill my stepmother for me?"

"I certainly wanted to. When she referred to me as the servant's girlfriend, I nearly threw an antique vase at her head. What a piece of work that woman is, she's as irritating as a pebble in your boot."

"Well, at least you're rid of her."

Jacob put his arm around Mr. Abbot. "I hear you've hired a replacement butler for my father. How is he working out?"

"Hinkle?" Abbot scoffed. "He's adequate as servants go, but he suffers from a horrible condition where he finds himself more amusing than he is."

Ethan brought all the luggage in and everyone retired to the sitting room where Abbot poured snifters of Delord Bas-Armagnac Napoleon.

"Ah, a digestif. You are a godsend," Jacob said. "So what do you think of it?" He motioned to the etching over the mantel.

"Salvador Dali. 1972. Titled: *Aurelia.* It's an interesting piece. Different from your usual sensibilities when it comes to the art world."

"I have a curiosity regarding the melting clocks," Jake admitted.

Timothy was watching the couple. "So are you two here to stay?"

Bea smiled, the crow's feet wrinkling the sides of her careworn face. "For as long as Jay will have us."

Jacob looked up from the pile of mail he was sorting. "I refuse to have two senior citizens living in sin under my roof for long. Please plan a wedding and make Bea an honest woman."

Abbot nodded. "Betty has clear ideas of what she would like in that regard."

Jake touched the registered letter from the laboratory. "You know what this is, don't you?" he asked, holding up the envelope.

"Confirmation," Abbot replied.

Timothy and Bea looked at one another befuddled. "Of what?"

"I stole my half-wit, half-sister's chewing gum when we were dining together at the restaurant in Melbourne. Disgusting, I grant you, then I sent it to a lab for DNA comparison."

"Devious," Timothy said, chuckling.

"If those two Jesus freaks share my blood then I'm a monkey's uncle. I think my father is playing the long con. This plan probably went into effect as soon as I came out."

He ripped open the letter and quickly scanned the results.

"Well?"

"It's all been an elaborate fraud," Jacob said smoothly. "I have no siblings. *Mon Dieu*, my father could teach a masterclass in assholery."

Bea placed a hand on his shoulder. "I'm sorry he lied to you, Jay. He's a selfish old man."

Jacob looked distressed. "You know, I was starting to like him more since he'd gotten too frail to hit me. Now I can see that cancer has not only taken his health but it's also eaten whatever was left of his soul."

Abbot cleared his throat. "I did manage to procure the latest version of your father's will. The addendum he threatened you with does not exist. We have to assume he hired those two individuals."

"What leeches," Timothy said, disgusted.

"They may not know," Jacob theorized. "My father might be conning them too. Dad always loved to play both sides against the middle. He was undoubtedly fucking their mother the horse trainer. But maybe Paul Weston is the only father they've ever known."

"What do you intend to do?" Abbot asked.

"Wait him out. I can play the long game as well as he can."

Bea was wringing her working-class hands. "Sounds like a very tangled web. Best to let the man die in peace thinking he's gotten his way."

Jacob suddenly saw the large box in the corner of the room. "It came!"

He ran over and started unpacking it.

"What is it?" Timothy asked.

"Our telescope."

◆ ◆ ◆

The Edwardian home that Jacob renamed Brigsley Manor was built in 1907. There was access to the roof from a short staircase and a small door in the attic. A narrow widow's walk traveled the entire length of the building.

"This is perfect," Jacob said, carrying the Meade telescope and tripod onto the walkway. Abbot helped him get it situated.

"We've had a fair amount of rain lately," he said, glancing skyward. "You'll need to bring the mechanism back into the attic after every viewing."

"I believe you're right. But the tripod can remain on the roof covered with a tarp. That will make future excursions easier to manage."

Bea and Timothy were cowering in the attic. "You should come out here. It's quite safe, and the view is magnificent," Abbot called to the open door.

"I don't want to fall off the roof," Bea said nervously. "Heights give me a fright, as do close spaces like this damned attic."

Jacob was adjusting the scope. "Boy, that apple didn't fall very far," he muttered.

"I heard that," Timothy said, crawling out the narrow door. Soon they were all standing and admiring the view of the river and the spires of the colleges.

"This would be cozy with a few chairs," Bea mumbled. "There's more room than one would expect up here."

"The Meade LX600 is a fabulous scope. It has a Starlock autoguiding system as well as the AutoStar II GOTO system with more than 145,000 night-sky objects programmed," Jacob quoted.

He'd managed to locate Jupiter low on the horizon and allowed each of his companions to see the gas giant up close.

"Amazing," Bea exclaimed.

"I want to try to show you the Eagle Nebula."

Abbot squinted at the night sky. "Also known as the pillars of creation. Seven thousand light-years away."

"Imagine it," Jake said, almost breathless as the telescope mechanically moved into position. "The light that's reaching us tonight is ancient."

"When we look at the stars we are seeing light that, in some cases, has taken thousands of years to reach us. We are gazing into the distant past." Abbot remarked. "It's possible to see supernovas that happened millennia ago and are no more because the light is just reaching the Earth. It's a bit like time travel."

Timothy and Jacob hugged one another as Bea observed the nebula.

"This makes our astrological forecasts feel all the more real," Bea stated.

Jake grunted. "You do know that astrology is all rubbish, don't you?"

She looked confused. "What are you talking about?"

Jacob watched her sympathetically. "Well, to begin with, there are thirteen constellations, not twelve. But three thousand years ago the ancient Babylonians found that inconvenient because of the calendar, which also made no sense. Why is October the tenth month when it should be the eighth? December is the twelfth month when it should be named the tenth. The mists of time have confused much we take for granted. I would have been born under the thirteenth sign, Ophiuchus, the serpent-bearer. It's situated behind the sun from November twenty-ninth to December eighteenth."

"I don't know where you're getting your information, Jay..."

"This is from NASA."

"That can't be right," Bea mumbled, confusion knitting her brow. She'd gotten bothered and made her way back through the small door and back into the house.

"Must you?" Abbot said harshly. "She enjoys that nonsense. It gives her comfort. Pulling the rug out like that is mean-spirited. I thought I taught you better, but discretion has never been a flower that grew in your garden, young man."

Abbot left the two boys alone on the roof so he could tend to Betty. Timothy hadn't uttered a word, but he did sigh loudly.

"Go ahead and say it. I deserve it."

The boy took another quick peek through the telescope.

"No one likes a know-it-all, *serpent-bearer*..."

CHAPTER 76

Disappearance

Timothy promised he would meet with the police, so Jacob and Sir John accompanied him to Oxford Town Hall. Elsie and Forrestal were standing with Bridges when the boys walked in.

"I don't understand why you find it necessary to further harass my clients when you have the man you are looking for in custody," Sir John complained.

"Tying up loose ends," Bridges answered. "We'd all like to get back to our lives."

"Where's Skip?" Jacob asked Elsie.

"Probably the library."

"So, Mr. Ashlock," Forrestal began. "We went to the address you gave us. The occupants had never heard of you or Dr. Thomas Pe."

"What?" he said, shocked. "Who was there?"

"A nice Italian family. They've held the mortgage for more than twenty years."

"I don't understand. Was the Italian's first name Fausto?"

Forrestal consulted his notes. "Yes, that's right."

"Well," Tim said meekly, "he might remember me as Timothy Abbot."

"Why would you be using that name?"

He looked at the palm of his hand. "It's a long story."

Bridges snorted. "It doesn't sound like a long story, it sounds like a short alias."

"Seriously, Bridges?" Jacob mocked. "Timothy *Abbot* as an alias?"

"Nevertheless," the DCI said.

"Carl, you're about as sharp as a bag of wet hair."

"We also searched every roster and directory at each college at Oxford. There is no Dr. Thomas Pe, in Asian Studies or anywhere else."

Timothy blinked and took Jake's hand. "I don't know what to tell you."

"Then answer this: Has Julian Adler ever made advances toward you?"

"Of course," Timothy freely stated. "I'd wager practically every lad in the orchestra has batted away the maestro's wandering hands."

"Did you ever feel threatened?"

"No."

Jacob leaned across the desk. "You have to wonder why a tired, old queen like Adler is slaying pretty young girls. Has he confessed to the murders?"

"Why do you ask?"

"Curiosity."

Elsie gave Jacob a quick smile. "We're just trying to unravel the mystery."

Jacob glanced at the doctor. "Have you ever noticed that the words ravel and unravel mean the same thing?"

"Dear Lord, just what we need, more etymology," Timothy mumbled.

She moved her wheelchair closer. "It's like bone and debones."

"Precisely. Or the words caretaker and caregiver. Flammable and inflammable. They should be opposites but they are synonyms."

Bridges gave them a frostbitten look.

"You'd make a good journalist, Mr. Weston," Forrestal said.

"I'd rather light myself on fire."

"I hope you're flammable," Bridges muttered.

Sir John waved a hand in the air dramatically. "I'm sorry we couldn't be of more assistance."

They got up to leave. "It was lovely to see you again, Carl, regardless or irregardless of the reason," Jacob laughed, and then leaned toward Elsie and whispered, "Let's chat soon."

She nodded.

Timothy thanked Sir John as he entered a cab bound for London. Jacob took out his phone and texted Skip. "I need to speak to Loge before you and I are back on the suspect list. I find it interesting that it's been several weeks since there's been a murder."

"Maybe killers take holidays as well," Timothy joked.

"Are you doing all right? What do you think happened to Dr. Pe?"

Timothy zipped his hoodie. "I think Miranda made him disappear. I'm going to go find her. I'll meet you back at the house later."

"You're driving to Greenknoll? Do you want me to come?"

Timothy shook his head. "It's probably better if I see her alone."

CHAPTER 77

Echidna

J acob walked through the south colonnade entering the library that bore his name. He found Skip Loge tucked away in a second-floor reading room. Jake shut the door so they could speak privately.

"You look like the statue of a bronze god," the detective remarked. "I take it Australia was warm."

"It was lovely."

"Are you any relation to Garfield Weston, the man this library was named after?"

"What do you think?" Jacob said, resigned. "My name is on everything from shoes to sausage grinders."

They sat close together. Skip had a pile of books on Greek mythology as well as other texts on folklore scattered around.

"They're thinking of removing the shrunken head exhibit in the Pitt Rivers Museum, which was quite a popular attraction. There've been complaints by the indigenous South American people."

"Are there a lot of indigenous South Americans attending classes at Oxford?"

"You ask an insightful question, Detective. By the way, you've got the wrong guy locked up," Jacob said casually.

"I think so too," Loge admitted. "Although Julian Adler

belongs in a cage for various and sundry other reasons."

"Are you wearing nail polish?" Jake asked, looking at Skip's hands.

"It's clear."

"Yes, I can see that. Timothy and I painted our toenails red in Australia, though I think we require a recoat."

Skip cracked open a book, showing Jake a picture. "I've got that beat by a country mile."

"There's more to you than meets the eye. So what is your theory on the killer?"

He stretched. "There's scant doubt in my mind that Timothy is at the center of everything. This killer feels rage and is directing it toward him. Perhaps the goal is to hurt—certainly, he is smart enough to see that Ashlock is being implicated. Timothy was our prime suspect for a time. Maybe the killer's goal is to see him put away for crimes he's innocent of committing. There's an evil kind of revenge motive in that thinking—and revenge is a powerful incentive. Certainly, the murderer has been successful in causing suspicion and pain."

Jacob nodded thoughtfully. "I hear what you're saying but I don't completely agree. I think he's jealous. He's removing everyone that stands in the way. All the competitors for Timmy's affection. I would seem to be a likely target if either theory is true."

Skip tapped his pen nervously against the table then opened his laptop. "I'm going to suggest an outrageous theory, so please don't think I'm insane."

Jake grinned. "Detective, I lived for almost a year in a haunted cottage. I can handle weird."

"Oh yes, White Oak, you've reminded me. Your old headmaster died in a strange and rather fiery explosion."

Jacob thumbed through one of the books. "Yes, I know. God has a wicked sense of humor, and not to mix theologies but, karma is a bitch."

The detective watched him closely. "So, you don't think there was any human intervention? Something like a Thomas

Sweatt scenario?"

"I don't believe they found any evidence of foul play," Jacob said lightly.

"And after that incident, you transferred immediately to Eton?"

"Better swim team, not to mention safer." He paused and smiled. "Ask me no questions and I'll tell you no lies."

"I've already decided I'm going to like you and Mr. Ashlock, so perhaps we should leave your dead headmaster in the past.

So, back to the matter at hand. First the simple facts. We have four murdered girls and not a single piece of strong evidence against the killer. No DNA, no witnesses, no latent fingerprints, fibers or trace evidence, and not a frame of him on any camera—and there are loads of cameras around Oxford. That itself is odd. Add into the mix that the murders have a ritualized or stylized pattern. The ancient Greek Theta, the removal of clothing. I believe this killer is old—perhaps very old."

"Some kind of spirit or demon? Is that where you're headed?"

"Yes. I even got a tip from someone saying as much. I discounted it at the time, but it stayed with me as a possibility."

"If it wants Timmy all to itself, why wouldn't it kill me first? I'm his boyfriend."

"An excellent question. Perhaps it has other plans for you."

"Such as?"

"Possession. If it becomes you, Timothy will love it forever."

Jacob furrowed his brow. "Certainly can't let that happen. We need to throw a fly into the ointment. How can this thing be killed?"

Skip pulled several books on mythology closer. "I'm thinking it's something like *Echidna*. She was a monster that was half-snake and half-woman and became the mother of many other monsters. Maybe she wants Timothy for breeding purposes."

Jacob's eyes widened. "We were attacked by a snake on our vacation. One with a nasty attitude. Now it feels like that animal was commissioned."

"She may be attracting her pets towards you, even unintentionally. It's like a succubus, but something about Timothy is drawing it closer. There's a deep attraction."

"He is quite attractive," Jacob said, grinning.

"The bad news is that it can't be killed with anything of this earth. Fire and silver may slow it down slightly. It's very old and, as we know, quite strong."

"That is not encouraging."

"There is a story I translated from Greek about a monster like this being slain with a weapon that was not forged on earth," Skip noted.

"Where do I buy one of those?"

"When we started the investigation we were amazed by the killer's strength, which made us assume a big, muscular man, but if it's one of these non-human entities it could look like anyone."

"You're thinking it might be a woman."

Loge nodded. "It could even be a little girl."

CHAPTER 78

Saint Jude

Timothy drove the Range Rover to Greenknoll in search of Miranda. He stopped by the pub and the bartender told him where her caravan might be located.

Being so close to White Oak made him nostalgic, wondering if boys were living in Brigsley Cottage this year. He could just make out the church steeple and the top of Kyler as he walked across the field. A dozen gypsy encampments sat beside the Tydell River, then he saw a small girl beating a rug hanging on a clothesline.

She spotted Timothy and went running to meet him. "Finally."

He laughed. "Finally?"

"I told Skip Loge to tell you to come. I've been waiting for weeks."

"Ah, well that message never made it through. You could have called."

She spun like a helicopter. "I knew you'd show up sooner or later."

"What did you do to Dr. Pe?"

She giggled. "Don't worry about dear Thomas. He's still one of the cunning folk, we just took him off the grid for a while. He was naughty, so we hid him."

Timothy stared at her. "Impressive. Is this what Dr.

289

Krage called *time mending*?"

The girl smiled and avoided the question. "Is the young detective wearing dresses yet?"

"Not that I know of."

She winked. "He will be."

"Do you know why I'm here?"

"Of course, Silly," she laughed, taking his hand and leading him toward her tent. He waved at the two women who cared for Miranda. "You're being stalked by a nasty piece of business. That's what you get for time traveling, it's like waving a red cape in front of a herd of bulls."

Timothy sat on the grass. "It's killing my friends, and I'm worried about the people I've got left."

"You should be. Fascinating that it hasn't killed Jake yet, you'd think he'd be on the top of that list."

Timothy looked aghast, then closed his eyes.

"Must be saving him for some diabolical scheme," she mused. "It's not like he hasn't already been dead."

"I've come here begging for help."

She reached into her bag and came out with pieces of jewelry. "Take these two bracelets. You and Jake should each wear one on your left wrist."

"Copper?"

"Yes, and topaz. A very powerful combination."

"How much?"

"Twenty quid," she said innocently, as Timothy reached for his wallet. "Each."

He rolled his eyes.

"Hey, a girl's got to make a living."

"What will they do?" he asked, turning the bracelets over in his hand.

"It's an ancient amulet for warding away evil in every form. It will chase away bad spirits and prevent magic from being cast onto you."

Timothy immediately put one on his wrist. "And will it keep this thing at bay?"

Miranda laughed. "No. Probably just piss it off, but at least it will help you identify it. This entity will find these annoying and foul. You must be careful though, just by wearing the amulet the demon will know you're on to its wicked game. It's old and smart, and a monster can always sense when it's been recognized.

You're a special lad, Timmy. It isn't just the traveling, it's your energy that has attracted the beast's attention. You could be a mender, if not for this jealous thing chasing you. It wants you all to itself."

"Can it be banished?"

"No," she said with finality.

"What about killing it?"

"That would be quite an impressive feat."

"Sounds like I need a Saint Jude medal, he's my mother's favorite saint."

The girl rolled her eyes. "It isn't a hopeless cause yet, but some prayer wouldn't hurt. You still need something else. Follow me."

She took his hand as they weaved their way past colorful tents and wagons, finally getting to a teepee with a small fenced area. "Jasper," she called, "I have a buyer."

A flaxen-haired boy of thirteen peeked through the flaps and smiled. "Oy, Miranda, let him take his pick."

The boy released half a dozen fat puppies, each as blond as Jake. Timothy laughed and got down on his hands and knees. He rolled around with the pups as they scampered and yelped.

"Tell me why I need a mongrel dog, Miranda, as magnificent as this lot are."

She crossed her arms. "Because dogs have keen senses and loyal hearts. A dog can warn you of the presence of a demon. They know the difference between humans and others."

"Very well. Jasper, hold all the pups back."

The boy corralled the wee nippers and Timothy sat

crossed-legged a dozen feet away. "Release the hounds!" he shouted.

The puppies ran and played, they chased one another and rolled on the grass. They surrounded him, but one gave Timothy special attention, bounding straight for him, resting her head on his lap.

"This must be the winner," he declared, lifting the puppy and cuddling her.

"Smart of you," Miranda said, "to let the dog make the choice. She will be a loyal companion until the end of her days."

CHAPTER 79

Tess

It was almost nightfall when Timothy arrived back home. The puppy had slept on his lap for the entire trip. He gently placed the snoring dog on the car seat while he went inside.

"Timmy," Jacob said, bounding down the stairs.

"JP Weston, I have a gift for you."

They hugged. "I adore presents. How was your trip down memory lane? Was the gypsy girl helpful?"

Tim took out the bracelet and put it on Jake's left wrist. "She was."

"Well, that child always did like you better than me. Is this copper? I'm not arthritic yet, though that probably is in my future. The stone is pretty though."

"It wards off evil."

"Does it? We should have had these when we ate dinner with my family," he joked.

"I left a package in the car, could you grab it while I wash my hands."

"Of course, *Caro.*"

Timothy spied from the window, watching as Jacob discovered her. He held the dog to his neck, breathing in the new puppy smell. When he came back into the house he was over the moon.

"Abbot, Bea!" he yelled. "Come meet the new girl in town!"

"Do you love her?" Timothy asked.

"More than life itself! This will be good practice for when we have children. Does she ward off evil too?"

They laughed. "She's a furry early warning system."

Jake hugged the pup again. "A canary in a coal mine."

Abbot and Bea came rushing in to see what the fuss was about. "Who's this?"

Bea held out her arms and took the puppy. "She's glorious. What's her name?"

Timothy smiled at his boyfriend. "Your call."

Jake looked closely into the big brown puppy eyes. "Everyone, this is Tess."

"I like it," Tim said.

"A dog is quite a lot of responsibility, master Jacob."

"You won't have to lift a finger, Abbot. Timmy will do all the hard work," Jake promised.

Bea put her hands on Jacob's shoulders. "I know you think I'm just a superstitious old woman…"

"Bea, I apologized for that snarky outburst— twice."

She waved a hand. "Timothy is a chime child."

"A what?" Abbot and Jacob said in unison.

They looked over and Tess was asleep in Tim's arms.

"He was born on a Friday at midnight, chime hours. He has access to things that are hidden from others. Musical talent, the ability to see the dead and fairies, to speak with them and come to no harm. To love and control animals and to heal others."

"Hmm, never heard that one before, but it makes sense to me. Explains a lot of things," Jake said calmly.

Bea shook her head. "Oh, so that you can believe."

Jake laughed. "I've got quite a lot of canine supplies to buy online now."

"Tess and I are going to the kitchen—I'm cooking a dessert for everyone tonight," Timothy announced.

"What sort of dessert?"

"*Mousse au Chocolat.*"

Abbot leaned in toward Jacob. "If Monsieur Dezo knew you were giving out his secrets he would boil you in oil."

Jake scoffed. "That man is a cheese-eating surrender monkey, who cheats at poker. I may publish it for the whole world to enjoy."

CHAPTER 80

Aqua Shard

"Try to behave tonight," Timothy pleaded. "This is a big deal for Billy."

"Mr. Ashlock, I don't know what you're talking about. I always behave, and this whole double-date idea was mine in the first place."

"Sweet Jesus," Timothy muttered.

When they arrived at Aqua Shard, Billy and Madelyn were already waiting, sipping cocktails.

"My, my," Jacob purred. "Lord Redgrave is the first to arrive and he's already getting the prettiest girl in the room tipsy."

Redgrave's cheeks started to redden as Timothy hugged him.

Jacob took the girl's hand and kissed it. "Madelyn, I presume."

"Mr. Weston."

"Call me Jake, we're all going to be fast friends."

Timothy hugged Maddy next. "You've no idea what you've signed up for tonight," he whispered.

"Don't be a goose," she scolded, kissing both his cheeks. "I've been looking forward to it."

"I adore this place," Jacob announced, looking out at the London skyline. "I've booked my favorite spot for us!"

They were ushered to a glorious window table in the private dining room looking out at London Bridge.

"He loves to show off," Timothy whispered to Maddy.

"I like the way he treats you. Are you happy?"

"Incredibly."

"Billy told me you're engaged."

Timothy pulled at his collar. "That's meant to be a secret."

"What are you two girls talking about?" Jacob asked.

"Orchestra gossip," Maddy lied.

Billy held the chair out for her. "And are you drinking gin?" Jacob asked, pointing to their glasses. "That's so British. What are those things called?"

"Maddy's cocktail is named, *God's Own*, and I'm having a *Corpse Reviver.* They're made with Tanqueray Ten," Billy said proudly.

"How vile."

"I think gin is the only British thing you don't like," Timothy said.

Jacob waved the waiter over. "To be honest, I'm not overly fond of Shepherd's pie either. I think I went off gin because it's my father's favorite."

He ordered two Spring Punches which were made with Kettle One and Veuve Clicquot.

"How did you lads like Australia?" Billy asked. "You're as brown as a bear, Jake."

"It was amazing," Timothy bragged.

"I lost my race, and we were attacked by an extremely nasty viper, but other than that it was aces."

"You should have seen it," Timothy said, eyes wide. "We're naked in a sleeping bag and Jake managed to slice the thing's head off as it lunged for me."

"You're a hero," Maddy said, holding up her drink.

"Stuff and nonsense. I acted on pure instinct. We were both terrified."

The starters arrived with Billy choosing seared Orkney

scallops and Jacob and Timothy sharing marinated yellowfin tuna. Maddy opted for Hereford beef tartare.

"You have to love a lady who likes raw beef," Jacob said, stealing a morsel from Maddy's plate. "So where did you two lovebirds meet?"

Billy put his arm instinctively around her. "At a pub. She walked right up to me and said hello."

Timothy pressed Jake's foot under the table.

"How romantic. Which pub?"

"Rusty Bicycle," he said, tucking into his scallops. "I was there with some of the..." he leaned over the table, "climbers and rowers."

"Billy and I are in the Night Climbers," Jacob whispered to Maddy.

"Yes, I gathered."

"I hear you're quite involved in the Women of Oxford movement."

She nodded as their entrees arrived. "It's vital. Four women were brutally attacked. I never would have guessed that our conductor was the killer."

"Me either, he doesn't seem the type. You must have been terrified," Jacob said, patting her hand. "It's a good thing Redgrave whisked you off to Scotland."

"It was wonderful there."

"Bit brisk though? What is there to do besides drink and complain about the weather?"

"We made out all right," Billy muttered. "Maddy comes from strong stock. She doesn't mind the cold, loves the outdoors and she's a crack shot."

"Ah yes, hiking around the highlands killing unsuspecting animals. I'd forgotten how the gentry loves that."

"What's a holiday if you don't kill a few things?" she joked.

"I'd be careful of this one, Redgrave."

Madelyn noticed the matching bracelets on the boys. "Those are lovely. Is it topaz?"

"Yes— a gift from Timmy."

"So thoughtful," she said, tucking into her spring lamb. "How did you boys meet?"

Jacob smiled, remembering back. "I met these lads when I first moved to England. We all attended White Oak."

"I thought you were at Eton," she said to Billy.

"We went there after, the headmaster at White Oak was a nutter. I told you Timmy and I have known each other since I was eleven."

Jacob and Timothy were sharing the chateaubriand, while Billy was having a beef fillet with mushrooms. Jake ordered a Barolo Bussia from Piemonte because he knew Timothy loved it.

"This wine is delicious," she mentioned.

"Timothy loves a fine Barolo."

He took Jake's hand. "Mr. Weston knows everything about wine. I've gotten quite an education."

"Wine in, wisdom out," Jake laughed.

"I'll drink anything," Billy said.

"So since the butcher is caught, I don't suppose you'll be having any more marches or candlelight vigils," Jake said, baiting her.

Maddy glared. "I think the Women of Oxford still has relevance as a movement."

Jacob was trying to get a rise out of her. "I don't know. I think highly specific groups tend to divide us up, rather than bring us together."

She laughed in his face. "You should be more enlightened, Mr. Weston, since you are a member of a marginalized group."

"Are you referring to homos?"

"Exactly, I'm sure you're a vocal advocate regarding gay causes and rights, just as you should be."

"Well, I'm not a zealot."

Timothy grinned. "He's decided to swim in the Gay Games."

"Precisely!" she shouted.

Jacob gave Timothy a frown, "Hey, whose side are you on?"

"Neither."

"Your group seems a bit sexist to me," Jacob told her.

"Then you're a douchebag, Mr. Weston."

He laughed openly at the obscenity. "I'll have you know it's taken me years to progress from vain teenager to opinionated Oxford douchebag. But my stance on the sexist stance of your group is unchanged."

"Seriously? And how many women are members of the Night Climbers of Oxford?"

Billy laughed. "She's got you there."

CHAPTER 81

Just In Case

"Do you think it will last?" Timothy asked.

"What? Redgrave and that tart? Heavens no. She's going to crush him like a bug on a windshield. Some things in life aren't meant to last, they're ephemeral like snowmen and sandcastles."

Tim sighed. "I don't suppose there's any value in saying something."

Jacob threw an arm around his shoulder as they settled into the den, the fat yellow puppy between them on the couch. "He's already too far gone. Being in love is sort of like having a broken nose—messy, usually painful, and entirely obvious."

"I feel rather guilty concerning Billy. When you were gone he was my best friend in the world."

Jake stoked the fire and went to where a stack of packages was waiting. "You should find a way to tell him or do something special. He'll be needing his friends around him soon enough. Madelyn is extraordinarily beautiful, but I'll tell you this: when I started to needle her about the movement she gave me a look so cold it could frost a cake."

"I've seen her in action. She has a rather short attention span when it comes to boyfriends," Tim stated.

"Unlike you, she wields her beauty as a weapon." Jacob unwrapped a book. "Hey look, Ian Thorpe sent us his cookbook.

It's titled: *Cook for Your Life*. Filled with all the recipes that keep him healthy and fit, and he signed it too!"

"Probably not a lot of calls for butter in there," Tim joked.

"Will you still love me when I'm old, fat, and bald?"

Timothy smirked. "I don't imagine you'll ever be bald. Hair restoration has made great strides, look at Sir Elton."

"True. That's one less worry, but you're a musician so you'll keep getting better with age and practice. I'm an athlete, so all the things that made me special will deteriorate with time. What will I have left when I am soft and slow?"

"Hmm, nearly unlimited funds and a superior intellect?"

"*Caro*, you always know just the right thing to say to me."

He opened a large cardboard box that contained a smaller metal case and a letter. "Look at this," he said, removing the device.

Timothy jumped up. "Where did that come from?"

"Dr. Pe had time to make it to the post office before he disappeared into the ether. He sent it to us with a strange recipe, and a note that reads: *Just in case.*"

"In case of what, do you suppose?"

Jacob held the device out, examining it. "I guess in case one of us dies."

CHAPTER 82

The Fellowship

The Night Climbers had gathered at the Rusty Bicycle to discuss and plan their next exploit. Everyone was already drinking and getting rowdy.

"I shouldn't be here," Timothy said with Tess sitting on his feet. "I'm not a member of your secret club."

"We haven't started the meeting," Jacob scolded. "You can at least stand one drink with these pirates."

The puppy was a popular attraction as every boy came over to greet the furry sidekick. When Doug Turner came by, Tim clapped him on the back.

"Say, Doug, I don't know if you're aware but I play the guitar as well as the violin."

"Do you? What sort of music?"

"That's what I wanted to talk to you about. I'm thinking of putting together a blues and jazz trio to play at the Hatter. Do you think you might be interested?"

"Sure, mate, why not?"

"Maybe we can get together at the house and jam next week?"

Doug seemed excited by the idea. "Text me. It sounds like more fun than the Bach we've been rehearsing."

Billy cornered Jacob near the fireplace. "One more game, that's all I ask." He began setting up the chessboard.

"Redgrave, have you ever actually beaten me at this game?"

"Once I have, yes."

"Was I steaming drunk at the time?"

"Entirely," Billy nodded. "And you passed out midway through, but a win is a win."

"Okay, milord, prepare to be slaughtered."

Casey Larson was watching them play.

"Weston, I wonder if I could ask you for a huge favor," he said, pulling up a chair.

"I'm a pushover for gorgeous crew lads. What can I do for you?"

"It's embarrassing."

"In that case, I'm all ears," Jacob grinned. "Don't worry about Lord Redgrave here. He can keep a secret."

Billy nodded distractedly as he studied the chessboard.

"There's a meeting tomorrow at Corpus, a trial of sorts, on my behalf. They think they caught me cheating last term and one of the proctors is petitioning to have me sent down."

Jacob's demeanor became more grave. "That's serious, my friend. What can I do?"

"I need an advocate to speak to the congregation regarding my character. I know your name and reputation could make the difference."

"Consider it done then, sport. Just name the time and place."

Larson heaved a sigh of relief. "What will you tell the kangaroo court?"

Jacob glanced at the game and made a final move. "Checkmate, milord."

Billy wordlessly stepped away, while Jake looked up at the rower. "I'll explain that you have an unquenchable spirit and that Oxford would be less grand without you."

"You'd be saving my life," Casey said. "If I get sent down my fate will be selling shoes in my father's shop for the rest of my life. I am a fairly decent artist though..." Casey's mind wandered at his few prospects without an Oxford education.

"Well I will be expecting a lap-dance for my troubles," Jake said.

Matthew Colton arrived with Adam Harper and Austin Smith-Fordham. "All right lads," Harper shouted, let's gather in the back room."

Timothy got up, adjusting the dog's collar. "We'll wait for you outside."

◆ ◆ ◆

Tess sniffed the chilly air while Timothy sat on a bench. "Do you smell a storm coming, girl?" he asked the pup, who wagged her tail appreciatively.

After a few minutes, Billy joined him. "Aren't you supposed to be plotting your next summit?"

Redgrave pet the puppy between its ears. "I'm sure they're going to pick the Magdalen Tower. It's the tallest in Oxford. They want a good perch to watch the ladies march."

"Is that where Madelyn is tonight?"

Billy nodded. "She carries a lot of responsibility for the group. It's important—the vigils and speeches. It was her idea for the march."

"You seem to really be crushing."

Redgrave tossed a pebble into the gutter which made the puppy bark. "I know she's out of my league."

Timothy grasped his shoulder. "On the contrary, she's lucky to know you." He took his bracelet off and placed it on Billy's wrist.

"I want you to have this—it will protect you from evil."

Billy smiled. "You're giving it to me?"

"Absolutely," Tim said softly. "I can't explain it, but in another life, you and I are best friends."

He gazed into Timothy's eyes. "I find that easy to believe."

CHAPTER 83

The Magdalen Bridge

Timothy woke with a start. He was dreaming of a massive snake slithering up his body and sinking its fangs into his neck. He glanced over at Jake, softly snoring, and carefully climbed out of bed. Tess watched from her puppy crate and whimpered. He took her out and kissed her head, whispering, "Let's go see the river."

It was just before daybreak and he'd decided to walk down to the bridge and practice. He needed to clear his head before classes started.

It's funny, he thought, *my playing is so much freer, and more expressive since the accident. I wonder why?*

❖ ❖ ❖

Casey Larson reached up and pulled his custom-made Oxford Shell from its perch in the boathouse. His fate would be decided before lunch and his only hope was that Jake and the other advocates would convince the judges not to send him down.

It is what it is, he thought. *Best not to dwell on it.*

He had learned a valuable lesson from the ordeal: it's better to fail as an honest man than to pass and be labeled a cheat.

He put his EarPods in and cranked up the music. He should have picked the road that led to becoming a dancer or a tattoo artist.

Casey placed the boat into the chilly water and padded barefoot back into the boathouse to get his backpack, and that's when he saw her emerge from the shadows.

"Hey! You're up bright and early. Did you want to go on the river?"

He grinned and rushed in, arms wide for a hug, not noticing the blade in her hand until it was too late. The steel flashed in the morning light as she reached for his throat.

Casey choked on the warm blood, flailing his hands wildly. *It's so red*, he thought, watching his life spill onto the deck.

She stood there defiant, arms folded, waiting for the boy to die. "You?" he managed to gurgle before dropping to his knees.

She laughed wickedly as his spirit departed. "You didn't actually think it was that queer conductor, did you?"

When Timothy heard the screaming from across the river, the déjà vu struck him like a cold slap across the face. "Casey," he whispered. Tess began barking wildly, pulling at the leash.

He quickly packed his things, grabbed the puppy, and ran up High Street toward home.

CHAPTER 84

New Clues

Bridges had reassembled the team and looked visibly distraught. "So what the hell is this?"

"Carl," Dr. Kelly said, "this boy bled out fast. His carotid was sliced clean by something very sharp, probably a scalpel."

"Does Adler have a partner?"

Skip was typing on his laptop and wearing makeup. The look was subtle but it hadn't gotten past Bridges. "Doubtful, Chief, and so you know, I always thought the conductor was a red herring."

"What about a copycat?"

Elsie blinked. "It's a valid thought because this is similar but also different. This victim is male and capable of putting up a fight—he was one of our main suspects. And yet, there is no sign of a struggle. Larson knew the killer, and that person may be taunting the police by killing off our suspects."

"It's unusual for a serial killer to alter the gender of his targets," Forrestal said.

"Kid, what do you think?"

"A photo of the symbol was leaked onto the web weeks ago. I've been comparing the forensic images of the markings from previous victims and the current ones we took today and they are extremely close. If it's a copycat then it's a good one."

He cleared his throat. "There's still something that all the victims had in common...Ashlock and Weston. Larson was close to them both. Jacob was slated to defend him today because Corpus Christi College was going to send Casey Larson down for cheating."

Forrestal leaned forward, his purple tie brushing the desktop. "Mr. Adler's lawyers are already demanding the immediate release and exoneration of their client."

"Screw that," Bridges replied.

Sergeant Eddings put his tablet on the DCI's desk. "There's a CCTV image of Ashlock playing the violin near the Magdalen Bridge."

"Was he alone?"

"No," Eddings answered. "He has a labrador puppy now."

Carl sighed.

"We should visit those boys and shake that tree again. And Dr. Courtemarche, we need to have a chat."

"Yeah?"

"Has one of our murder suspects offered you a million dollars?"

"What?" Leta Kelly gasped.

"He's going to be donating funds to start a charitable foundation. No money has changed hands yet."

"Then you haven't accepted a bribe and committed a crime—yet. We can't allow you to take that money."

She looked at Skip, betrayed at last, but he shook his head. "No one gave you up, Doctor, but just because a suspect asks us to turn off the recorders in an interview room doesn't mean we comply—sometimes we just turn off the red light and let the machines run."

Elsie pulled her shoulders back and puffed out her chest defiantly. "Really? Then find yourself another shrink, Carl. I quit."

She turned her chair and gazed at Skip and Leta with tears in her eyes. "I'm sorry," she mouthed, wheeling out of the conference room.

Bridges looked closely at Detective Loge, "Kid, what's the deal with the makeup?"

CHAPTER 85

Tea with the Docs

When Timothy arrived back from class everyone was sitting in the drawing-room having tea. "Ah, the man of the hour," Jacob said.

He was surprised to find Doctors Matthews and Courte-marche sitting with his mum having tea and cakes. "This is an unlikely gathering," he mused.

"I called them together," Jake admitted. "We're having an informal symposium."

Timothy looked suspiciously at his boyfriend. "And why am I the man of the hour?"

The puppy ran to each woman sniffing, wagging, and having a grand time.

"That's a very happy dog," Dr. Kay said.

"There's never been a more spoiled animal," Bea re-marked, tossing a tennis ball across the floor.

"We're discussing memory— repressed, blocked, and otherwise. Jacob told us that you suffer from localized dis-sociative amnesia."

"Does he?" Timothy stared at the boy. "I'm not sure what those terms even mean, but I didn't think we were airing our laundry. Why don't we talk about Jacob's madness?"

Elsie scoffed. "His pathology is far too easy."

"Let's hear it," Timothy demanded.

She pulled her wheelchair in and placed a cake on her plate. "Have you ever noticed how he touches people when he talks to them? It's as if the distance has to be closed off before he can communicate. It's physical."

"So, I'm a hugger, what dark secret does that reveal?"

"Empathy, even with people you don't like all that much. You seek a connection."

"Bravo," Jacob said, touching Tim's face with the back of his hand. The boys looked at each other. "I just want to know if you can get some of that time back."

"Okay, fine," Timothy said, resigned. He poured himself some black tea. "What do you ladies want to know? I haven't had a mid-afternoon emotional collapse since before our trip."

"You've been troubled by dreams though?" Kay asked.

"Yes."

"Do you feel that you are starting to remember traumatic events?"

Timothy shrugged. "The dreams are a jumble. Facts and fiction interspersed. But to be honest, I remember all the traumatic events of my life."

"Name a few for us."

Jacob rubbed Tim's back. "My brother's suicide. Unwanted sexual advances by teachers and others who I trusted, not to mention when my boyfriend drowned."

"What? Who are you speaking of?"

"Jake here, of course."

The boys turned to one another and nodded. "Maybe they can help," he whispered.

"He isn't suppressing bad memories, this is something else. Timothy doesn't have gaps in his memory—he remembers things happening differently. He has memories, just not the right ones."

"They feel like waking dreams in my personal reality, so no one else shares those fragments of time," Tim said softly.

Dr. Kay perked up. "Brain injury can be responsible for that. My original diagnosis was partial anterograde amnesia, but we may have to modify that. Many therapists believe that repressed memories can be regained through therapy or simply through elapsed time, but the prevailing wisdom is that this also fosters the creation of false memory."

Elsie wheeled her chair towards the window and Tess ran after her nipping at the wheels. "He could also be delusional. This could be some kind of psychic break, although I'd rather not speculate too far in that direction since he was recently a suspect in a criminal investigation."

"Couldn't he be remembering things from a past life?" Bea asked, which caused the doctors to chuckle.

"Even if that were true, it would be impossible to prove," Elsie said.

"What about hypnosis?"

Dr. Kay looked sternly at Jacob. "You don't truly believe this is past life memory seeping into his current existence, do you?"

"No. He's remembering an alternate reality. A separate timeline that's standing in the way of him being able to recall this one. Those old memories are blocking that time period— just over a year of his life— but I think somewhere deep down he still has those lost memories. Maybe hypnosis can restore the erased tape."

When the doctors had left Bea began clearing the tea service. "You boys should have just come right out with it."

Jake looked quizzically at her. "With what?"

"Timmy traveled back in time and saved your life. Any idiot could figure that one out."

The boys glanced at one another and started to laugh.

"You're a corker, Bea."

"By the way, your new bathtub arrived. The plumbers installed it while you were out."

"Wonderful!"

"What?" Tim asked.

"I bought a copper bathtub. It's very chic. I had it put in the guest bathroom we never use."

"Hmm."

Jacob smiled weakly. "Copper soaking tubs were all the rage among the eighteenth-century French monarchy, Marie Antoinette had one at Versailles."

"Did she?" Timothy said sarcastically.

Jacob put the leash on Tess. "The pup and I are going down to the covered market before it closes."

"Buy some fruit and vegetables if anything looks good," Bea shouted.

"I'm visiting your friend, Mr. McNett, the silversmith. He's finished a project for me."

CHAPTER 86

Fortis Fortuna Adiuvat

T he Ashmolean Museum housed over forty thousand artifacts collected over three hundred years, from over a hundred archaeological sites, including Tutankhamun.

Jacob had disguised himself in coveralls and was slowly moving a mop around the exhibits. It was nearly time for the museum to close.

The gentleman who had been reading his newspaper casually got up and approached the boy. "Interesting employment for the son of a billionaire."

Jacob spun quickly around and saw Matthias smiling. "Dr. Krage, what are you doing here?"

"Helping. Did you imagine you were going to waltz in here, pick a lock, and walk away with a priceless artifact?"

"My scheme was slightly more complicated than you make it sound. I'm going to switch the item so no one misses it."

He chuckled. "It's an interesting piece. The dagger has a golden handle and sheath, but the blade is made of what appears to be iron, but quite unusual metal since it hasn't tarnished even after three millennia. It's not known if the material had a religious significance, but the Boy King seemed to be a collector of *iron from the sky*. Did you get your replica past the metal detectors by coming through the employee entrance?"

"Yes," Jacob replied. "They need to install one back there. I bet the workers are making off with all sorts of things."

Krage rubbed the stubble on his jaw. "Not everyone has criminal intent. Your prize is sitting on a pressure-sensitive plate, there are also silent alarms should the glass be opened and a camera pointed in that direction."

"I didn't plan for all that. I guess I could just smash and grab and hope for the best."

"Ah, *Fortis fortuna adiuvat*, fortune favors the bold. But let's not be hasty. I have a device in my pocket that can release a pulse disabling all electronics for two minutes, which is how long it will take for the backup system to reboot. Unfortunately, that includes the lights. Will you be able to accomplish your goal in complete darkness and within that time frame?"

Jacob smiled. "Easily. But Dr. Krage, if I may ask, why are you helping me? And how did you know I'd be doing this?"

"It was on Timothy's explicit orders. He would refuse to join my team unless we give you a sporting chance to defeat this evil entity."

Jacob stared at the glass case. "So you and I have been here before."

"Many times."

"And what is the usual outcome?"

Matthias lowered his gaze. "Most of the time you die."

"Most?"

"About seven out of ten times the creature kills you."

Jacob dried his sweaty palms on the coveralls. "Never tell me the odds. The only world I care about is the current one."

"It's a strong, ancient, and clever beast. I'm frankly surprised that you ever succeed. It's drawn to Timothy like a moth to a flame. It can sense his presence."

"Who is it?"

"Now, now," Matthias chided. "I thought you loved surprises."

"Okay. Will you at least tell me if the meteor knife will

work?"

"It has to touch the heart. Your one advantage is that the entity thinks it will live forever. Arrogance, that is its *hamartia*."

"A fatal flaw. Then it can be killed—it's not immortal."

Matthias nodded. "Nothing is eternal. Sooner or later time catches up to us all."

A chime sounded signaling the imminent closing of the museum. "Let's do this."

"Can you hear the environmental machinery?"

He tilted his head and could make out the air conditioning system humming like a beehive. "Yes."

"It will make a clicking sound right before the system turns back on. You need to be finished with your task by the time you hear that."

Jacob grasped the lock picks inside his pocket and moved directly in front of the glass cabinet. "Do it," he whispered and the lights went out.

◆ ◆ ◆

By the time the clicking began and the lights flickered back to life, Jacob was away from the cabinet and Matthias was preparing to leave. They nodded to one another.

"I can protect Timothy while you battle the monster."

"That would be appreciated."

"There's a scientific mystery around that artifact in your pocket, you know. Experts are still confused."

"Confused about what?"

"That knife was found buried with Tut— but the Egyptians didn't start using iron to make things like knives until about a hundred years after his death."

CHAPTER 87

Puppy Dreams

The boys were preparing for bed. Jacob had built a huge fire in the hearth and the puppy had fallen asleep on the rug nearby. They watched the dog twitch and make whimpering noises as she slept.

"Puppy dreams," Jake whispered, holding the stolen knife in his left hand, then smoothly flipping it up and catching it by its golden handle.

"What do you suppose she sees?" Tim wondered. "Do you think she's remembering her mum?"

"I think we all dream of our mothers once they are no longer with us."

Tim touched the cold iron of the knife. "Will this work?"

"I know it will."

"I've been thinking about the murders."

"That's understandable. You knew every victim."

"It's more than that," Timothy explained, his voice low and tight. "I can see what the pattern is."

Jake leaned in. "You can?"

He gazed down at the dog, nodding. "I slept with them—every single one."

"What?" Jacob said, astounded.

He shook his head. "Not in this timeline—in my alternate. A series of one-night stands, but that's the pattern. It can't be a coincidence. I knew it as soon as Casey was killed. That happened in my alternate too, but he was the first casualty."

"So Miranda was right. You drew this creature's attention and it followed you across time and space."

The boys peered at one another in the flickering firelight and shadow. After all this time, Timothy had learned the unique language of Jacob Weston. He could interpret the silences, read them like tea leaves.

"I should be the one to kill it," Tim whispered. "It won't hurt me, but you are in danger."

Jake laughed in his face. "You couldn't harm a fly."

"I beg your pardon, but I did put more than a dozen bullets into our old headmaster."

Jake laid back. "Killing something with a knife is a horse of a different color, and I am a master of legerdemain. Besides, Skip seemed to think your admirer was saving me for some kind of possession scenario."

"What?"

"Yeah, if I suddenly seem strangely not myself I hope you will have the strength to place a bullet into me."

Timothy looked stricken. "I am certainly not that strong."

"Then you'll have to persuade Mr. Abbot. For once the butler will actually have done it. By the way, you'll need to write out a list."

Timothy gently picked up Tess and placed her into the crate next to her blanket. "A list of what?"

"All your one-night stands, you naughty boy. The Butcher is a jealous spirit—we'll need to give those names to Skip so he can keep a watchful eye."

Tim sighed. "You're right of course. What a humiliating task. I'll look like such a trollop."

Jacob reached out and slapped his butt. "You were sad and lonely, so you acted like a dog with two dicks," he laughed. "I imagine your life must have been pretty dull without me."

Tim mussed Jake's long blond hair. "You say it in jest, but it's mostly true. I lived under a dark cloud. There was a void I couldn't fill—but I did my best."

"Dr. Krage has promised to look after you while I do battle."

"Did he?"

"He can hide you where the monster won't be able to smell you—and if I should fail in my task, he has a nice job offer that should keep you busy."

CHAPTER 88

Bridge of Sighs

T he Night Climbers, all dressed in black, made quick work scaling the iconic bell tower at Magdalen. They sat atop watching, waiting, and drinking. Unfortunately for everyone, it looked like rain.

Jacob consulted his map of the parade route. "The ladies will soon be making their way up to Rose Lane and veering to the left onto High. From there, their route takes them close to Merton."

"This tower will be a bitch to get down in the rain," Matthew noted.

"We'll be rappelling from the northern side," Harper replied. "It's child's play. Has anyone seen Turner?"

With everyone in blackface, it was difficult to know who was absent. "He never misses a climb."

They were drinking Nonino Grappa which Jake felt would have the perfect warming effect against the inclement night. "To Casey," he toasted. "He left this world, and all of us too soon."

The boys cheered. "To Casey!"

"I suppose this puts a crimp in the hose of the Women of Oxford's holy crusade," Matthew Colton said to Billy.

"What are you on about?"

"The Butcher is starting to kill off lads. He's showing

321

himself to be an equal opportunity murderer. That seems to play against Missy's theme of oppression and objectification of the fairer sex."

Jake put his arm around Redgrave. "Perhaps they'll let us join the movement now— but that name has got to go."

They saw the light of all the candles in the distance. "It's quite beautiful," Harper stated.

"A decent number of them as well— must be near sixty strong."

"I'm worried about her," Billy whispered, nudging Jake. "Being so visible in this movement. It feels like she's taunting the bastard."

"I wouldn't be overly concerned, she's in a large group." Yet Jacob had to wonder if in that alternate world Maddy and Timmy were getting horizontal refreshments. Perhaps she was next on the Butcher's list.

As the girls passed by the tower it began to rain, sputtering out all of their candles. "Gentlemen, since the weather is upon us, I hope you will join me in pissing off the tallest tower in Oxford," Jake said, unzipping his fly.

And laughing that's exactly what the boys did. When the grappa was finished and the singing and revelry had mellowed, they started to set ropes for their descent.

The girls had made it to New College Lane, a darker and damper parade than anticipated, but still strong in spirit. It was then that the boys heard the whistles. Dozens of frantic, high-pitched alarms came from the direction of the parade.

Jacob scurried to the ropes, rappelling down the 144-foot tower in less than two minutes, then he sprinted toward the march. He had the meteor knife in a hidden pocket.

When he reached the Bridge of Sighs, Jake saw the body. A rope was tied around the ankles and the corpse was tossed from the open window of the covered bridge, suspended so that he dangled upside down from the overpass to the narrow lane below. The musician was nude.

The theta had been carved into his chest, but the symbol

was much larger than on the previous victims. Blood had settled around the single bullet hole in his forehead.

Douglas Turner, the drummer, and the boy who never missed a climb was dead.

◆ ◆ ◆

In the street it was pandemonium. Girls were screaming, or crying. Many were blowing their plastic whistles causing more alarm and noise. People had pulled out their phones and started taking photos and videos of the scene and posting it live.

Skip Loge was one of the first officials to arrive. He assessed the scene and spotted Jacob through the crowd of onlookers. He rushed up to him. "Are you insane?"

"Why?"

"You're dressed like a cat burglar. Do you want to be arrested?"

Billy caught up, looking much the same way. He was yelling like a madman for Maddy.

Jacob realized that Skip was correct, and he didn't want Tut's knife to be found during an impromptu search by the police. "You're absolutely right," he said, fading away into the crowd.

Billy found Maddy crying in a doorway. "We're going!" he shouted, grasping her hand.

CHAPTER 89

The Vigil

A lthough officially the Trinity term had begun, few students attended a single lecture. Most of them just touched base with their tutors and remained hidden in their rooms.

The student newspaper, the Cherwell wrote that more than a third of the student population was not at Oxford or anywhere in the vicinity. People were running scared. Since the deaths of Larson and Turner, everyone was walking around shell-shocked.

"We can't just mope around waiting for more bodies to drop," Jake said.

"It's been a week. What do you propose?"

He was lying prone on the floor with Tess on his stomach. "I don't know, Babe, but I am bored rigid waiting for the monster to come out of hiding. I believe I'll have poker on Friday."

"Friday?" Timothy said, surprised. "You know that's the night of the prayer vigil."

Jake sighed loudly. "I prefer to play cards with the lads rather than stand out in the cold listening to all that sanctimonious blather."

He began texting his card-playing troupe. "Those that are keen can say a few prayers and show up here to gamble and drink afterward."

◆ ◆ ◆

Bea and Abbot set out a lavish buffet for the party, while Jacob busied himself setting up the poker table and counting out chips. Timothy had taken Tess for a walk by the river.

"Not attending vespers for your lost friends?" Abbot asked.

"No, I prefer to honor my comrades in my own way. And I meditate every morning now, that's the closest I want to get to supplication."

Abbot brushed the felt tabletop. "I couldn't help but notice that master Timothy has been wearing your mother's ring."

"Nothing gets past you."

"Details matter."

"I gave it to him in Australia. It's to signify my intention to marry, but not until long after you and Bea have tied the knot."

Abbot nodded. "You're still quite young."

"True, but I promised my father that I would wed."

The butler grinned slightly. "I doubt that was the coupling he envisioned."

"Well, we Westons love surprises."

"And what are your thoughts regarding the Butcher?"

Jacob shuffled the cards. "I believe we're as prepared as we can be. Protecting Timothy and this household is my foremost concern."

Abbot wiped his hands. "You do love puzzles, don't you, my boy?"

"I do indeed. All the best bits in life are mysteries."

CHAPTER 90

Poker Night

T he boys were gathered and Jacob had attempted to make everything special for the first poker night of Trinity.

"Larson and Turner are gone. I'm gutted," Matthew said. "I sleep with the door locked and a baseball bat next to my bed these nights."

"Which is why we must carry on in their honor," Jacob contended.

"Is Billy coming?"

"He said he had to make an appearance at the vigil for the sake of Maddy, then he'll be on his way."

Austin and Adam came in with Ethan. Everyone began tucking into the food. "Bea's put out a nice nosh up," Ethan said.

"She's only happy when everyone is eating," Tim said.

"So have the coppers been bugging you?"

"No more than usual. I meet with Detective Loge every few days. I like talking to him."

"Do they have any fresh clues?" Cotton asked.

"They say they are looking into alternative methods and motives."

"Very cryptic."

Jacob began dealing cards while Timothy and Tess sat watching from the couch. Billy arrived about a half-hour later.

"Lord Redgrave," Jake said. "How was the vigil?"

"Bloody boring, and cold. You were wise not to go— there's a fair amount of angry, militant women at Oxford."

Jacob frowned. "I do believe Missy and some of those other girls like kicking a hornet's nest. Were there prayers offered for Casey and Doug?"

"Not specifically, but I believe they were meant to be thrown in whenever anyone mentioned the fallen." Billy began making himself a sandwich and pouring a glass of wine.

"Billy," Timothy asked, "why aren't you wearing the bracelet I gave you?"

He looked sheepishly at his friend. "Yeah, sorry about that, mate. Maddy hated that I was wearing it. She said that it smelled like Venice at low tide and threw it into the rubbish bin yesterday."

Jacob immediately perked up. "Did she?"

Timothy's eyes widened.

"So, Redgrave," Jacob began carefully. "Your family has dogs in Scotland, don't they?"

"Heaps. Hunting dogs mostly. We have horses too."

"And how did Madelyn get on with them?"

Billy scoffed. "She didn't. Most animals frighten her. She was attacked by a neighbor's dog when she was a child."

Jake got up from the table. "I need everyone to go into the cottage and sit with Mr. Abbot and Bea. Billy, listen carefully— You need to text Maddy. Tell her Timothy is sick and is asking for her to come to his bedside. Can you do that for me?"

"Why?"

"It's difficult to explain, but your girlfriend may not be what she seems."

Just then there was a knock at the door that startled the boys. Jacob ran up the stairs to find Matthias Krage shaking out his umbrella and raincoat.

"This is the way it usually happens," the physicist said. "Where's your boyfriend?"

CHAPTER 91

Alternatives

Timothy and Matthias were crowded into the small upstairs bathroom as Dr. Krage filled the copper tub with warm water.

"So it was Maddy all along?"

"Yes," Matthias answered. "She's an old and extremely powerful entity. You have an energy that she finds irresistible."

"I don't want to travel back in time and change anything in this world. I can't risk losing what I have here."

Matthias nodded. "If we are moving through time and space your spirit will be lost to the creature. It will confuse her senses and give Jacob a better chance at success. We won't be mending or changing time, merely observing some alternate worlds. It will be good for you to see some of the many possibilities and paths your life could take."

"What about the Heisenberg Uncertainty Principle?"

"Hmm, you boys have been brushing up on your physics. That principle states that anything that is observed is changed by the very act of observing it. It's only true to a minuscule degree. The rain doesn't change the way it's falling just because we are watching it."

Timothy lightly touched the bathwater. "Won't you need to cook up some of that earthy psychedelic potion to knock our spirits free?"

"That won't be necessary." He removed a small tin of pills from the pocket of his jacket. "One of these will have the same effect. Now if you wouldn't mind climbing into the water, we haven't much time to hide you."

◆ ◆ ◆

Timothy lowered himself into the tub and held one of the pills in his hand. "What's in this?"

The doctor winked. "It's a concentrated form of the brew which Pe gave you. *Ayahuasca*, the soul vine."

He swallowed the pill and rested his head back against the tub.

"We're protecting you from the beast, who will not be able to sense your spirit while you are on this journey. But this will also help you to understand your purpose on Earth and the true nature of the universe. I will guide you in seeing the possibilities."

"You're like the *Spirit of Christmas Yet to Come*."

"Dickens knew that the choices we make in life have a wide-ranging effect on the world around us."

Once again Timothy felt the sensation of free-falling through space, watching prisms of color shift and vibrate, but the experience this time was far more subdued and controlled.

Dr. Krage stood beside him, holding his hand. He showed the boy various moments in time, not only from his own life but from the world stage. Presidents and leaders, palaces and landmarks.

"Sometimes we bring back timelines that have been muddled by the tampering of others," he winked as they revisit Jacob's funeral. "While other times we attempt to divert the river of time on a larger scale."

"You interfere with destiny?"

He shrugged. "Five years ago a disturbed person detonated a bomb next to the statue of David in Florence, destroying it. There was a debate among the Menders after the event. We could easily prevent this senseless vandalism, but perhaps that act of terrorism inspires others, for good or ill. It's difficult to determine."

"But you decided to save the artwork," Tim said, squinting toward the lights.

"Yes, in this case, we felt the world was a better place where Michelangelo's David still existed. It's impossible to eliminate every evil act, nor should we—but occasionally we tip the scales slightly."

"The group makes choices for the benefit of mankind?"

The physicist nods. "It's a daunting and subjective calling. When you observe dozens and dozens of worlds which have only slight variances the choices seem more obvious. It was difficult for us to allow you to save your boyfriend, for instance."

"Why?"

"It was something that touched us personally. As a Time Mender, your voice and actions help balance our cause, but you also deserve the chance to live a quiet life, filled with love. You were willing to risk everything to be with Jacob, so that has to count for something. Miranda can sometimes glimpse future possibilities, and your road together is never easy."

They watched an amazing sunset over Byron Bay. Two old men were sitting in lounge chairs drinking. "Don't spoil any surprises for me," Timothy pleaded.

"If Jacob is clever and strong enough to slay the beast then my group will leave you to live your life however you choose, but if he should fail, you must consider joining us."

"What are his chances?"

Matthias put on a brave face, "They aren't great, to be honest—but Jacob Weston has a stout heart and you can never count him out of a fight. He can often surprise us all."

CHAPTER 92

The Roof

S he knocked politely as if she was dropping over for tea. Jacob quickly sent a text off to Skip before opening the door. He saw Madelyn standing in the rain.

"Hello, Maddy. Timmy has been asking for you."

"I don't believe you, Mr. Weston, but I'm here nonetheless. Aren't you going to invite me in? I know you know my secret."

He smiled tensely. "Can you only enter if someone invites you?"

"Don't be a moron," she said pushing past him and into the foyer. "For the moment I can't sense him, so where is the boy, and how have you managed to hide his presence?"

Jacob walked toward the fire. "Both good questions, which I do not intend to answer."

She stared at his bracelet. "Take that vile thing off before I rip it from your arm."

He removed the copper amulet and placed it on the mantel.

"How did you discover my true nature?"

Jacob snickered and poured himself some scotch. "This is Oxford," he said, talking with his hands. "There are tons of books on Gods and monsters."

She narrowed her eyes. "Then you must have learned

that I am unstoppable and immortal."

He said nothing.

"I can sense the others, you know. So close. I can smell their fear. Little Lord Redgrave is nearby, I would know his stench from a mile away," she laughed wickedly, shaking the water from her hair.

"Careful, Billy is a dear friend," he replied, wondering if she could also sense the terror rattling around his chest like a marble in a tin cup.

"I'll ask you again, where is my Timothy?"

He peered into those strange violet eyes. "He's gone into his favorite hiding place."

Jacob climbed the staircase toward the attic with Madelyn closely following. "Tell me why you've been killing so many innocent people?"

She scoffed. "They all got what they deserved—I'm only protecting what's mine."

He walked through the dusty attic to the door leading to the roof. "Why Timmy? What makes him the object of your desire when you can have anyone you want?"

"You should know the answer better than most. He has a rare soul— a light, beautiful quality that is lovely and unique."

Jacob stepped out onto the roof and into the rain. "We agree upon that, Miss Drepa."

She followed him down the narrow path. "What are we doing here? Where is he hiding? What foolish game are you playing?"

"All in good time," he answered.

At that moment Abbot lunged out from where he was crouching near an eave.

"Abbot," Jacob shouted, "don't let her near you! She has the strength of ten men."

Madelyn advanced toward the butler while he inched backward along the railing. In a single fluid motion, he pulled his Walther PPK from the holster at his shin and aimed it toward her chest.

"Miss, I must ask you to keep your distance." He cast a glance over the side toward the ground below.

"Unless you've loaded that revolver with silver bullets, I'm afraid it will be useless."

Madelyn gave Jacob a withering stare. "Clever boy."

She brandished her own small pistol, and fired twice at the butler, missing each time. He took cover behind one of the brick chimneys, firing his gun from a crouched position and hitting the girl in the center of her chest. Maddie merely shrugged off the bullet, although it did manage to ruin her clothing.

"I liked this frock," she muttered, glancing at the damage. She bolted forward toward the old gentleman and just as she was upon him—he jumped off the roof.

"One down," Maddy said gleefully.

Tess was at the door, barking, and growling, trying to protect her master. "I'll toss your little dog right after that old man. I hate animals."

"What?" Jacob gasped. "You wouldn't kill a puppy."

"Try me."

"*Mon Dieu*, you truly are a monster." He managed to grab the dog by the scruff of the neck and push her back toward the door. "Tess, stay back. Down!" he commanded.

"I'm going to offer you a deal, Jacob since our Timothy is so fond of you."

"Does your bargain involve taking possession of my body?"

She cackled again as lightning struck dramatically in the distance. "You've been doing your homework, so I'll advise you to go along with the plan or I'll kill every living thing on this property and take what's mine anyway."

Jacob surrendered, kneeling on the roof, and bowing his head. "Be quick about it then, I don't have all night."

She took his right hand, holding it in a vice-like grip, and began chanting in Greek, invoking ancient magic. Her flesh started to shimmer and turn into banded snakeskin.

"Stop what you're doing!" Miranda shouted from the doorway. Bridges and Skip stood behind her.

Madelyn spun around, furious at the interruption, her violet eyes hooded, a forked tongue darting from between her lips. "You don't belong here, Time Mender. This one is a sacrifice..."

But the distraction gave Jake just enough time to reach up with his free hand, pulling out the meteor knife and thrusting it deep into the monster's chest.

"Fuck you, Maddy," he yelled and twisted it toward her heart.

She looked down, shocked, the blade buried up to its golden handle. Madelyn clawed at the weapon, hissing and screaming, the shrieks loud enough to shake the house. It was the first time the monster had known pain. Jacob jumped back toward the door as she writhed on the ground in agony.

Her true body was revealed, half snake and half woman. The greenish scales rippled across her neck and arm, mingling with the white flesh of the girl. There was a blinding flash like lightning hitting the house, then an acrid yellow smoke rose from her body as she rolled frantically along the roof, hissing, and cursing, raindrops sizzling as they touched her strange skin. Madelyn suddenly combusted in a tremendous fireball shooting sparks and embers twenty feet into the wet night air.

The knife clattered down at Jake's feet where he wiped it on his trousers and slipped it back into his pocket, while the creature dissolved into a puddle of rancid smoke and ash, leaving only the smell of sulfur behind.

It was then that Jacob realized Skip was wearing a long dark wig and a blue evening gown. "Did my message catch you at a bad time?"

Skip weakly nodded. "I was on a date."

"Where do you keep your gun now?"

"Inner thigh, next to the garter."

"Well, you do you, honey."

Tess was circling the fetid stain which was still sputtering and smoking in the storm. She growled at what little remained.

"What the actual fuck just happened?" Bridges yelled.

Jake threw an arm around the crusty DCI. "I just killed the Butcher of Oxford, my friend. Case closed."

The group stared down at the spot where Madelyn was destroyed. "But, I don't understand..."

"We tried to tell you, Chief. It wasn't altogether human," Skip said.

"Exactly how are we supposed to write this up in a report?" Bridges grumbled.

"Abbot might have a few ideas on that score, and if you'll excuse me, I think my dear friend may be injured. He fell quite far, landing in our shrubbery."

The ambulance arrived to take Mr. Abbot to the hospital. Bea was sitting beside him in the laurel hedge, holding his hand.

"Didn't MI6 teach you not to fall off roofs?"

"Madam, I didn't fall, I deliberately jumped."

"Mr. Abbot, you broke your leg," Bea stated emphatically. "James Bond never broke his leg."

"Well, I'm nearly sixty, and James Bond is a fictional agent."

Jacob nodded at the former spy. "Quick thinking on your part."

"Were you able to dispatch the beast?"

Jacob knelt. "The job is done, we're safe. I'm going to wake Timmy and then we'll come to meet you at the hospital."

"You're quite an extraordinary young fellow, master Jacob."

"I had a good teacher."

CHAPTER 93

Wake Up Call

He unlocked the bathroom door and found Timothy unconscious in the copper tub, Dr. Krage still holding his hand. Matthias heard the hinges squeak and smiled up at Jacob. "Congratulations. Is Miranda here?"

Jake nodded. "She helped me by distracting the monster. Thank you."

The doctor released Timothy and stood, "I'll leave you boys to it then." He touched Jacob's shoulder. "Make your lives extraordinary."

The puppy came barreling into the bathroom slipping on the tiles and panting. She sniffed at Tim's hand draped over the side of the bath.

"Wake up, *Caro*. I need you," Jacob whispered.

Timothy's eyes slowly blinked as he tried to focus. "Hey," he said through the fog. "You managed it."

"Easy peasy. Southpaws always have an advantage in battle, did you know that? The opponent doesn't expect an attack from the left side. It's actually where the word sinister comes from--*a sinistro*, 'from the left' in Latin."

He sat forward in the tub to kiss him. "You do have blinding, jammy luck, Jake Weston."

They laughed, carefully placing the pup into the water. The boys watched as Tess instinctually swam around. She loved it.

"I can only be the best version of myself if I have you there to guide me," Jake whispered.

"I feel the exact same way about you."

CHAPTER 94

MI6 & Walking Sticks

Mr. Abbot sat in his hospital bed, glasses perched on his long nose. "It's merely a broken bone, I should be discharged immediately."

Bea patted his hand. "You fell forty-five feet, my dearest. They are concerned about concussions and blood clots and all sorts of other dangers."

"Ridiculous," he muttered.

Bridges arrived bearing a small bouquet. "For you, sir."

Abbot considered the white tulips. "Thank you, Inspector. I didn't know you cared."

"I wonder if I might have a word alone."

Bea raised her eyebrows at the detective. "I suppose I can go look for a vase. I'll be right back, Luv. By the way, your sister is here—she's coming to check on you."

"Dear God," Abbot said. "You'd think I'd had a stroke." He looked at the waiting detective. "Yes, so what can I do for you, DCI?"

"I have a police report to write and press releases to issue, as well as college chancellors and deans to deal with, and we have a rather unusual chain of events here. Weston mentioned that you might have some ideas in that regard."

Abbot chuckled. "I don't think the truth will serve the greater good in this instance," he said, taking out a pen and jotting down something for the detective. "Call this number," he said, handing him the slip of paper. "When you are asked for a code, say, *Limelight.* MI6 will take care of the rest."

"What the bloody hell will they do?"

Abbot considered the question. "Probably produce a corpse who will become your captured Butcher. They'll give him a plausible history and a name, undoubtedly a foreigner who's difficult to trace. You may even be awarded a medal for apprehending and killing him."

"So that's the way governments do things?"

Abbot frowned. "You can't have the populace believing in monsters, demons, and aliens roaming around the UK. I mean, you want them to be superstitious, but you don't want to confirm their deepest fears. Sometimes we need to keep secrets so the world can have peace, as well as closure."

"Thank you, Mr. Abbot."

Jacob and Timothy knocked at the door.

"Do come in," Abbot called. The boys stared at Bridges.

"I told you we were innocent," Tim said with a wink.

"I was just doing my job."

Jacob pulled the detective to one side. "I hope you'll let Miss Loge continue in her police work. She's a credit to the force."

"Listen, I don't care if the Kid is in a dress or a suit of armor as long as he, or she, brings that big brain to the task at hand."

"You're a good sport, Carl. And what about Elsie and our project?"

Bridges looked away. "I wouldn't know anything about that, and if I did, I'd probably support it."

"Dr. Kelly has you wrapped around her little finger, doesn't she?"

Bridges just shrugged. "There's no place I'd rather be."

Abbot's sister Rachel came parading into the room with a much younger man in tow. He was gorgeous. "Blakes!" she announced. "We were so worried!"

"This is a nightmare," the butler whispered.

Bea had returned and was placing the tulips into a glass vase she managed to find. Rachel and Bea hugged, then introductions were made all around.

"Davis," she said to the young man. "Do go fetch us some tea while I catch up with my brother."

Jake and Timothy were grinning, while Bridges excused himself to make his calls and wrap up the strange case.

"He's my driver, and massage therapist."

Bea and Abbot exchanged worried glances.

"Yes, I know, he's frightfully young. I have no illusions and I know it won't last. But you know what they say..."

"Oh dear God," Abbot muttered.

"What do they say, Rachel?" Jacob asked.

"Thirty goes into fifty more times than fifty goes into thirty."

The boys guffawed.

"White tulips," Jake noted. "Those signify respect."

"From the DCI," Bea said.

"Interesting. You know dreaming of tulips is symbolic of new beginnings, and happy changes."

"Then I hope I start dreaming of tulips," Timothy said.

Bea produced her present. "I was saving this for a special occasion, but you need it now." She handed Abbot the gift wrapped in brown paper.

"Sometimes just surviving is a special enough occasion."

Mr. Abbot unwrapped the handmade walking stick.

"This is very kind, but I do not require a cane, madam."

Bea scoffed. "It's a walking stick, you old goat."

Rachel admired the silver work. "Blakes, it looks exactly like the stick that Papa used to carry everywhere."

He finally smiled, touching the silver eagle. "It does indeed. Thank you, my love."

CHAPTER 95

Copper Tub

Seven months passed before the lure of the copper tub became irresistible. Jacob carefully procured all the necessary ingredients, then waited for an afternoon when Timothy was out with the orchestra. November brought Thanksgiving and his birthday which were always so nostalgic. The memories had been calling to him like a siren's song.

He added salt to the bathwater.

If there was a chance, the slimmest possibility of saving her life, then he had to try.

The soul vine had been brewed, he mashed it into a paste and added a bit of Barolo.

Tess watched as he disrobed and stepped in.

He shook the device and lowered it into the water.

Tess whimpered, sniffing at the air and sensing danger. The hackles on her back were raised as she licked her lips nervously. She was nearly a fully grown dog and would jealously guard her master, though it seems she was advising against his travel plans.

Throwing all caution to the wind, Jake Weston ate the strange potion and tumbled down the rabbit hole.

Miranda closed her eyes and staggered. "Did you feel

that?"

Krage and Pe rushed over, helping her to sit down. "What?"

Her heart was beating impossibly fast. "A ripple—a big one. Close to us. Someone we know is moving through time."

The three held hands trying to pinpoint the source but as soon as they touched, Dr. Krage disappeared.

Miranda stared at Pe. "Well, that can't be good."

❖ ❖ ❖

He woke in his childhood bedroom in New York at sunrise. There was a double knock and Abbot strode into the room.

"Master Jacob, you mustn't dawdle this morning. Your mother expects you downstairs for breakfast in fifteen minutes. She's taking you into the city and you need to be out by seven o'clock."

"Abbot?"

"Yes? What's the matter with you? You look lost."

He stared down at his small hands, jumping out of bed on feet that didn't quite fit. "How old am I, Mr. Abbot?"

The butler was opening the drapes and letting the early light into the room. "What a silly question. You are twelve, soon to be thirteen. Welcome to adolescence."

Jacob scrambled to his desk and pulled out a sheet of paper and a pen. He immediately began writing. "I'm going to need your help. You have complete access to my trust fund, correct?"

"Of course."

"We'll be setting up a corporation. The JP Weston Corp. I'll need you to be the CEO since I'm so young."

The butler looked skeptical. "Very well. And what will our corporation be doing?"

"Speculating in the equities market."

"Fascinating," Abbot replied. "And do you know which companies you'd like to invest in?"

The boy was still scribbling down notes. "Funny you should ask. Here's a list of sixteen companies—a few of them don't exist yet, but we'll want to jump into their IPOs. Divert as much of my capital into our new corporation as you can without raising suspicion from the family. We should be able to start on about a million dollars without anyone taking notice."

"You're serious about this?" Abbot asked, looking over the list of names.

"I am. You must trust me on this. Start the process immediately."

◆ ◆ ◆

He bounded down the stairs and heard his father speaking on the phone, so he quietly stepped into the private den. It was strange to see the man so young and healthy again. Paul Weston finished his call and turned to regard his only son.

"Jacob. Off to the city early, are you?"

"So it would seem."

He turned his back and shuffled some papers. "Take care of your mother while I'm gone. I'll be back in a week."

He crossed his skinny, pre-teen arms. "She knows about you—about the affairs. We all do."

Weston spun around sharply. "What did you say?"

"She's the best thing to ever happen to you, and you are a cheat and a liar. Some people never know what they have until it's gone."

His hand moved like lightning. The slap was so hard and well-placed that when it landed it hurled Jacob across the room, tumbling him into a bookshelf.

"Don't ever speak to me that way again."

◆ ◆ ◆

When he was dressed he came into the drawing-room where his mother was patiently waiting. She gasped when she saw the welt on his face.

"Jake! My God. Did he just do this?"

He fell into her arms and hugged her tightly. He had nearly forgotten the smell of her perfume.

"It doesn't matter," he cried.

"What did you say to set him off so early?"

Jacob gazed into her pale blue eyes, memorizing the softness of her hair and her dimpled smile. "I told him the worst thing I could think of—the truth."

"Go to the kitchen and have Dezo whip you up some eggs. I want a word with your father before we go to the city."

Janett Weston stormed into the den slamming the oak door behind her. Paul rolled his eyes. "The mama bear here to protect her cub," he mumbled.

"Listen to me carefully. If you raise your hand to our son again I will leave you, and trust me when I tell you that I will take half your empire out the door with me."

"Idle threats."

She smiled, inspecting her French manicure. "We know the same lawyers, and frankly they like me better. So why don't you pick on someone your own size."

He put a few ice cubes into a glass and poured himself some gin, with tonic and orange juice. "He's soft, Janett. He cries like a little girl and spends all his time drawing or reading books. You're turning him into a mama's boy."

She stared at the drink. "It's a bit early, isn't it, Hun?"

"I'm still on Tokyo time."

She stood close to her husband. *His breath could peel the wallpaper,* she thought. "I'd rather have him reading books than becoming a bully."

He laughed in her face. "I've been chatting with Caldwell. There's a very fine boarding school in New York. Trinity-

Pawling. It's only sixty miles away. I think we should enroll him."

She scoffed. "What? Don't be ridiculous, I won't hear of it. Our son is twelve years old and belongs right here under our roof. God knows Harvard and Stanford will be calling for him soon enough."

"Janett, at least give it some thought. It's not like I want to ship him off to Europe."

"Darling, the answer is no."

"Then I'm going to have Abbot find him a trainer to toughen him up. Jacob needs to learn to defend himself, frankly, he's the type of boy kids like me used to target."

She looked distraught, but in some ways, she knew there was truth in what he was saying. She nodded her head curtly.

"And he needs to pick a sport. He's going to grow too large to become a jockey."

She glanced out the window towards the garden. Her daily migraine was starting early so she quickly took two pills attempting to stave it off for a few hours.

"He likes to swim," she finally acknowledged.

CHAPTER 96

Sapphire

They arrived at the Empire State Building well before the observation deck was opened to the public. A young gentleman in a burgundy jacket escorted them up. "You'll have it all to yourselves for at least fifteen minutes," he said.

Janett thanked the man, slipping some folded bills into his hand. It was a clear, crisp day and all of New York was laid out before them.

"Mom, it's amazing!"

They took a few selfies, smiling and mugging for the camera while trying to hide Jake's bruised cheek.

"Listen," she said, pulling her cashmere scarf close around her neck. "I can guess what you said to your father this morning. Don't poke the bear on my account, *Caro*. I've made my bed and I have no illusions about who I married."

Jacob stared at her. The woman he saw was wise, brilliant, and caring. "I've something important to tell you, Mum."

She looked intrigued as they sat on a bench watching the sun moving up over Manhattan. "I'm all ears."

"I meet someone," he said. "He will come into my life when I'm sixteen. He's the most amazing person I've ever known. Clever and beautiful and, you'll love this, he's a musician. A gifted violinist. His name is Timothy James."

She listened to the story silently nodding and smiling,

her deep dimples showing. "How do you know this boy will come into your life?"

"It's fate. Destiny. I wanted you to know that I won't be alone and that I'm happy. Do you believe some people can know the future?"

She tilted her head, her short blond hair blowing in the breeze. "I think some people get glimpses, but the future is always changing."

She knew so much truth.

"I have a present for you," she said quietly, taking the sapphire ring off her finger. The sun hit the stone showing the clear six-points. "It's a star to guide you. It has never let me down."

Jacob got up and took his mother's hand. "We have to go now."

"Where? They aren't expecting us at Le Bernardin until noon."

"We may have to miss lunch. I've scheduled you for an MRI at New York-Presbyterian Hospital."

"What? Whatever for?"

He met her gaze. "I don't want to scare you, but you may have an aneurysm laying in wait. I want to see if we can't stop it in its tracks."

"I don't understand."

"I've had Mr. Abbot call ahead. Please just believe me on this."

◆ ◆ ◆

To their credit, the doctors were concerned at the length and severity of the headaches she'd been experiencing and decided to proceed with the MRI. The experts were amazed and alarmed to find the problem, just as the young boy had predicted.

They scheduled the operation immediately. Jacob massaged her neck as he waited for them to take her into surgery. Tears streamed down his face.

Janett saw how upset her son was. "What's the matter?"

He looked at her, a boy who had already lost his mother once. "I'm scared."

She smiled and there was nothing but peace in her voice. "Don't be scared, my blue-eyed boy, I'm not scared."

◆ ◆ ◆

Abbot arrived with Paul Weston.

"Where is she?"

"They've taken her into surgery already."

Abbot hugged the boy and moved him toward the hallway. "So, your guess was correct?"

"Yes."

"You're having an interesting day, aren't you master Jacob?"

He shrugged. "Did my father cancel his trip?"

The butler straightened his cuffs. "He postponed it. The jet is on standby. Now would you like to explain to me how you are stock-picking and life-saving? Did you suddenly become clairvoyant?"

The tow-headed twelve-year-old who is nineteen puts a small hand on the gentleman's shoulder. "I know you were MI6, my friend, and you hide a great many strange truths, and here is another— I've traveled backward through time to try to save my mother. I'll be going back where I belong soon, so I wonder if I might just take this moment to thank you for everything."

Mr. Abbot had the slightest grin on his face. "Is there anything you'll be requiring in the near term?"

"Make sure I keep up with the swimming. In time I'll learn to love it. Also, make sure I get sent to school in England. By the way, you're going to want to stick to your diet—you'll meet a lovely woman in a few years."

"Will I? What's her name, if I might be so bold."

The boy gave him the lopsided grin. "You know how I love surprises, so I won't spoil yours. It starts with a B, though."

Jacob fell asleep in the waiting room next to Blake Abbot. When he woke up he was twelve again, and he'd lost an entire day.

CHAPTER 97

Consequences

When Jake awoke the first thing he noticed was that Tess had left her post. That's odd, he thought. She must have needed to go for a wee.

He vaulted out of the tub to be sick, spending several minutes purging himself of everything left in his stomach. Once he felt slightly more human he stumbled naked into his bedroom.

It was early and he barely noticed that he was sharing the massive bed when he crawled under the covers. The boy reached over and snuggled close. "I was getting worried, Jake. Where have you been?"

He pulled back, surprised. "Cotton! What are you doing here?"

Matt smiled. "Well, it's Thursday, isn't it? I've just popped by for sex."

"What?" Jacob asked, grabbing some sweatpants. "Is this our usual thing?"

Matthew sat up. "Since you bought the house. What's the matter?"

Jacob was starting to wake up, shaking off the haze from the drug. He was wearing his mother's ring again, so he could feel the panic sinking in its teeth.

What have I done?

"So, you and I are boyfriends?"

Cotton laughed, crawling naked out of bed. His body was amazing. "That's not a word I thought was even in your vocabulary," he replied. "We decided to keep it FWB until after the Olympics."

"Olympics?"

Jake looked down, touching his side. The scars were gone. The car accident never happened.

"Cotton, look at me!" he demanded. "Who's coaching us?"

"Dylan Lir, of course."

"And you and I both qualified for the Trials?"

"Easily," he answered, reaching for Jacob's shoulder. "What's going on with you?"

"Umm, I'm having trouble remembering things."

Cotton looked concerned. "Did you hit your head? Maybe it's a concussion. Shall I take you to the doc?"

"No, I'll be fine. Clear some things up for me though. Where is Mr. Abbot?"

"Your butler? I guess he's in New York with your dad."

He sighed. "What about Timothy Ashlock?"

"Who?"

Dear God.

"Has anyone been killed?"

"Killed?"

"Yes, have there been any murders lately?"

"Don't be daft, Weston. No one's been murdered at Oxford for decades." Cotton began to get dressed. "We should grab some breakfast and get our asses to practice."

"I'm going to miss today, classes as well. I need to rest and sort some things."

Cotton tightly hugged him. "Call me if you need anything."

"Hey," Jake whispered, "where's my dog?"

Cotton stared into his pale blue eyes.

"You don't have a dog."

◆ ◆ ◆

Jake looked through the photos on his phone and barely recognized anyone. Casey Larson was there, Cotton and the swimmers. Adam Harper and the Night Climbers.

No Ethan. No Billy. He scrolled further and further back. He went to Eton, not White Oak. He never knew Fulton, or Rothwell, or even Miranda.

He called the gentleman. "Abbot, I need your help."

"Master Jacob. How are your practices going?"

He sighed. "I wouldn't know. I don't know anything. I've made a terrible mistake, I'm afraid. Tell me, is my mother alive?"

There was a long pause. "She died when you were twelve. You managed to get her to the hospital, but she had a stroke on the operating table."

He crumpled to the floor like a marionette with its strings suddenly cut and began to sob. Some memories beg to be forgotten. "I need you to come to England for a while."

"I understand completely."

"Do you?"

"Of course. Time travel is a nasty bitch."

Jacob sat on a bench reading Marcel Proust's *À la Recherche du Temps Perdu* in the original French. He'd chosen the perfect spot to spy on the musicians leaving the rehearsal hall without being noticed.

His pulse fluttered when Timothy appeared in the doorway. "Hello gorgeous," he whispered.

Timothy was holding her hand as they left. They chatted for a moment in front of the building, then kissed before going their separate ways. Madelyn had finally snagged her prey.

She walked toward the bench Jacob was sitting on. He quickly put his nose into the book and remained stock-still. She walked within inches without a hint of recognition.

He got up and followed Timothy down Holywell street. "Ashlock!" he shouted, causing the boy to stop in his tracks and turn suddenly.

"Yes?" he answered, smiling tentatively.

Jacob caught up to him. "I wonder if I might have a word."

"Who are you?"

The question crushed Jacob's heart, confirming his darkest fear.

"I'm Jake Weston."

He extended a hand and when the boys touched the déjà vu sent a shockwave through Timothy's core. He nearly dropped his violin case.

"Have we met?"

Jacob had to forcibly restrain himself from smothering the boy with kisses.

"Do I seem familiar?"

He chuckled. "Very. I may have even seen you in a dream, as odd as that must sound to a stranger."

"I don't find that odd in the least. I know you as well as I know my own shadow. I could sketch every freckle from memory." He reached out and moved the boy's curls. "I'm glad your ear is unscathed."

Timothy frowned at that statement. "My ear? Well, this was a strange encounter. Nice to meet you, Mr. Weston. I'm afraid I must be off."

He began to walk away.

Jacob leaned against a building. "Your mother's name is Betty, you grew up in Hackney, you had a brother named Henry and you're wicked fucking good on the violin."

Timothy turned and stared at him, blinking. "You could have found that information any number of ways—and what do you mean, had a brother?"

"Henry. He died, didn't he?"

"Of course not. He lives in France with his wife. They have a baby boy—my nephew, Jean-Marc."

Jacob looked confused. "Extraordinary. In the dream, are you and I dancing during a meteor shower?"

His eyes widened. "How can you know that?"

"Because you promised me you'd never forget it. It's a memory from another time, Timmy, not a dream. It's proof of the persistence of memory."

"I don't believe you."

"Etta James was singing, *At Last* when we started to kiss." Jacob pointed to a nearby pub, "Let me buy you a pint, please. For old time's sake."

He gave him the persuasive lopsided grin, and he swore Timothy recognized it.

"Okay then, one pint *for old time's sake.*"

They entered the Eagle and Child Pub. "You know Tolkien and CS Lewis used to come here to discuss their work," Jake explained. "This place is steeped in literary history."

"Yes, I know."

"Do you?"

He rolled those beautiful hazel-green eyes. "You're not the only one with a brain, Mr. Weston."

"Here and I thought you were just another pretty face."

"Not just," he said, sipping his ale. "And for the record, I'm not gay."

"I know, *Caro*. I just thought in my case you might make an exception."

"I'm engaged to be married, so I'm afraid my time mucking about with strangers is over."

"Well, you're not married yet. And you just might be fibbing about not liking boys."

He noticed a flyer on the bulletin board inside the pub, a planned social justice speech sponsored by the Women of Oxford.

"What is it you want from me?"

His expression melted like butter in a hot skillet. "I just want you to remember us. I've lost something I can't live without. I need to meditate more because sometimes I jump head-first without thinking about the consequences of my actions."

"I don't know how I can help with any of that," Timothy answered.

"Kiss me!"

"What?"

"There's no one in this back room but us. Kiss me, please."

"You're daft, Weston."

"Timmy, you have to give it a chance to work. I know you are special, a Chime Child, and there's some piece of that alternate that touches you still. There's an echo, a faint residue.

We've all met people that we immediately feel like we've known forever. If you're open to the mystery of time, you can recognize old friends in the eyes of strangers. We travel in troupes. Alternates, past lives, an endless circle intertwined—and you and I have known each other as well as any two people can. Please, Ashlock, just kiss me."

He didn't argue further, merely leaned across the narrow table. He held the back of Jacob's neck and slowly pulled him closer. The thought crossed both their minds: *Can a kiss bring back a lost history?*

Timothy closed his eyes and slightly opened his mouth. The kiss was long and true, and sweet memories filled Jacob's mind and heart. Brigsley Cottage in the rain, swimming at Ducker, dancing in Australia, and eating in Paris. The laughter and tears. The music, the wine, and so much love.

Timothy blinked his eyes and smiled.

"Well?" Jacob asked.

"That was very nice—but I don't know you. I'm sorry."

CHAPTER 98

Future Plans

Jacob ran through the forest near Greenknoll looking for her. He sprinted toward the tents. She saw him coming.

"Miranda, I've got to talk to you."

She looked up at him scowling and slapped him hard across the cheek.

"Hey," he yelled, rubbing his face. "What's that for?"

"You use a device without so much as a by your leave? Do you know how big a ripple you caused? It's a massive headache. Dr. Krage just resurfaced in Munich. We were afraid you bumped him right off the timeline—and that would be truly problematic. We are still trying to sort it."

He sat on the grass, his head in his hands. "I brought the dreadful machine back to you. I can't believe I used it. I'm so sorry. I didn't think I would hurt anyone."

"Everyone thinks they're an exception to the rules. What were you trying to change?"

"I was attempting to save my mother. It always seemed rather unfair to me. She left just as I was becoming interesting to be around. A futile attempt on my part."

She nodded. "It's a bit of a Pandora's Box, isn't it? Especially for a curious mind like yours. You love living life on the high wire. I always say, if you sit in the barber chair long enough, you're going to get a haircut."

"You've got that right," Jacob said. "Let me ask you this though: If I never lived at White Oak, then you and I have never met. How can you know me?"

"I'm a Time Mender, you tosser. One of the cunning folk. I can keep more than one set of alternates in my head simultaneously, even when someone like you comes along and throws a wrench in it."

She sighed. "So you fucked things up for yourself?"

"Well, some things, yes. Other things are actually a bit better."

"That's always the way."

"Timothy's engaged to be married to the monster, who's alive again, and he doesn't know me! I'll be as lonely as the moon without him."

"That complicates matters. He's in danger though, she'll eventually get bored and kill him. Give me your hands, it will be faster."

She closed her eyes while grasping him.

"Hmm, Timothy won't recognize me either. He must be having flashes though. Snippets, dreams."

"He is."

"We can't allow him to be near that creature. It's too dangerous. Timothy has an important role to play in this world and that thing will suck the energy right out of him."

Jake tossed a pebble across the meadow. "It was strange. The creature, Madelyn, stood three feet away and didn't seem to know me."

Miranda smirked. "The object of her desire is Timothy. Her memory in this timeline must be completely entwined with his. You caught a break there, but if he starts to remember you, so will she. If it knew you were a threat you'd probably already be dead. So what are you going to do?"

"I guess I'll just have to kill her again and then sweep Timmy off his feet. Luckily, I didn't return that dagger."

She looked into his pale eyes. "Matthias, Pe, and I could mend this. It would be simple enough to return to the day you traveled and steal back the device before you had a chance to use it."

He considered the suggestion. "Timothy's brother is alive in the current timeline, not to mention I'm back in Olympic shape. Every ending is just another beginning in disguise. Let me see if I can't right the wrongs here and now. Keep your plan on the back burner in case everything goes tits up with the monster."

She smiled. "The two of you are quite the couple. Troublesome, but fun. You're the sort of pair that makes everyone around you feel rather invisible."

"I thought when he kissed me he'd suddenly remember everything."

She laughed in her high-pitched, little voice. "You've been spending too much time reading Grimm's. What do you plan to do next?"

"Hire two dear friends that won't recognize me. A housekeeper from Hackney and a driver from Manchester. I wonder if I could ask you for a favor?"

"Certainly."

"I'm thinking of getting a dog—do you know where I might find a puppy that needs a loving home?"

She whistled and Tess came running across the meadow, leaping at Jacob and licking his face excitedly.

"She knows me!" he cried. "How's that possible?" He hugged the dog close, sobbing into her thick blond fur. "I thought I'd lost her forever."

Miranda winked. "Dogs don't reckon time the same way we do. They live in the moment and their memory is tied to their heart. All you need is love and a good dog, and this one will always belong to you and Timmy. So how do you plan to win him back?"

Jake Weston smiled. "I'll buy an old violin and make him Mousse au Chocolat."

EPILOGUE

Dezo's Secret Mousse au Chocolat recipe:

INGREDIENTS

3 1/2 ounces bittersweet chocolate
(do not exceed 70% cacao), chopped (Jake uses Scharffen Ber-
ger or Valrhona chocolate)

3 extra-large eggs (preferably organic and very fresh),
separated, room temperature

pinch of Himalayan salt

2 1/2 teaspoons superfine sugar, divided

3/4 cup chilled heavy whipping cream

* may use: 1 tablespoon espresso or strong coffee
            1 tablespoon cognac
            Fresh raspberries for garnish

RECIPE PREPARATION

Place chocolate in a double boiler and stir until it is melted and smooth. Remove from heat. Add egg yolks to melted chocolate and whisk until very smooth. (add espresso or cognac here and whisk)

Using an electric mixer, beat egg whites and add a pinch of salt in another medium bowl until peaks form. Gradually add 1½ teaspoons of sugar, beating constantly until whites are glossy and medium-firm peaks form.

Using a rubber spatula, fold ¼ of beaten whites into the chocolate mixture to lighten. Gently fold the remaining whites into the chocolate mixture just until incorporated. (do NOT over mix, mousse should look streaked)

Divide mousse among four bowls. Cover and chill until set, about four hours.

Beat cream and 1 teaspoon sugar in another medium bowl until peaks form. Spoon whipped cream atop mousse.

Add raspberry garnish.

ACKNOWLEDGEMENT

I believe in thanking the folks that support and encourage my writing. It can be a lonely business. Also, thanks for letting me name some of my characters after you.

Dylan Bruno, Chris Bruno, Will Kir, Thomas Pe, Bridget Lee, K'Lyn Matthews, Jesse Barnes, Collin Boetel, my Chinook Lane gang, my family at the Crow's Nest, Blake Adams, Matt Pekel, Rachel Luckhurst, Matt Bell, Barbara Fogerson, Karen Swan, Richard Nolthenius, Eric Hoang, Carla Barbosa, Lee Mark Hamilton, Kevin Majdic, Jon Michaelsen, Harry Styles, Justene Adamec, Laura Rochelle, Jan Jessup Schattner, Susan Hoisington, Chris Hemsworth, Timothée Chalamet, Josh LePage, Adam Harper, David Commons, Janet Rader, Robbie Dice, Erik Thomas, Patrick & Payson McNett, Ethan Rill, John Colistra, Alan & Dona Love, Kevin Clarke, Betty Ashlock, Justine Iadiano, Mark Tydell, Clayton Takacs, the folks on Goodreads, Michael Bruno, Lisa Simon, the Eddings Family, Jason Fuller, Austin Smith-Ford, Sam Russo, Jason Webb, Leigh Ann Wallace, Marissa Miller, Cheryl Renner Imada, Matt Hanks, Sharon Cox, and to Travis with the amazing tattoos.
(also in fond memory of Cassidy, Matthias, Billy, Betty and Janett)

ABOUT THE AUTHOR

Marko Realmonte

is a novelist and screenwriter living in a sleepy, Central California beach town. He shares his life with a loyal Labrador, great friends, good wine and the blue Pacific.

He's currently working on an LGBTQ Fantasy novel, titled, The Wizard King

Contact the author at markorealmonte@gmail.com

www.markorealmonte.com